YЯAM

THE SUMMONING

MARY

THE SUMMONING

HILLARY MONAHAN

HYPERION
LOS ANGELES | NEW YORK

Copyright © 2014 by Hillary Monahan

All rights reserved. Published by Hyperion, an imprint of Disney Book Group. No part of this book may be reproduced or transmitted in any form or by any means, electronic or mechanical, including photocopying, recording, or by any information storage and retrieval system, without written permission from the publisher. For information address Hyperion, 125 West End Avenue, New York, New York 10023.

Printed in the United States of America

First Hardcover Edition, September 2014

First Paperback Edition, August 2015

1 3 5 7 9 10 8 6 4 2

V475-2873-0-15166

Library of Congress Cataloging Control Number for Hardcover Edition: 2014004254

ISBN 978-1-4231-8693-9

Visit www.hyperionteens.com

SUSTAINABLE FORESTRY INITIATIVE

Certified Chain of Custody
Promoting Sustainable Forestry
www.sfiprogram.org
SFI-01054
The SFI label applies to the text stock

This one's for the horror guy.
Enjoy, David.

September 2, 1863

Dearest Constance,

I regret to inform you that you are an abysmal sister. You snatched the only handsome Boston lawyer to ever grace Solomon's Folly, thus relegating me to a life of wedded torment with a sheep farmer or some other dullard. I will forgive this grievous insult, but please remember my graciousness come the holidays.

I wonder how long it will be before Mother suggests you take me to the city so I may seek my own gentleman. Am I terrible to confess that I would enjoy the sights more than romance? She may have married at seventeen, but I do not feel so compelled. It is likely my impatience speaking. An endless parade of soft words, flowers, and idiocy sounds quite grating.

Upon reconsideration, the flowers would be nice. I would be content so long as my ardent gentleman gifted me with flowers and had the good sense to leave immediately afterward.

You asked about my wellness, and though I do not like to complain, I must indulge this one time. Your departure was the first in a series of disappointments. Last month, our beloved Pastor Renault moved to a congregation in the Berkshires. I wish him the best, but miss him already. He had such a kind, loving manner.

The new pastor is as pleasant to me as Cain is to Abel. I'm convinced Philip Starkcrowe was sent to test my faith. He is tall

and bird-boned with pitch-colored hair and eyes like night. He is
young for his station, too—perhaps a few years beyond twenty.
It is strange to see him donning the robes. He looks as though he
wears the clothes of a man much larger than himself. He is a boy
tromping about in his father's boots.

His voice is good, and his sermons are certainly impassioned,
but there is darkness to his words. Where Pastor Renault spoke of
God's love, Pastor Starkcrowe talks of God as an angry shepherd.
We are sinful sheep bound for everlasting torment. I'm surprised
he doesn't make us sing our psalms with mournful baa's in lieu of
honorifics.

There's also the matter of his hypocrisy. You once jested that
Mother is a princess torn from a storybook, but the pastor looks
upon her like he has never seen a fair-haired woman. I may be
innocent, but I am not ignorant, and there is an earthiness to
his gaze that unsettles me. It unsettles Mother, too, though she'd
never say as much. She is far too kind.

I, however, lack such grace. After Sunday's sermon, the pastor
came to thank us for our devotion. While speaking to Mother, he
stared too long at her—pardon my crassness, Constance—but
he stared too long upon her necklace. It was so bold! I tried to
hide my disapproval, but I must have failed because he turned a
furious eye upon me. He drew me before the congregation then,
and with that loud, fire-and-brimstone voice, proclaimed that
"while Mrs. Worth has a pleasing disposition, I cannot say the
same for her youngest daughter."

I may lack your sweetness and Mother's etiquette, but I never
thought myself so monstrous. It was mortifying. Everyone in the
church heard him. Elizabeth Hawthorne had the nerve to smile

at my embarrassment! You would think being schoolmates for years would garner me some affection, but she will not forgive me for that Thomas Adderly nonsense. It is not as if I welcomed his advances. He has onion breath and warts on his hands, yet Elizabeth still believes that I lured him away from her affections.

The rejection must devastate her Hawthorne pride. They do not breathe the same air as the rest of us commoners, don't you know.

I loathe the privilege money affords some people. I rest well knowing that you will never struggle, but if you become an inflated harpy like Elizabeth, I will strangle you in your sleep, Constance. On this I swear.

Since the pastor's histrionics, showing my face around town has become a nuisance. Just yesterday, Mrs. Chamberlain clutched her cross when I was in her presence like I could afflict her with a fiendish curse. I was tempted to hiss at her to see if she would hide beneath her bread counter. Mother would have murdered me, but I daresay it might have been worth it.

I apologize so much of this letter is ill news, my sister. Mother does say I spit vitriol when I am riled. Perhaps next time I will be a more uplifting correspondent. For that matter, perhaps I'll find a suitable sheep farmer in the meanwhile and will write of my impending nuptials!

I love you and miss you,

Mary

1

"Bloody Mary.

"Bloody Mary.

"BLOODY MARY."

Jess's voice echoed like we were in a cave. Darkness has a way of making everything seem bigger and more claustrophobic at the same time. Four bodies crammed inside Anna Sasaki's basement bathroom meant we were each nudged up against something cold and hard. Jess got the vanity, I got the toilet, Kitty was at the tub, and Anna had the linen closet door.

"Bloody Mary.

"Bloody Mary.

"BLOODY MARY."

The lights were off in the windowless room. According to Jess, Bloody Mary had to be summoned by the light of a single candle. Ours flickered on the edge of the sink below the mirror.

Though no one moved, and I barely breathed, the flame danced a jig on its wick as if held by invisible hands.

The whole thing felt eerie, despite my logical reasoning that the summoning was ridiculous. I'd played Bloody Mary at slumber parties with these same girls when we were twelve. Trying again in high school seemed a waste of time—but there was a strange exhilaration to it, too. The lure of the unknown. It was a good scare, the kind you got walking through a haunted house. The anticipation was far worse than the reality.

I bit my lip and stared at the mirror. Jess claimed there was a right way and a wrong way to summon Bloody Mary. This time we were doing it the right way. Positioning mattered. Salt mattered, too, because it purified against evil. Water mattered. Hand-holding mattered. Even the number of girls mattered. Before, the idea was to scream Mary's name in the dark and scare yourself pretending to see a ghost. This was more deliberate. More believable. This time, it felt like we knew what we were doing.

The mirror stayed vacant for at least thirty seconds. I didn't need to look at the shadowed faces beside me to know they were staring as intently as I was. It was so quiet. Seconds ticked by. The longer we waited for something to appear in the mirror, the less convinced I became it would. The thrill of calling Bloody Mary dwindled. There'd been goose bumps on the backs of my arms when Jess first said the name, but now they were gone. A sinking feeling of disappointment rippled around our summoning circle.

I was about to ask *Are we done yet?* when I saw a flash in

the mirror. I blinked, sure that it must have been one of our reflections. Then it happened again. A light streaked behind the mirror—a star across a night sky. Kitty's hand flexed inside of mine. She'd seen it, too.

The mirror filled with fog, like condensation after a hot, steamy shower. But the fog was on the other side. The *wrong* side. Droplets of water streamed down the glass, cutting black rivulets through the gray.

Kitty twitched again and I clamped my fingers down on hers so she couldn't jerk away. Jess had warned us about breaking the circle. We had to hold position or we'd be putting ourselves in danger. Bloody Mary hadn't gotten her name because she liked hanging out with teenage girls. To keep her at arm's length, we needed protective wards. The first and most important ward was the handhold.

Behind the mirror, the fog changed from a thick paste to a swirling mass of charcoal smoke. My goose bumps returned and my heart beat so hard, I thought it would pound through my lungs and splatter on the floor.

This couldn't be happening. I tried to think of ways Jess could have manipulated the glass, but I'd checked the mirror before we started. The frame was solid bronze, the mirror far too heavy for a single person to lift. There wasn't space for a movie projector in the room, and Jess didn't have the tech skills anyway.

No, this was legitimate ghost activity, and there I stood, witnessing it with my three best friends. Anna murmuring under her breath. Kitty wheezing louder and louder. Jess saying, "Come on—come on," over and over again.

"Look, Shauna. Look," Jess said. I looked. A black silhouette emerged through the fog, walking toward us down a tunnel that ought not exist. No, not walking—*shuddering*. There was no fluidity to the movements. It was one jolting, shambling step into the next, like a zombie movie monster.

Blood rushed to my face. My toes curled inside my sneakers. Bloody Mary was real and she was walking toward the glass! I didn't know what to do; I wanted to run away, but I desperately wanted to stay, too. It was horrifying and exhilarating, like that first big whoosh on an upside-down roller coaster.

Then she rushed us. An unnaturally fast blur of madness barreled our way from inside the glass. Her hand struck the mirror on the other side, though there was no sound to punctuate the strike. I yelped, the desire to crouch and hide warring with my mind's insistence to absorb every last detail.

Most of Mary was masked by the fog, but her hand was as clear as my own. Her fingers were long and twiglike, with twisted, swollen joints. A sheaf of gray, shriveled skin hugged each appendage, peeling away from the tips. A deep gouge bisected her palm from pinkie to thumb, revealing her rotten, ragged flesh. Tarry blood seeped from Mary's wound, smearing the glass in streaks of blackish maroon.

Gross.

And it got grosser when Mary curled her fingers over to rake them down the glass, her nails in a state of decay. Some were broken off at the nail bed, others had snapped into sharp, serrated razor tips. I expected to hear a shrill squeal from the mirror, but there was nothing. My mind filled in the audio track with nails on a chalkboard, the imagined sound sending another ripple of fear through my body.

I was so consumed by terror and fascination that I had forgotten about Jess, Kitty, and Anna. I should have been more careful. When Mary lifted her second hand to the mirror, this one just as desiccated as the first, Kitty jolted next to me like she'd been struck by lightning. She tried to wrench away, forcing me from my stupor. My fingers dug into Kitty's sweaty palm to keep her steady, but I felt her pulling. She'd become a hundred-and-seventy-pound eel at my side, and there was only so long I could keep control of someone so slippery.

"Kitty, stop," I whispered.

"No. Nooooo," she groaned, another violent twist nearly pulling my arm from the socket. I doubt her resistance was conscious on her part. Kitty knew the dangers of breaking the handhold as well as the rest of us, but she was panicking. I clutched her wrist to anchor her to the group.

"Jess," I hissed. "Do something."

"What? Oh . . ." Jess said, seeing Kitty struggling beside me in the dark, Anna manhandling her on one side, me on the other. Before Kitty could escape the circle, Jess's voice rang out strong and clear through the bathroom.

"I believe in you, Mary Worth!"

The hands and blood vanished immediately. The fog dissipated, as though a gust of wind had swept it away. We were left in a dark bathroom with an empty mirror and a flickering candle.

We never saw Mary's face.

2

It started with the letter.

Jess had gone to Solomon's Folly during April school vacation to stay at her grandparents' lake house. Solomon's Folly—or the Folly—is a sleepy old town without much going for it beyond its strategic access to other, more interesting places. Go south on the highway and you're on Cape Cod. Go north and you're in Boston. Farms, trees, and a lot of creepy graveyards constitute most of the town. Our hometown of Bridgewater isn't much more exciting, but at least fast food and a movie theater exist here.

I'd spent half the summer at the lake house last year, canoeing and grilling and getting bitten by mosquitoes with Jess, my best friend since before I could remember. We met in kindergarten and have been friends ever since. Even when she'd graduated from "the girl I was in Girl Scouts with" to "blond, blue-eyed beauty queen," we'd stuck together. I'm good-looking enough with my red hair and dark brown eyes, but Jess is a stunner. The all-American-girl-next-door flavor of stunner. The rest of us pale in comparison.

I declined the invitation to the Folly that April so I could perfect the art of laziness at home. I was working my butt off to make honor roll, and with four advanced placement classes, it wasn't easy. Junior year is college transcript year, and if I wanted to go somewhere that wasn't the University of Loser, I needed good grades for scholarship money. April vacation was the last chance I had to relax before finals came crashing down.

Jess had been positively industrious by comparison. Sometime during her vacation, she'd rediscovered the Bloody Mary legend. The letter from Mary Worth to her sister, Constance, was her sales pitch. The photocopy of the original was her way to get us on board with the summoning.

"There's a rumor that Mary Worth is Bloody Mary," Jess said, dropping a pile of papers into my lap as I devoured pizza in Kitty Almeida's downstairs media room. We were gathered around a glass-top coffee table, me on the center cushion of the couch, Kitty seated to my left, and Anna perched on the floor by Kitty's knees. Jess hovered behind us, looming over my shoulder like an oversize parrot.

"You mean that stupid game we played a million years ago?" Anna asked between bites of pizza. She had tomato sauce on her face. I threw a napkin at her so she could clean up. "Thanks," she murmured, wiping her chin, then tying back her hair. Anna's dad is Japanese, her mom is Irish. From Mom, she'd inherited a stocky build and freckles. From Dad, she'd gotten pretty brown eyes that she hid behind a pair of gold-framed glasses and perfect black hair that felt like water and hung to her waist.

"Yeah, the one where you nearly puked because I slapped the bathroom door when you were inside? Remember?" Jess asked with a snicker. It took me a minute to pluck that memory from the banks. It had been a slumber party at the McAllister house to celebrate Jess's twelfth birthday. Someone got the brilliant idea to play Bloody Mary. Every one of the ten girls there went into the bathroom individually, shut out the lights, and called for Mary. And every one of us insisted we saw something creepy in the mirror—except we hadn't.

Poor Anna was the last to go. By then, Jess had grown bored of the game and decided to up the ante by grabbing the doorknob and shaking it to make Anna think the ghost was there. Anna hadn't puked, but she had cried, and we'd all had to tell Jess what a jerk she was at her own birthday party. She'd always had a talent for being the biggest ass in the room. I loved her, but that love came with a great responsibility, like whacking Jess whenever she got out of line.

"Yes, that one. And thank you for reminding me!" Anna said. "This conversation is now a total waste of your time."

"Wait. No, hold on. Read the letter." Jess reached down to grab the papers from my lap, waving them under my chin. My choice was either to accept them or suffer the torment of a thousand paper cuts. The script on the pages was small but legible despite the cursive flourishes. Someone had taken great care to make it as neat as possible, and glancing at the signature on the last page, it was evident that someone was Mary Worth. Little black ink spots dappled the corners of the paper, and there were shadowy rings in places that indicated the original letter had some water damage.

When Kitty swooped in to read over my shoulder, the motion a little too "starving seagull on popcorn" for my taste, I shooed her away and read it aloud. The language was stiff, but the September 1863 date explained the tone. This was Civil War–era stuff, all "Four score and seven years ago," and somewhere, my U.S. history teacher totally appreciated that I'd immediately linked the year to the Gettysburg Address.

"Whoa, this is over a hundred and fifty years old? Where'd you get it?" Kitty asked.

"Solomon's Folly," Jess said. "The town claims to be the source of a lot of urban legends. At least, that's what my grandfather says. He's a little weird, but sometimes he says cool stuff."

Jess was failing to mention that they suspected Grandpa Gus was in the early stages of dementia, but I wouldn't bring that up in front of the other girls. Jess loved her grandfather, even if he sometimes forgot his pants and wore a kitchen colander as a helmet for fun.

"That's neat," Kitty said, taking the letter to skim it. When she was done, she slid it onto the coffee table between two pizza boxes, narrowly avoiding a run-in with a puddle of grease. "It'd be cool if it's really Blood Mary's letter."

Anna shrugged. "There's nothing in that letter that screams

'scary ghost chick.' Husbands and pastors and mean girls? So what?"

Anna was being harsh, but that edge was part of her personality. She was blunt to a fault.

"Well, it could be Bloody Mary," I said. "I mean, yeah, there's the possibility it's not, but if everyone in town says it is, why is it so ridiculous to consider it?"

"Seriously," Jess said. "Have a little imagination, Anna. Grandpa had me talk to my great-aunt Dell. She's as weird as he is, by the way, Shauna. Like, seriously creepy old lady. Anyway, she filled me in on the summoning details. She says there's a real way to do it. I think she was trying to scare me, but I want to try it anyway."

"So do it. Why do you need us?" Anna pressed.

"The summoning has to be four girls, that's why. Otherwise I'd ask Marc and Bron—" Jess cut herself off with a muttered curse. She wasn't supposed to mention Bronx. He'd dumped Kitty three weeks ago, and Kitty had spent every day since weeping and listening to their song while one of the three of us stroked her hair and told her it was okay.

The problem was that Bronx was best friends with Jess's boyfriend, Marc. Jess couldn't exactly ditch Bronx in a show of solidarity, and so there was static. It wasn't like Jess talked about Bronx a lot, but saying his name was enough to make Kitty go slouchy and cast her eyes to the floor.

I had to swallow a groan. After three weeks, Kitty's kicked-dog routine was getting old, but my irritation was tempered by the knowledge that her melancholy wasn't a manipulation tactic. She had zero self-esteem. Kitty was a solid forty pounds heavier than the rest of us and she seemed to think it made her disgusting. Bronx had certainly liked her curves, but Kitty saw herself as the ugly duckling no matter how many times I pointed out her stunning green eyes and gorgeous caramel-colored hair.

Jess didn't have the same kind of patience. She'd done her best to overlook Kitty's moroseness, but lately, Jess rolled her eyes to the ceiling and gritted her teeth. "It makes me feel like a bad friend," she'd told me in confidence, "like she thinks I'm trying to hurt her, and I'm not." I understood Jess's perspective. Intentionally or not, Kitty was laying a major guilt trip on Jess's shoulders. If she could stop being passive-aggressive, they'd probably be fine, but that wasn't Kitty's way.

Looking between the two of them, I knew we'd skated onto thin ice. Kitty was shriveled in the chair next to the television while Jess's mouth pinched into a grimace, her eyes narrowed to feline slits. Kitty was about to get a massive blast of Jess fury to the face. I *really* didn't want to have to pick up those pieces, so I grabbed the pages of the Mary Worth letter and waved them over my head, a red flag before the bull. I knew it'd at least distract Jess from the imminent danger of a meltdown.

"This. We should do this," I said. "The Bloody Mary thing. It'd be cool."

Anna caught on to my great distraction plan and hauled herself up from the floor to reach for the letter. "Sure, why not?

It's not like anything will happen. But if it'll shut Jess up, I am totally down for it."

Jess ignored the jab. She was too busy erupting into excited, ear-piercing squeals, like we'd crowned her prom queen for the second time this year. She vaulted the couch to throw herself into the seat beside me, her arms snaking out to jerk me into a spine-crushing hug. She may have been a skinny chick, but she could give hugs that'd make a grizzly bear squirm.

"Awesome! Kitty, you in?" she asked. Kitty was nodding her head before Jess even got the question out. Depression or not, Kitty fell into line with the rest of us because that's just what Kitty did.

If I had known that days later we'd be watching Bloody Mary scratch at Anna's bathroom mirror, I might have thought twice.

3

"That shouldn't have worked," Anna said, slumping on the floor between the toilet and the wall. Her hands kept raking through the hair at her temples like it needed to be patted into place. "There is no way that should have worked. How? How did it work?"

Kitty nodded her agreement from inside the tub. After we'd broken the handhold and turned on the light, Kitty jumped inside the bath to lie down, her head tilted back like she wanted the shower to rain a better reality over her. She was stiff with fear. Her eyes bulged, a flush stained her cheeks. Her right hand was white-knuckled on the side of the tub, like she needed something solid to hold on to while she reconciled the impossible thing that had just happened.

"But it *did* happen," Jess said gleefully. She pulled a red notebook from her backpack and perched on the bathroom vanity, her butt in the sink, her back to the salted mirror like it hadn't just had clawed ghost hands menacing it. She recorded every detail of the summoning, including the time and which cardinal points people stood on when Mary appeared. There were papers glued to the first few pages of the notebook, presumably the letter she'd shown us. Jess was keeping everything in one tidy place for all her Bloody Mary needs.

"How are you not even a little bit bothered by this?" I asked. I didn't look as rattled as Anna, and I wasn't catatonic like Kitty, but I had my own issues. My head pounded like a one-man band was doing laps across my forehead.

"I am freaked out a little, too, but it was so cool. Wasn't it? It was awesome!" Jess insisted. She grinned at me and rubbed her shoulders like she was cold. Maybe she was a little more bugged out than I gave her credit for, though it still took massive stones to sit on the sink with her back to the mirror like that. "Bloody Mary. We did it. Like, really for real. How awesome is that?"

"Awesome in the broadest sense of the word, maybe," Anna returned. "I'm not so sure what we just did was smart. Some stuff is better left to books and movies. The reality is too...I don't know. It's too something. And that something isn't necessarily good."

"No way," Jess said, hopping down and turning around to scoop the salt off the vanity. I wished she wouldn't do that. It made me feel safer to have it around, but she'd brushed it aside before I could make my mouth form the request to keep it there. The headache was wreaking havoc on me. "We've done something only a handful of other people have ever done. We've done something historic. Yes, it was scary, but she's a ghost! Ghosts are *supposed* to be scary."

I started to see Jess's point. It had been exciting until it turned terrifying, and even then the terror was pure adrenaline. I'd only felt uncomfortable when Kitty began her freak-out dance beside me. "I guess," I said. "I just got . . . I feel a little sick. I got scared it'd go bad at the end. We never really talked about what would happen if we screwed up."

"There's no point discussing it if we're not going to screw it up. Which reminds me. You," Jess said, whirling on Kitty. Jess leaned over the tub so far, her profile was hidden behind a veil of blond hair. The only thing I could see from my position on the floor was Kitty's bewildered, slightly gassy expression.

I swallowed a groan. Why had I brought it up? I knew Jess would go after Kitty sooner or later. I didn't have to make it sooner. I braced, ready to intervene if Jess got bitchy. For all that she was my best friend, she had a mean streak, and Kitty was the poorest equipped of our group to handle Jess when she was riled.

"What'd I say about the handhold?" Jess demanded.

"I'm sorry. I got scared," Kitty replied. I watched her sink farther into the tub, shrinking away like Jess was going to unhinge her jaw and swallow her whole.

"I said there were three things we had to do. One, line the mirror. Two, light the candle. Three, and most importantly . . ." Jess let the thought linger.

"Hold hands, I know," Kitty said. "I'm sorry."

"Sorry won't cut it if you screw it up next time. Hold it together, or if you can't, I'll have to get someone else." Jess's hand reached down to pat Kitty's shoulder. It was supposed to be a reassuring gesture, but Kitty flinched like Jess was going to beat her to death.

"Wait, there's a next time now? You want to do this again?" Anna asked. I was guessing she was less interested in a repeat performance than Jess was. Or I was, to be fair. I was curious about the rest of the Bloody Mary package. I wanted to see what was attached to those hands, but there was no way Anna would listen to me.

Jess, however, stood a chance of convincing her. Jess was one of the most charismatic people on the planet when she put her mind to something, and even the iceberg that was Anna Sasaki would melt in the wake of an impassioned Jess speech. Jess wasn't stupid. She didn't get great grades like me or Anna, and she spent most of her time texting instead of paying attention in class, but she was clever. She understood people. If she wanted us to do something, she'd appeal to us in whatever way would get her results.

Jess slithered past me to sit down in front of Anna. The bathroom was so small their knees touched, but that didn't stop Jess from worming her way in so Anna was forced to look right at her. "How are you not seeing how amazing this is?" Jess asked. "I know it was scary, and scary is usually bad, but this is different. It's a miracle that it worked. Doesn't that excite you? That you're doing something other people can't? I bet fewer people have seen Bloody Mary than have . . . I don't know. Climbed Mount Everest. Or gone into space."

"Well, yes." Anna groaned, leaning her head against the tiled wall beside her. "It's scary. I'm also not sure it's safe. She clawed the glass. What if she's violent?"

"She's violent on the other side of the mirror. She can't hurt us while our hands are held. We control the summoning, we control her. You know?" Jess grabbed Anna's hand, giving it a long, reassuring squeeze. "One more time. What can it hurt?"

Anna jerked away with a sigh. The moment I heard that sound, I knew Jess had won. "Fine. Fine! But if something happens to me, I'm going to come back and haunt you. I will haunt you when you pee. I will haunt you when you're making out with Marc. I will make you miserable for the rest of your life."

"How's that different from any other day of the week?" Jess flashed Anna a grin before whirling around to look at me. "Tomorrow for another summoning, yeah?" She glanced between me and Kitty. Both of us nodded, though mine was more enthusiastic. Kitty was afraid, but Jess had already given her the out if she didn't want to come along. There were more than enough second-string friends to replace her. Laurie Carmichael and Becca Miller came immediately to mind, two girls from Jess's softball team who followed Jess around like puppies.

"Cool. One thing, though." Jess whirled in a circle so she could look at all of us, her finger pointed at each of our faces. "No parents. My mom would flip if she knew what I was up to. They won't believe you, anyway, so unless you want to look stupid, keep it quiet."

I hadn't considered telling my mom, but Jess had a point. If I told my mother that I'd conjured an evil ghost in a mirror, she'd probably look at me funny before asking if I needed to see a doctor.

"Right," I said, Anna and Kitty nodding along with me.

"Good. Okay, I've got to get home for dinner. You coming, Shauna?" Jess asked.

"Sure," I said. My mom had worked doubles since Monday, so Jess had dragged me home with her every day this week. Mrs. McAllister always seemed happy to have me, and I always thanked her profusely for the meal, feeling like a charity case.

"Let's go," Jess said, slipping out of the bathroom. She handed me my backpack as I followed her into the hallway.

I could hear Kitty and Anna talking quietly behind me. I poked my head back inside the bathroom to say bye to them. They waved, both looking tired and scared, and in Anna's case, a little irritable. She had her glasses off and was rubbing her eyes. Her hair had escaped its clip and had slithered over her shoulders like a black waterfall. Kitty had cried so much, her eyeliner had smudged down her cheeks in black tracks.

"See you two tomorrow," I said.

"Later," Jess echoed, and we climbed the front stairs to get to the driveway. Jess drove a hybrid car so green, it practically glowed in the dark, but she liked it and that was all that mattered. I climbed inside and buckled my seat belt, my hand already looping around the handle in the ceiling. One too many car rides with Jess had taught me to hold tight or risk massive head trauma when she took corners.

"Can you call your mom and make sure it's okay that I come over?" I asked when she climbed in beside me. "I don't want to crash again without asking."

Jess nodded and pulled out her cell. Two minutes later we were headed back to her house, four neighborhoods away.

⚬⚬

The whole "honorary McAllister kid" status was fine until Todd, Jess's seven-year-old brother, decided to annoy me like I was his real older sister.

"Shauna, guess what?"

"What?"

"No, you've got to guess."

"Uhhh..." I said, concentrating on putting my napkin across my lap so I wouldn't have to answer.

"Shaaaauna. You have to guess!"

"Todd," Jess warned, slapping a wad of green bean casserole onto his plate so hard, bits of it splattered over the front of his blue T-shirt.

"Eat your dinner before it gets cold," Mrs. McAllister said. She leaned over the table to stuff a buttered biscuit in his mouth to muffle him. "I'm sorry, Shauna. 'Guess what' is one of the lovelier things he picked up in school. Oh, Jess, Marc called while you were out. He said he couldn't get your cell. Give him a call after dinner."

Jess had shut off her phone when we were summoning Mary

so we wouldn't have any interruptions. Marc must have called while we were incommunicado.

"Thanks," Jess said.

The thing I liked best about coming to Jess's house, besides the food, was the noise. Being an only child with a mother who worked all the time meant my apartment was tomb-silent. Sometimes it was okay. I could hear myself think to get my homework done, I could read or go online without any interruptions. But it was isolating, too. Here, with Mr. McAllister's loud deejay voice, Mrs. McAllister's propensity to drone on about anything that came to mind, Jess's phone ringing off the hook, and Todd's unbridled energy, I was distracted. I let the family's whirlwind swallow me.

"How was studying today, girls?" Mr. McAllister said with a mouthful of green beans I really wished he'd kept to himself. Apparently, instead of telling her parents she'd convinced her best friends to summon a deranged ghost, Jess had told them we were studying. Her parents should have known better. Jess didn't know the meaning of the word *study*.

"We didn't get as much done as we'd like. We'll probably finish up after dinner," Jess said, the lie sliding smoothly off her tongue.

"Then I don't want to hear the TV on." Mrs. McAllister gave us a pointed look. "And this isn't going to be an all-night thing, either. Bed by midnight, Jess."

"Can you talk to me like an adult? Seventeen, not seven." Jess hunched in her seat, stabbing her chicken like it was the dead bird's fault her mother nagged her.

"Maybe if you hadn't spent all last term on the phone with Marc, you wouldn't have gotten C's and D's on your report card. You're far too smart for bad grades, and softball's only going to get you so far."

The amazing thing about Todd, besides his ability to get anything in the universe stuck up his nose, was his complete lack of survival instinct. For some ungodly reason, he picked that exact moment to launch into a string of whining that was so high-pitched and irritating, I couldn't understand a word he said. Eventually, I figured out something about giant robots and dinosaurs and going to the movies, but it had practically required a translator and a Todd-to-English dictionary to reason it out.

"Saturday, Todd. Your father already told you that. Whining's not going to get you there any quicker. Now finish your dinner," Mrs. McAllister said.

"But Moooooom. I want to gooooo."

"Oh, my *God*, will you shut up about that stupid movie? It's all you talk about. You're so annoying sometimes," Jess snapped. The combination of Kitty's flip-out, her mom's scolding, and Todd's Toddness had frayed Jess's last nerve. I knew it was coming, but I'd hoped to be clear of the shrapnel before the bomb went off.

Mrs. McAllister's hand jerked out to grab Jess's wrist, her expression dark. "Knock it off. Seventeen, not seven, remember?"

"Whatever."

"Not 'whatever.' It wasn't so long ago that you were throwing tantrums, and you'd better believe we didn't treat you like you just treated your brother. Check the attitude."

"Apologize," Mr. McAllister said.

Jess rolled her eyes. "Fine. Sorry, Toad."

"Jessica!"

"...Sorry, Todd."

Dinner conversation petered out after that exchange. I helped clear the table, meticulously scraping each plate before putting it into the dishwasher. Jess was already halfway up the stairs to her room when I asked if I could be excused. Mrs. McAllister smiled and nodded, her voice getting louder when she said, "Your friend *still* has better table manners than you, Jessica."

Another one of Jess's *whatevers* floated down the staircase.

I grabbed my book bag from the floor of the kitchen and followed Jess to her bedroom. In the McAllister stairwell, there was a decorative mirror hanging among the family portraits. I caught a glimpse of my reflection mid-step and a shiver racked my spine. For all that I'd come down from Bloody Mary during dinner, seeing that glass made the unrest slither back. I ran the rest of the way to Jess's room, my eyes pinned to the floor.

The second the bedroom door clicked behind me, Jess pulled out the red spiral notebook from her backpack and looked over her Bloody Mary notes. I sat on her bed and grabbed a stuffed pony Marc had won for her at the summer carnival last year. It rested on my stomach, and I bent its ears back and played with its hooves while Jess plunked down in front of her computer, her hand shaking the mouse to clear her screen saver.

I could see the reflection of my sneakers in the sliding mirror doors of Jess's closet. I averted my gaze.

"You okay?" I asked, knowing she was upset with her mother.

"I will be. My family's irritating."

"I think all families are."

"Yeah, well, mine wins a prize," she said. She thumbed through her Mary notebook, past the photocopied letter she'd pasted to the first few pages and the notes she'd taken after Mary appeared. She read a few lines, typed something into her Web browser, and began reading from her monitor. I squinted to see, but it was too far away and I was too lazy to get up to snoop.

"I'm trying to find out about Mary Worth. Like, who she was. All the books I've found had mixed reports on Bloody Mary. Some say she was crazy and killed her children, some say she was a vampire. Others say she was a girl who died in front of a mirror and she got trapped inside it."

I'd heard these stories before and I nodded, making the stuffed pony dance at the back of Jess's head to amuse myself. "That's an old folklore thing. They used to cover mirrors in a house when someone was dying or dead. They thought the glass would swallow their souls," I said.

"Yeah, that," Jess said, her head jerking around toward me. I dropped the pony back onto my chest. "We'd have to find out if there was a mirror nearby when she died."

Jess clicked a few more Internet links, and I stifled a yawn against the back of my hand, my eyes straying to her alarm clock. I may have been a little tired, but I was still wiggly and nervous over Mary. Sleep wasn't coming anytime soon.

"I do have to study tonight," I said. "I have a McDuff essay on the Battle of Antietam due, so I can't stay late."

"That's fine. I'll bring you home soonish. So what did you think of Mary?"

I rolled onto my hip to look at her, my head perched on her mountain of pillows, my arm wrapped around the carnival pony. "What do you mean?"

"I mean, did you have fun? Did you like summoning her?"

"I don't know if 'like' is the right word, but it was fun. Terrifying, but fun." I fussed with the pony's ears again. "I wish Kitty hadn't scared me more than I already was."

Jess whirled around in her desk chair, her head falling back against the headrest of her seat. "Right? If she does it again, she's out. I've got way too much invested. Like, I got the letter, I went and talked to Aunt Dell at the library. I even called this woman Cordelia Jackson, who supposedly summoned Bloody Mary a billion years ago. She didn't want to talk to me, but that's beside the point. I worked for this. I don't want Kitty screwing it up for me."

I realized then I'd never asked Jess what would have happened if Kitty *had* broken the handhold. Stranger, it hadn't occurred to Anna to ask, either. "What happens if she does?"

Jess lifted her head to peer at me before letting out a long sigh. "Nothing confirmed, but she can scratch at people, grab them. That's just a rumor, though! Like I said, Aunt Dell was trying to scare me when I talked to her, but obviously there was some truth to what she said if the ritual worked. Cordelia survived Bloody Mary, so—"

"Survived?" I interrupted. That wasn't the verb I was expecting. *Summoned* maybe, or *encountered*, but *survived* made it sound like our lives were in peril if we kept messing around with the ghost, and frankly, I wanted to see her, but I wasn't willing to do it at the expense of my life.

"Well, yeah. Cordelia's here to talk about it, so that makes her a survivor. We're survivors in the same way. It's just too bad she hung up on me when I called her." Jess leaned forward in the chair to look at me, her hands balanced on her knees. "It was just a word, Shauna. If Kitty screws up, I'll send Mary away. I summoned her; I can dismiss her. She *has* to listen to my voice. That's how it works."

4

At one in the morning, I was too tired to work on my Antietam paper and too nervous to sleep. Jess dropped me off at eight, and while I'd done all right with the Bloody Mary thing when the McAllisters were around, the moment Jess drove away I was left with the thought of those ghoulish hands, the creaks and groans of an old building, and my imagination. I jumped every time a pipe rattled or my ancient upstairs neighbors went to the bathroom.

The post-summoning jitters afflicted everyone but Jess. Anna had glued herself to her dad's side all night and refused to go downstairs. Kitty had brought Kong, their Doberman, inside to sleep with her.

Jess, however, insisted she was fine. She texted me little tidbits of information she'd found online about Bloody Mary.

Jess: *Mary 1st appeared in the US in the 1960s.*

Me: *Why did she wait a hundred years?*

Jess: *Dunno. Still lookin.*

I didn't know how to respond, so I left it at a *cool*, all the while trying to keep my head on straight whenever Mrs. Zajac upstairs paced her way from her bedroom to the bathroom and back again.

It still struck me as weird that Jess wasn't the slightest bit freaked out. I finally asked her how she was so calm.

This is science, she texted. *Like an experiment.*

Not only was this *not* science, but real science was terrifying. Hadn't she ever cut a cat open in Mr. Sanno's anatomy and physiology class? That was Frankenstein-level horror, but when I said as much, Jess texted back *lol*.

I forced myself into bed at half past one in the morning. Fifteen minutes later, my mother came home from her closing shift at McReady's. The squealing door and the movement in the halls should have bothered me, but her presence quelled my nerves. She was my own fleshy night-light. I heard her pad toward my room and open my door to check on me; I closed my eyes and feigned sleep. Fleshy night-light or not, if she saw me up this late, she'd lecture me. Lucky for me, fake sleep translated to real sleep and I managed to drift off.

When I woke to the bellowing of the alarm clock, I heard my mother rummaging around in the kitchen. I oozed out feeling like I'd been hit by a garbage truck. I must have looked that way, too. Mom gave me the hairy eyeball over the top of her newspaper.

"You look exhausted. Are you okay?"

"Hey." I shuffled to the coffeemaker to get myself a cup, loading it with milk and sugar.

She pushed a chair out with her foot. "Want some waffles? They're frozen, but I'm a little short on time."

"You worked a double yesterday. I can get them myself," I said.

"You're still my kid. Let me pretend I'm good at this parenting thing." She put the newspaper aside and walked to the toaster, popping a pair of cardboard-looking waffles into the metal slots. She pressed a kiss to the top of my unshowered head as she passed me. "Why are you so tired?"

For a moment, I thought about telling her about Bloody Mary, but I had given my word to keep silent. I didn't *have* to do as Jess said, but the truth was, I wasn't sure how Mom would take it. I'm not one of those kids who's into darker stuff. I don't love horror movies, I don't talk about ghosts or aliens. I don't even read my horoscope. If I started babbling on about ghosts in mirrors, Mom would think something was seriously off with me.

"History paper took me longer than it should have," I said.

"No fun. I hope you weren't up too late." Her fingers drummed on the counter as she waited for the waffles to pop. The dark circles under her eyes made her look tired. Eighty-hour work weeks would do that to a woman. She was pretty in spite of it, though; prettier than me, anyway. Where I'm short, she's tall. Where my hair goes to frizz in the rain, hers stays curly and glossy and bounces around her shoulders. She has flawless, model-like skin. I'm riddled with freckles from forehead to toes. I'm not ugly, but my mom's in a different league.

"A watched pot never boils," she said under her breath,

turning away from the toaster to rummage around for maple syrup, a plate, and a fork. "Oh. I've got tomorrow night off from McReady's. You up for tacos and chick flicks?"

"Sure."

"Awesome. There's a Sandra Bullock thing I've been meaning to see, and I can hit a drive-through on the way home." The toaster popped. She pulled the waffles out, tossing them back and forth between her hands so she wouldn't burn the tips of her fingers. I watched her smear them with butter and maple syrup, my stomach grumbling. She served me the plate and dropped a paper towel over my head like a hat. I grinned, not bothering to move the paper towel even when it slid down to cover half my face.

Mom winked at me and drained her coffee cup. Her eyes flicked to the clock on the wall, a deep furrow appearing in her brow. "Shit, got to go. I should have been out of here five minutes ago. See you later tonight?" She lunged for her purse on the counter, jogging through the kitchen and living room to get to the door faster. Her hands slapped at her jacket pockets in search of her keys.

"Bye, Mom," I yelled after her with a mouth full of waffles. It came out more like "bah mot," but she understood, wagging her fingers in a wave.

"Bye!"

Her feet pounded down the steps of our apartment building a minute later. A door slammed and a car engine roared to life. When I looked back down at my waffles, I realized my appetite had left with my mother. I pulled the paper towel from my head and went back to my room to get ready for school.

$$\sim\!\!\infty\!\!\sim$$

The morning was one boring class bleeding into the next. I turned in my homework, bombed a math quiz because simple addition was beyond my tired brain, and shuffled to the cafeteria like a zombie. By the time I found my usual lunch seat, Jess was already waiting for me, Marc at her side and Bronx at Marc's other side.

Marc Costner was everything Jess ought to be dating—popular, arrogant, athletic. She was also smarter than him, which worked out well. I couldn't see her with someone smart enough to tell her to shut up when she ran her mouth. Jess was a pretty girl, and pretty girls were supposed to date cute guys like Marc. Sandy brown hair, green eyes, and a broad, square jaw.

Bronx wasn't quite that good-looking, but he wasn't unattractive by any stretch. He had black hair that curled around his ears and golden tan skin. His eyes were the color of good fudge. He was stockier than Marc, but not fat. He was the star football player on our team. When he hit other guys, they fell over, and when other guys hit him . . . well, they fell over. Bronx was a big dude.

Anna and Kitty weren't there yet, which was probably good. Kitty was going to lose her mind when she saw Bronx, and I hadn't had enough caffeine to deal with her drama yet. I grunted my hellos at Jess and the boys before dropping my bag onto the floor and lurching to the lunch line.

Once I had my food, I could see Kitty and Anna in the doorway of the caf, looking at our table as if sitting there would give them Ebola. They spotted me and I lifted my fingers in a feeble wave. Anna darted toward me, Kitty dragging behind her.

"Are we not supposed to sit with you?" Anna said in greeting. Despite her own sleepless Bloody Mary night, she'd been perfectly pleasant to me in the two classes we'd shared this morning. But seeing Bronx and Marc at our table now, all that pleasantness was gone. She looked like she could breathe fire.

"You can sit wherever you want," I said, dropping my gaze forlornly to my pizza. Hopefully she'd let me eat it before it got cold. The way she ground her jaw, I wasn't sure that was going to happen. The sad part was, I hadn't gotten that caffeine yet, either, so I was operating on two and a half exhausted brain cells screaming for a can of Coke.

"Well, it upsets Kitty. Jess is making problems," Anna said.

"Is she? Jess is allowed to sit with her boyfriend at lunch. We're fully capable of finding another table." I glanced over at Kitty. She looked like a deer about to be flattened by a bus. "I'll move my stuff and the three of us can sit together somewhere else. I'm sure Jess will understand."

Kitty took a moment to think the option over. While I waited, I finagled the cafeteria tray into the crook of my elbow so I could shove my pizza slice into my mouth. I loved the girl, but some things had to come first. Not dying of starvation was one of those things.

"We can sit there," Kitty said after a minute, her chin notching up. She wanted to look tough, like she could handle the situation, but the effect was ruined by the slight twitch in her cheek.

"Are you sure?" Anna pressed.

"Yes. I can't avoid him f-forever." Kitty tugged her arm away from Anna and went to make her usual salad. Anna followed her, and I took the opportunity to flee back to my seat. I positioned myself opposite of Jess so Anna and Kitty could sit on my right. This way, Jess and I acted as a Mason-Dixon Line where the northern boys and the southern girls never had to meet. They could stare at one another if they wanted to—I wasn't the eyeball police.

"Hey, Shauna. How you doing?" Bronx asked, smiling at me over his carton of milk. He had four empty ones on the table in front of him, and I glanced at my crappy sugar cola with guilt. He got vitamin D. I got stuff that would take the rust off of a car fender.

"Good. Tired."

"Oh? You out late last night?"

"Not really, just studying."

"I did that once. It hurt my brain," Marc said. He slung his arm over Jess's shoulder and made kissy faces at her until she gave him one of her fries. He bit her finger, and they shared a nauseating giggle.

Bronx smirked and shook his head. From the corner of my eye, I saw him glance behind, his eyes locking on Kitty. His face hardened and then fell before he leaned across the table to half whisper, half yell to me. He didn't want everyone to hear him, but the din of the cafeteria was so loud, it was hard to be inconspicuous.

"She doing okay?" Bronx asked. "Jess said she's had a bad couple weeks. I wasn't trying to . . . you know. I feel bad."

Jess eyed him and then me. I peeked past Jess's shoulder and saw Kitty coming our way, Anna at her elbow. This wasn't the time to talk about this, though I did want to know why a seemingly decent guy would dump his girlfriend with no warning. Maybe if he explained himself, Kitty could wrap her mind around it more. It'd give her closure or something.

"Not now. Text or call me later," I said.

"What?" he asked, the cafeteria suddenly noisy.

"Text or call me later," I repeated. Only I said it too loud and Kitty was close enough to hear. She looked between me and Bronx, and I knew something terrible had just happened.

"It's not like that," I said to Kitty, and she nodded, but she wouldn't look at me. All evidence that she was going to be brave about Bronx was gone as she scampered to the seat farthest away from him. Anna cast me a look, but it wasn't unfriendly. It was pity. Kitty knew me better than to think bad stuff about me, but when it came to Bronx, Kitty wasn't thinking straight. All Kitty knew was I'd been friendly with Bronx because he was her boyfriend, but there was no Bronx-and-Shauna dynamic. Now there suddenly was, and it scared her.

It was Jess who broke the uncomfortable silence—and managed to make the situation more awkward. I hadn't thought that it was possible, but Jess shouldn't be underestimated. "Oh, come on," she snapped, rolling her eyes at Kitty and then over at Bronx. "Like Shauna would do that to you. I can get your being upset, but do you think she's going to hop on Bronx's junk the moment you're off it?"

While I appreciated that Jess was defending my honor, I wanted to hide under the table for the rest of my life. The urge to crawl into a hole wasn't made any better when Marc whispered to Bronx, Bronx nodded, and they vacated the table.

"Jess, don't," Anna snapped.

"Don't what? Point out that Shauna would *never* do that to Kitty? Ever? Come on. You know she wouldn't," Jess said.

I felt that I should speak up, maybe assure Kitty that it was okay, but Anna picked up a piece of broccoli and flung it across the table at Jess. It hit her forehead and tumbled down into a puddle of ketchup. "Yes, I know she wouldn't. And Kitty knows she wouldn't, but it's still too raw. Don't be a bitch."

"It's been three weeks. Three weeks!" Jess got up from her seat to sit down across from Kitty. "We love you—I love you—but this has got to give. If you're so crazy upset that you can't deal with Bronx talking to your friends, or him being around or whatever . . . I don't even know. I'll start sitting with Marc at lunch and the four of us can hang out after school. But I'm not going to watch you psycho yourself into thinking Shauna's out to get you. Okay?"

Kitty nodded, but still she said nothing. Anna glared daggers at Jess, and Jess arched an eyebrow. There was no other way to interpret that gesture. It was an invitation to escalate this into an argument. Jess and Anna normally poked each other like sisters, but with all the weirdness at the table, it couldn't go anywhere good.

"Enough," I said. I'd been toying with my cookie, but I put it on the corner of my tray so I could address them with my serious face. "I would never hurt you, Kitty. If I talk to Bronx, it's to find out what's up—that's it." I glanced at the other side of the table. "And Anna, Jess—it's over. Let it be over. We've got plans later. I think we're all tired and a little on edge, yeah? So let it go."

Anna gave a curt nod. Jess shrugged and retrieved her book bag from the floor. Her expression was flat and irritated. For all that she'd bull-in-a-china-shopped that conversation with Kitty, she was making an effort to rein in her temper. Jess grabbed her tray and walked off to go sit with Marc and Bronx, abandoning the three of us to a quiet, joyless lunch.

5

I was staring out the window at the empty football field for most of my last class and missed the assignment my English teacher had given. At the last bell, I darted for the door. Yes, I'm a good student, but there are days I need to get away from school and give my brain a break.

I quickly shoved my books into my locker, though I still managed to be the last one to the parking lot. I stiffened seeing my friends together by Jess's car, expecting more static, but the hours apart must have mended the rift. Kitty was talking, Anna was nodding, and Jess was smiling. I wouldn't question how it happened. I was too relieved.

"Let's do this," Jess said when I approached. She opened the trunk of the car so I could throw my bag in with everyone else's. Kitty and Anna slid into the backseat while I buckled myself into the front. Jess peeled out of the parking lot with a spin of wheels and flying grit.

Anna had the house to herself until her parents came home from work, so we crashed at her place for the second day in a row. Anna opened the front door while Jess rummaged around in her trunk for supplies. There was a big box of kosher salt, a beeswax candle, a compass, and the red notebook.

Kitty and Anna went upstairs to take a small break before we got started, but not Jess. She went right at it. She dropped her stuff in the sink and removed the pictures from the wall—a Sasaki family portrait from some camping trip and a *Starry Night* lithograph. She hadn't done this the last time we'd summoned Bloody Mary. I watched her stack the pictures on the bottom step, curious.

"It's a precaution. The frames are shiny. Like, you can see yourself in them," she said. "I don't want Mary to come through in a weird place."

I grabbed the portrait to look into the brass frame, my distorted reflection peering back at me. "Does it work like that? Like, she can be summoned somewhere other than a mirror?" I asked, horrified at the idea of Mary's appearing in places she didn't belong.

"I won't take any risks. I told you I was being safe."

I watched Jess arrange the candle and grab the salt before flipping open her notebook. Everything she did was so organized, and I tried to find solace in her system, but my stomach clenched. The ritual worked *because* Jess was so careful. These precautions weren't for safety so much as for success.

I wanted to bail right then, but leaving would infuriate Jess. I'd be mad at myself, too, I supposed. "I had the chance to see

Bloody Mary but I settled for her hands" felt pathetic. I didn't want to be that person. I took a deep breath and replaced the family picture on the step. One good look at Mary and I'd be done. I just had to swallow my nerves and go for it.

I could handle it. I'd be fine.

"Hey, can you go get me a water? I'm thirsty," Jess said, interrupting my thoughts.

"Sure," I said.

I could hear Anna and Kitty in the kitchen murmuring, and I wondered if they were feeling the same way I was, that maybe this wasn't such a good idea. I crested the top step and peered at them. They were standing side by side near the kitchen sink, their heads tilted together. Kitty looked pale; Anna looked angry.

"Everything cool?" I asked.

Kitty nodded; Anna scowled.

"I'm not so sure I want to do this again. I don't want to be afraid of my bathroom forever," Anna said.

"Do *you* want to be the one to tell Jess that?" Kitty asked. I pointed at Kitty as if to say *That* before opening the fridge for Jess's water.

Anna shrugged. "I really don't care. She'd get over it. I just . . . I don't know. This seems like a bad idea."

"It's a terrible idea," I said. "But I do kind of want to see Mary's face. I mean, just to finish it. We never have to do it again."

Anna lifted her glasses to rub her eyes, her mouth puckered like she'd smelled something bad. A moment later her shoulders dropped and the glasses slid back onto her nose. She shook her head and shouldered past me to get out of the kitchen. "Fine. Let's get it over with, but I hate you all a little right now."

The three of us went downstairs looking like we were marching to our executions. By the time we crowded the hallway outside of the bathroom, Jess had finished with the salt and was skimming her notebook one last time, the compass in her left hand. I offered her the water and she pointed at the side of the tub, indicating I should leave it there.

"I'm making a small modification to the positioning this time," she said. "Kitty, you come stand here." She motioned at the spot Jess had taken the first time, next to the vanity. Kitty squeezed past her, frowning that she was now closest to the mirror. She opened her mouth to protest, but Jess cast her a sharp look and Kitty kept quiet.

"I can stand there," I offered, but Jess shook her head.

"No, you're going to be where you were. Kitty's going north to the vanity, Anna south to the tub, and I'll take the linen closet so I can see better." I'd still be holding Kitty's hand this time, just on the opposite side. I eyed her, hoping she wouldn't spaz out again. She looked nervous, but not nauseated like yesterday. Maybe that was a sign we were in the clear. Jess would be on her other side this time, too, and I knew she'd be a little better at reining Kitty in than Anna had been.

We wedged into our positions looking nervous and grim. I had a terrible case of the jitters, adrenaline pounding through my body. Jess leaned past Kitty to light the candle before flicking off the lights. Anna let out a shuddering gasp, Kitty groaned, and I held my breath as Jess fell into place opposite me. We were ready.

⚬⚬⚬

"Bloody Mary. Bloody Mary. BLOODY MARY," Jess shouted.

The candle on the vanity cast eerie shadows, our forms tall and distorted against the walls. Our hands were clenched together so tightly, our fingers trembled. This time, it took only seconds for condensation to cover the glass. A thick fog swirled, gray tendrils of smoke spinning in a maelstrom, before a black figure appeared, the vague outline of a woman. I braced myself, expecting more of the slow, shambling gait we'd seen last time.

SLAM.

Mary moved fast. One moment she was distant, the next her hands smacked against the mirror. Her fingers flexed, and then the clawing began, a shrieking squeal of razors cutting across glass. I jerked back, forcing myself to maintain the handhold. There'd been no noise during the last summoning. Now, the sound was undeniable.

"Why? Why can we hear her?" I asked, my voice warbling.

"I changed a few things around. Watch," Jess replied, her voice barely above a whisper as Mary's hands slid down the mirror. The fog thinned, and for the first time, I saw her. All of her.

She was dead. That wasn't a surprise, but I hadn't expected her to be *so* dead. Her mouth gaped open in a rictus grin, revealing a row of jagged, broken teeth that grayed along the gum line. Her face was gaunt, like her skin had been pulled taut somewhere behind her head. It reminded me of papier-mâché, when the first layers of tissue are on top of the balloon and the colors of the latex underneath are still visible. Except in this case, the balloon was her skull, and the tissue paper was her too-thin flesh. A spidery network of veins pulsed along her temples and upper cheeks.

There was a hiss as her tongue lolled out. It was pasty and white, covered in film and wiggling around like a worm. She raked it over the glass with an awful groan. Her lips were so receded that her teeth clicked against the mirror, the pointy stubs black and yellow with decay.

I tore my gaze away from her mouth and up to her eyes, fathomless black orbs sunk deep into her skull with no lashes, no brows. Patches of skin had peeled away along her forehead and chin. Her nose was nonexistent; the cartilage had rotted, leaving her with two socket holes that oozed a tarlike guck. Her hair was stringy tufts of black on a bumpy, pointed skull. Her cheeks were hollow with sharp, boney edges.

Beside me, Kitty squeezed my fingers for reassurance, and I did the same back, both of us transfixed by the jerky, erratic movements of the ghost behind the mirror. We could still hear the screech of her fingernails, along with something else—a raspy, rattling breathing.

"I . . . I can hear her. God." Kitty groaned.

"I know, isn't it awesome?" Jess asked.

Jess used "awesome" way too loosely.

We kept our eyes fixed on the mirror. Mary jerked her head to the side to eye Jess. Kitty and I were closer to her, but Mary wasn't interested in us. Jess had said that she controlled the ritual, that Mary only answered to the summoning voice. Maybe that meant Mary only wanted to see the person who called her, too.

I could see the excitement on Jess's face. Kitty, Anna, and I wanted to puke, but not Jess. She was happier than I'd seen her in ages. I watched her lean toward the mirror to get a closer look. I wanted to be that cool, that collected.

"Mary, can you hear us? We can hear you," Jess said.

Mary snapped her jaws and lunged at the glass. The mirror bowed out with her. Jess reared back with a yelp, the first sign of true terror I'd seen from her. Kitty and Anna screamed. I began to hyperventilate. I had no idea what just happened. A mirror was cold glass. It was solid. It shouldn't move. But this mirror had stretched like a liquid membrane, like Mary was pushing against a sheet of plastic wrap.

"Why? *Why?* Send it back. *Send it back,*" Anna wailed, tears streaming down her cheeks now. "Enough. I BELIEVE IN YOU, MARY WORTH."

"It won't work from you, it has to be me who dismisses her. Hold on a second," Jess hissed, licking her lips and squirming. I felt Kitty jerk around and I moved my hand up from her fingers to grip her wrist. If the mirror was moving, we were already in over our heads. Kitty breaking the bond would make the situation worse.

"Mary, if you can hear us, talk to us," Jess said, her cheeks flushed red, her eyes enormous in her face.

Mary edged forward, pushing herself against the mirror. She tested the gooey mass with awkward hesitance. Her fingertips pressed on the surface, a jagged fingernail poking through, ripples flowing outward from where it emerged.

Part of Mary was no longer in her world, but in ours.

"Oh, my God," Jess gasped, then barked with laughter. *How could she laugh?* I'd gone so rigid, you could have replaced my spine with a yardstick. Anna silently wept on one side of me, and Kitty had her eyes snapped shut, murmuring "no, no" and shaking her head.

"Talk to us, Mary. Tell us your story," Jess continued.

"What are you doing?" I asked as Jess leaned forward to talk to the ghost. Jess was so bold, so sure of herself. It was like she'd known what to expect from Mary, and if she had...

No. She wouldn't do that. She'd never set us up like that.

"I just want to talk to you. Can you speak, Mary?" Jess prodded.

Mary ignored her, popping another finger through the mirror and cooing as she sent a third, a fourth, and finally a thumb. My throat constricted as Mary's second hand quickly joined the first. They were now free of her glass prison and waving about, her fingers curling over like talons. Mary rasped and rattled, and when I saw the unnerving look on her face, I realized she was laughing.

What would a ghost have to laugh at? I had no answers. Well, no *good* answers, anyway.

"Mary, I...We want to know about you," Jess continued. "About your life. We read your letter to your sister, Constance."

The moment Jess said Constance's name, Mary froze. Pain seemed to cross her face, one gruesome expression followed by another. I heard a faint trill from her side of the mirror, like the high-pitched squeal of a mewling kitten. Jess took it to mean she could continue the questioning.

"Yes. We read about Constance!" Jess paused to collect herself. It was clear by her tone that the ghost's response thrilled her. I jerked my face Jess's way. She was shaking—almost vibrating. It wasn't fear pulsing through Jess's body, it was excitement.

"Jess, stop," I pleaded, but she ignored me.

"We read about Constance's marriage and her move to Boston. And how you thought you'd marry a sheep farmer. And we read about Pastor Starkcrowe and Elizabeth."

"NGGGGAH!" Bloody Mary dove at us, her chittering replaced by furious, punishing bellows. It was hard to tell whether the mention of the pastor, of Elizabeth Hawthorne, or of both had enraged her.

Mary's face tore through the mirror, twisting and writhing feet away from me. Her jaw snapped like a rabid dog's, a string of green saliva hanging from her maw like she hungered for flesh. The candlelight was dim, but I could see every fine line on her face. I could see the dead leaves strewn through her dripping wet hair and the pounding black vein in her temple.

And the smell. When Mary crossed into our world, she polluted the air with a scent too sour, too sweet, and too wet.

There was earthiness, too, like mud and moss. And rot. So much rot.

"Stop it! This isn't safe. Send her away," Anna pleaded. "Please, please."

"We're fine. She can't cross the salt barrier," Jess snapped. "It's moved out a little, but she still can't cross it. Look. *Look!*"

I looked. The salt line was there, but Jess hadn't put it flush to the glass like last time. The line was five or six inches away from the bottom frame of the mirror. Was Jess *trying* to coax Mary out?

If so, Jess and I were going to have some serious problems.

But first, the ghost.

6

Mary let out an angry shriek. We reared as far from the mirror as the tiny bathroom would allow, clinging to one another's hands in desperation. Kitty wriggled like she had during the last summoning. I slid my fingers up to her elbow, gripping hard as she gasped in surprised pain.

"J-Jess, I c-can't... make it stop," Anna stammered.

But Jess was relentless. As she watched Mary test her new freedoms, her smile was gone but her expression was no less intense.

Mary pushed her arms through the glass, her left hand reaching toward the wall, smearing her palm over the beige tiles. The sludge from her open wound drizzled down the crevices of the grout.

Mary rolled her head, shifting her gaze among the four of us, hissing and flicking her tongue. She peered down at the salt line and groaned before reaching her desiccated fingers toward it. The tip of her middle finger grazed the line. Mary screeched, snatching her hand back, like she'd been burned. She ducked behind the mirror with a growl, crouching so we could only see the top of her head and the few fingers she'd looped over the bottom of the mirror's frame. A puddle of water pooled on the counter from where she'd been leaning, tendrils of it snaking its way toward the salt line.

"Almost done, I swear," Jess said. "Mary, can you speak? Can you say something before you have to go?"

Mary's eyes darted to Jess's face. I watched her mouth open. Her lips twitched, like she was trying to make a word, and formed a cracked, misshapen little *O*.

"You can do it. Tell us," Jess said, encouraging Mary with the gentleness of her tone. Jess tried to move closer to the mirror, but Anna yanked back on her arm, keeping Jess pinned against the opposite wall. Jess snarled, but Anna kept her hold even when Jess jerked Anna forward, forcing them closer to the ghost.

Mary's mouth wavered, her lips still puckered. Despite my terror, I quieted. I wanted to hear Mary, too. Mary stood to lean from the mirror, her head popping through the liquid glass as she moaned. Her lips quivered and receded, showing her broken teeth and worm-riddled gums.

Puff.

Mary blew out the candle on the vanity with a tiny puff of fetid air, plunging us into blackness. We screamed, but it was Jess's voice that rang the loudest. "I BELIEVE IN YOU, MARY WORTH."

The bathroom went silent. My heart pounded in my ears, my temples threatening to splinter apart. I wanted to be somewhere where the light never faded. I wanted to erase the name Bloody Mary forever. I wasn't sure I'd ever forgive Jess. She'd put us up to this. She'd moved the salt line. Every awful feeling swarming inside of me was Jess's fault.

"Never. Never again. Do you hear me? Never again, Jess. You're lucky if I'll ever talk to you again." Anna sniffled and began to cry, heart-wrenching sobs.

Jess sighed into the darkness. "Come on, guys. We're fine," she said. "It was scary, but—"

"Turn on the light," I yelled. A rivulet of sweat coursed down my face and over my cheek. I was drenched in sweat. I dropped Kitty's hand to brush my forehead against the back of my arm.

I never should have let Kitty go.

A wail ripped through the room. Mary was there. Somehow, some way, Jess's dismissal didn't work. Maybe it was because the candle was snuffed out. Maybe it was because the salt line was moved, or maybe Mary's murky water had melted through the defense. Whatever the case, without the handhold in place, there were no protective wards left to contain the beast. Kitty scrambled away before I could stop her, stumbling into a wall with a pained thud. I was now closest to the mirror.

Closest to Mary.

Jess flicked on the bathroom light just as Mary's claws raked down my shoulders. It was razor blades through butter, bloody cuts splitting my flesh in crimson tracks. I tried to flinch away, but Bloody Mary reached around my front and jerked me off my feet, dragging me toward the glass, toward the world we had woken behind Anna Sasaki's mirror.

I was going in.

I tried to struggle, to wriggle and fight and slap at Mary's hands, but she'd hooked me too tight. There was no way out. The glass surface rippled and bowed as Mary pulled me in, headfirst, my face pointed at the ceiling. My back struck the sink. I screamed as Mary scraped me across the ledge beneath the mirror, fire shooting along my spine.

Behind me, there was only the ghost and the fog. Mary hoisted me again, and the top of my head crested the surface of the mirror. It slurped on me like a frigid, toothless mouth. Over my forehead, over my brows—the mirror swallowed me into its gullet. Gel flooded my eyes, plunging me into darkness. My friends' panicked screams cut off as my ears were drawn through the quivering glass.

From chaos to empty silence.

I cried out for help as the undulating liquid spilled into my mouth. Farther in, to my shoulders, my chest. The mirror gel had slipped to my waist and was spilling toward my hips. I held my breath as long as I could, until the desperation for air overwhelmed me. Instinct forced my mouth open again and that sour, brackish water rushed into my throat. I gasped, but only to choke. I was going to drown halfway between Mary's world and my own.

Until hands grabbed my feet and pulled. As I slipped back out of the mirror, Mary dug her fingers into my flesh, her nails shredding at my chest. I screamed, gagging as my lungs filled with fluid. A twisted game of tug-of-war pulled me back and forth between my friends and Bloody Mary. My world was shrinking by the moment. It wasn't until my friends gave another mighty haul that the stalemate ended. The ghost lost her grip, her claws torn from my flesh. I spewed onto the floor of Anna's bathroom like the mirror had birthed me from its foul womb.

Anna screamed then, the kind of terrified shrieks reserved for horror movies and personal tragedies. I forced myself up onto my knees, expecting my back to spasm with the movement, but shock had settled in. Though my vision was blurry, I could still see Bloody Mary heaving her way out of the mirror, her blood-smeared fingers clutching onto the frame. She lifted her leg over the bottom, her foot sloshing down onto Anna's floor like she'd emerged from a swamp.

Mary was out.

She chuckled as she forced her way into our world, her movements slow and lumbering one moment and fast and jerky the next. Stringy black hair hung to her elbows, the strands caked to her neck and shoulders. Pale, gray skin hugged her knobby bones, the flesh at her joints worn through. A tattered white dress covered her, splotches of my blood staining the fabric along the ragged sleeves and bust.

"I BELIEVE IN YOU, MARY WORTH! I BELIEVE IN YOU!" Jess screamed from her position near the linen closet, but the words did nothing. Our defenses were obliterated.

Mary's head tilted back as her nostril holes flared to scent the air. Anna shoved past Kitty to get to the door. The two of them fumbled with the knob, but it wouldn't turn. We hadn't locked it, but even if we had, it was to keep people out, not in. Something else was at work here.

I coughed and shook my head, wanting desperately to escape the bathroom, but I had to pause to let my body convulse, my lungs dispelling more of the rank liquid. I glanced up at Jess, hoping she'd stall Mary, but Jess was frozen, staring at the terror lurching our way. Anna was screaming and pounding on the door. Kitty was throwing her weight at the door, trying to rip it from the hinges, but not Jess.

Mary peered down at me and groaned, her hand lifting toward my head like she wanted to stroke my hair. I did the only thing I could think of to protect myself: I reached for the salt box on the floor and whipped a handful at Mary's face.

The moment the salt crystals struck her face, Bloody Mary thrashed and bumbled away, her flesh sizzling, sour-smelling smoke wafting off of her in oily clouds wherever the salt had touched. Mary clawed at her cheeks and forehead in a frantic attempt to remove the salt stuck to her wet skin. I clapped my hands over my ears to block out Mary's deafening wails.

"Go back, GO BACK!" I ordered, my voice cracking.

Mary dropped her hands and fixed her black eyes on me, her thin, leathery lips receding with a hiss. She swung her arm at my head. I took another handful of salt and flung it. She screeched and writhed, smoke fizzling off her body.

I threw more salt, trying to force a retreat. It seemed to be working. Mary turned to put her hands on the mirror frame and began climbing back inside, her foot perched on Anna's sink. Once she had good purchase, she leapt, the watery glass sucking her into its depths. Somehow, I was winning. I scrambled to my feet, my hand rapidly firing salt at the mirror. The gel thickened, the crystals suspended halfway between Mary's world and ours.

I'd hoped when the mirror swallowed Mary, she'd disappear, but she rose up to fill the glass again, the fog behind her whipped into a frenzy. Mary pushed her hands out like she'd grab for me, but there was too much salt embedded in the mirror. Her hands burned on contact. She wrenched them away and shuddered, smoke billowing from her palms, the tips of her fingers peeling like blackened onion skin.

7

I don't know what shook Jess from her stupor, but something
penetrated the fog. She relit the candle by the sink and grabbed
the salt from my hands, placing a thick line beneath the glass.
Whenever she got too close to Mary, the ghost lashed out, but
the mirror had solidified enough that Mary couldn't cross. The
salt thickened the glass to a tar-like consistency.

"Everyone, come here. Turn off the light. I want to try to
dismiss her again," Jess said.

"Oh, screw you. Like w-we're going to trust you again,"
Anna snapped just as Kitty gave the bathroom door another
shove. It popped open like it had never been locked. Kitty and
Anna thrust themselves into the hall, Kitty wheezing, Anna
thanking a higher power for getting her out alive. I glanced at
the mirror behind me. Mary remained, staring at me, hungry
for my blood. Her lip curled and twitched, her eyes devoured
my face, burning my features into her memory.

I could hear Anna sniveling as she climbed the stairs, but Jess's voice rang out, stopping her short. "If you don't help, this thing is going to live in your basement forever. Let's finish this." Anna erupted in stomps and a series of nonsensical threats—she was furious at Jess. But living in a house with an open link to Bloody Mary was sufficient motivation for Anna to return. She resumed her position, taking a moment to wipe her tear-stained face with a towel.

Kitty continued up the stairs, and Jess darted after her to drag her back down to the bathroom. They reappeared a minute later, Kitty stumbling in Jess's wake, her inhaler plugging her mouth, cheeks and eyes red. She looked puffy, too, like she had so many tears swelling inside of her, she might rupture.

Kitty pocketed the inhaler, and Jess herded her into position by the sink. Kitty stood there shaking, her tongue skimming over her lips. No one wanted to do this, but we reformed the summoning circle after Jess flicked off the light. I laced my fingers with my friends', this time leaning as far away from the mirror as I could.

I could still hear the wet rattle of Mary's breath from behind the glass.

There was little ceremony this time. "I believe in you, Mary Worth," Jess said, and we waited for the fog to usher Mary away. Except it didn't. Mary bashed her forehead against the glass, black smears of her blood streaking down in curling rivers. Her fingernails shredded at the pane, two nails snapping off, exposing raw, tender flesh—but Mary remained trapped inside.

She refused to go.

"I believe in you, Mary Worth!" Jess shouted again. Mary plastered her face to the mirror, giving us an unadulterated view of the mushy insides of her nostrils. It was Jess who had given all the summoning commands, but Mary's gaze fixed on me. I'd become the object of her fascination. I shuddered as she eyeballed me, her tongue slithering over the glass to lap at her own blood.

"Oh, my God. Gross," Kitty rasped.

"Wh-what if she never goes? N-never leaves?" Anna stammered.

Jess took a deep breath before jerking her hand away from Anna to break our bond. She braced, probably expecting the mirror to soften and unleash the monster again, but Mary stayed on the other side, her hands pressed to the glass as she stared at me. Jess relaxed, her hand smoothing over her blond head. "We'll figure it out. There's got to be a way to get rid of her. Shauna, are you okay? Does your back hurt?"

My back didn't hurt until Jess mentioned it—then it hurt *a lot*. Mary had scoured those talons over my flesh. A burning pain exploded across my shoulder blades. I swallowed a whimper, feeling faint. I wanted to sit down. I needed to sit down. I let go of Kitty and Anna and sank onto the toilet, my butt scooted forward so I didn't brush my back against the tank.

"I don't feel very good," I admitted.

"She should go to the doctor," Kitty said. Jess waved her off, crouching to peer at me. Jess's thumb and forefinger grabbed my chin, her sharp fingernails biting into my jaw.

"You're pale," she said.

"I'm always pale. Fresh off the slab," I returned, but the joke fell flat, especially when I glanced to my right and saw Mary hovering, her body half-hidden by the mirror frame. She was trying to follow me, but the glass would only let her get so far, so she wedged herself against the side.

Jess inspected my injuries. She leaned over my shoulder to tug my shirt away from my back, but the moment she pulled, I twitched. I was wet, and the fabric had adhered to my open wounds. The slight tug nauseated me enough that I placed my hand against the wall, using the cold of the tile to distract me from my queasiness. It wasn't until Jess let out a groan that I suspected the shirt wasn't stuck to me with water so much as with blood.

"She needs help," Jess said. "But a doctor is going to ask questions. Let's see if we can do anything first. Maybe, like, clean the cuts and bandage them? If it's still really bad we can make something up about an accident or...I don't know. Something."

I was furious with Jess but in too much pain to argue. We could fight later, when I wasn't about to bleed to death in Anna's basement.

"Let's get out of here," Kitty said as she turned on her heel and raced up the stairs.

"Good plan," Anna agreed, her eyes fixed on the mirror.

Jess wrapped her arm around my waist to help me to my feet. I sagged into her side. We shuffled from the bathroom like the slowest three-legged race ever, leaving Mary squirming and hissing in the mirror behind us. Jess managed to get me out of the doorway, but we had to stop when I got dizzy. The exertion made me want to throw up all over again.

"I'm not staying here. Not with her here," Anna proclaimed. I glanced back in time to see Anna grab a sheet from the linen closet and throw it over the mirror. It didn't hang quite right, and she darted in to adjust it so she couldn't see Bloody Mary anymore. When Anna neared the mirror, Mary growled like she knew Anna was there even though she couldn't see her. Anna looked terrified, but she persevered, tucking the sheet under the frame until Mary was fully hidden from view.

Anna closed the door and ran into the hall behind us, her face expressionless. "Let's get out of here. The house. I don't want to be here right now. Let's leave and then figure this mess out." She wriggled her way past me and Jess to go get Kitty.

I wasn't going to stop her. As much as I wanted my back tended, I wanted to get away from Bloody Mary even more.

∞

Kitty wedged a folded towel behind my back so I wouldn't bleed on Jess's car upholstery. Another towel covered the seat so my pants didn't drip everywhere.

We drove toward my house. Every time Jess took a turn, I tensed, and tensing flexed my back, which hurt. Kitty insisted I needed a doctor, but I didn't want to end an already traumatic day in the emergency room. Getting home, and safe, was my top priority.

We said little during the ride. We were too upset, too freaked out. Jess's brow was furrowed like she was deep in thought.

Kitty had her head tilted back with her eyes closed. Anna sat wide-eyed with rage. I'd never seen her look so mad and be so silent.

I was mad, too. I'd nearly gotten killed by Jess's game. I couldn't say for sure Mary had broken free because Jess had moved the salt line. I suspected as much, but really, we hadn't fully summoned Mary on our first attempt. Maybe she would have been able to cross over our way even without those extra inches between salt and mirror. Maybe the water would have come through and eaten away at the line like it had this summoning. There was no way to know.

I wasn't ready to drop Jess as a friend. Not yet. Jess was as upset as the rest of us. Whether it was because I'd gotten hurt or because everyone was going to blame her or because the whole thing had gone so wrong, I didn't know, but it didn't matter. Jess's misery bought her a little slack. Probably not with Anna, though. Or Kitty.

"I still see her. Like, even with my eyes closed, I see her," Kitty said from the backseat.

"Now imagine her in your basement bathroom forever. I'll be able to see her whenever I want," Anna returned.

Jess stayed quiet as she took the last turn to my street. She pulled into the building parking lot and eased into the guest spot. I went to put my hand on the door to let myself out, but Jess insisted on helping me. Pain cut across my shoulders, making me gasp. Jess held me still until I was steady on my feet.

"Her bag's in the trunk. Grab it. House keys are usually in the front pouch," Jess said to Kitty. Kitty ducked behind the car to rummage for my stuff. She pulled out my backpack and pawed through the front section for my keys. Anna plucked them from her hand and jogged ahead of us, first to let me into the base floor and then up into the apartment. Jess and I hobbled after her, Kitty behind us with her hands up to catch me if I fell.

Inside, the apartment wasn't much to look at—boring beige walls, matted beige carpet. The entrance opened into a living room with floor-to-ceiling windows and a small kitchen with a round table and four chairs. Past the living room was a hallway with a bathroom on the right and at the end, a split into two bedrooms. Mine was on the left, Mom's was on the right.

Anna headed down the hall to open my bedroom door, and Jess eased me inside toward the bed. She tried to get me to lie down, but I stopped to drop Anna's towel and peel off my shirt. Putting my arms over my head hurt too much, though, and Jess had to strip me down to my bra and underwear. I felt weird standing around almost naked, but the girls didn't care. Anna tossed my wet pants into the hamper and my shirt into the trash.

Jess helped me onto my bed. I sprawled facedown, and she lifted my hair to get it off my neck. From the doorway, Kitty gasped. At first I thought she was reacting to the cuts in my back, but instead she pointed to my mirrored vanity, her cheeks ballooning out.

"Something flickered. Her. I think I saw her," Kitty said.

My head swiveled and I braced to see Mary's face in the

glass, but there was only the reflection of Anna's head, Jess's back, and my pale pink drapes.

"We didn't summon her here. I don't think that's possible," Jess said.

Anna snorted. "Yeah, she's hanging out in my downstairs forever, remember? Thanks for that, by the way, Jess. Thanks. Not only did you nearly kill Shauna, you've made my house uninhabitable."

Jess whipped her head around to glower at Anna. She'd been quiet to this point, but by the look on her face, that was about to change. "Stop," Jess snapped. "We both know being angry won't fix anything. It's not going to make Shauna's back better. And it's not going to get rid of the thing in your basement. We can fight later, after this is over, but for now, cut the crap, Anna."

"Oh, so *I'm* the one who needs to cut the crap," Anna said. "Me, not you."

"Yeah, you. You're being a bitch. Shauna needs help."

Anna seethed. She stalked a few steps forward, her finger pointing at Jess's face, but Kitty reached out to grab her shoulders, reeling her in like a fish. Kitty turned Anna until she faced my vanity. Anna spun, but not without another shooting glare in Jess's direction. "What?" she demanded.

"J-just watch. Please?" Kitty pleaded, her voice thick with fear. "I swear she flashed by."

The two of them stayed stock-still, peering into my mirror, as Jess disappeared into the hall. I heard her in the bathroom opening cabinets and drawers. I craned my head to see what

Kitty was talking about, but there was nothing in the mirror other than their reflections. There were no shooting lights, no fog, no scary dead faces.

"I don't see anything," Anna said.

Kitty frowned and settled at the foot of my bed, the mattress shifting beneath her weight. She rubbed her palms down her cheeks and rolled her head around on her shoulders. "Maybe I'm seeing things. Sorry. I'm worked up."

"We all are," Anna said, sliding a hand to Kitty's shoulder and squeezing. "I'm going to jump at my own shadow for a long time."

Jess came back into the room with a wet facecloth, my mom's first aid kit, and some antibacterial ointment. She dropped everything on my nightstand except for the washcloth, which she pressed against one of my cuts. It burned like she filled the gash with molten lava. I gritted my teeth, willing myself not to cry out. My hands grabbed handfuls of the blankets beneath me, wadding them up into a tight ball.

"I'm covering this stupid mirror," Anna said a second later. She walked past the bed to tug my bathrobe from the peg on the wall and slung it over the vanity. It was probably for the best; when I got around to being vertical again, I'd planned to do the exact same thing.

Jess pulled away from the first cut and moved to the second in the same agonizing manner. It was an unpleasant few minutes, the room silent. I dropped my head when my eyes began to water. Jess stopped mauling me with the washcloth, but then came the ointment, and that was worse in some ways.

Her finger didn't go into the cuts, but it did press down on the tender skin around them.

"You're not bleeding anymore," Jess said quietly. "It's clotted. She got you good, but I don't think you need, like, stitches. I mean, we can go to the hospital if you want and say you got attacked by a cat, but..."

"A cat? Really? More like a freaking tiger," Anna said. I nearly laughed, but then Jess smeared my wounds with more ointment and I forgot how to be happy about anything, ever.

"She should risk the doctor. Bloody Mary's fingers were dirty and gross," Kitty said, her hand coming to rest on my calf. She gave it a squeeze before pulling up my blanket to cover my bare legs. "She could get a nasty infection. Remember that girl who got that flesh-eating disease on the news? They had to cut off her hands and feet."

"That's up to Shauna," Jess said, opening the first aid kit and pulling out a pair of the big Band-Aids. She tore the packages with her teeth and then placed them over my cuts, gently prodding them to lie flat. "But they are going to ask how she did it. We bring her in for stitches, she says a ghost attacked her, they'll think she's nuts or lying. If she's lying, then they're going to wonder why. Who's abusing her. Her mom? Her boyfriend? Us? It's just... I get why you're saying it, and if Shauna wants to go I'll drive her, but it's a big, ugly can of worms. We need to come up with something they'll believe before we go."

I glanced at my friends. For all that we didn't like admitting it, Jess was right. Bloody Mary was something the world should know about. She was something we should be able to talk about and warn people away from, but we couldn't. No one would believe us.

"I'll wait," I said, dropping my head down into one of my pillows. "If I need a doctor later, we'll go, but for now let's see how I do." Everyone nodded, all of us wearing matching frowns. Earlier, I'd feared my friends would be torn apart by what happened at Anna's house, but I realized then it wouldn't happen for one reason. We shared a ghostly burden.

8

Jess flung the red notebook onto the floor with a frustrated sigh. She'd been leafing through it in hopes of finding something that'd help with Bloody Mary, but she'd come up empty. It wasn't surprising; most of what she had in there was for making Mary appear, not disappear.

Kitty also tried to help by scouring the Web on my laptop. Searching for Bloody Mary yielded a bunch of Halloween sites, so she switched to a general ghost search. I was prone in bed with Anna wedged onto the mattress at my side while we looked for clues on her phone.

Sadly, the Internet failed us.

A lot of what we found involved sites charging exorbitant fees to purify a house against negative spiritual activity. Many claimed to be professionals, but it was hard to take them seriously when their Web sites had horror movie sound tracks and

blinking cartoon ghost banners. Also, their "real ghost" pho-
tography sections were typically floating orbs or mysterious
shadows. Nothing we found was Bloody Mary–caliber.

"I think I'll head home for a bit. Call Aunt Dell and maybe
try to talk to Cordelia Jackson again," Jess said. "I don't have
any leads, but they might."

"Why not call them from here?" Anna asked, her tone sharp.
"If we're suffering, it's only fair you suffer with us."

I could tell Jess wanted to yell by the way her molars ground
together, her cheek twitching like she had a nervous tic. Her
eyes swept to me for a moment before she took a deep breath,
her nostrils pinching together. "Because, smart-ass, I don't have
Aunt Dell's number on my cell."

"Who's Cordelia Jackson?" Kitty asked, cutting Anna off
before she could provoke Jess again.

Jess whipped her head around to eyeball her, her expression not altogether friendly. "She's a girl from Solomon's Folly
who summoned Bloody Mary a while ago. She hung up on me
last time I called, but maybe if I explained what happened to
Shauna..." Jess's voice trailed as she swiped her stuff off the
floor. "You cool if I go, Shauna? I'll call you tonight."

I nodded and glanced at the girls. I was afraid both of them
would ask for a ride home and leave me alone to suffer horrible
Mary paranoia and an aching back, but neither Kitty nor Anna
looked inclined to follow. Maybe it was a safety in numbers
thing. Maybe they were too mad at Jess.

"Drive safe," I said. Jess nodded, heading for my front door.

"Later," Kitty called after her.

Anna said nothing.

The front door clicked, and Anna shot up from the bed next to me with a shriek. She went to my doorway and peered down the hall, staring at the closed door like it had grown fangs and a tail. "Thank God. I want to smack her for being so stupid. I get it, we agreed to do it, but if we knew what we were in for? Yeah, no. No, never."

"I'm not sure Jess knew what we were in for, either," I said, slowly pushing myself up from the bed. "I guess we should have asked better questions." My wounds felt tight and sore, but I ignored the pain and forced myself onto my feet. Kitty reached out to steady me, and I cast her a grateful smile when her hand cupped my elbow. "Thanks."

"I have the right to be mad," Anna insisted. "You can't tell me I don't."

"You do. I'm mad, too," I said. "I will be for a while, but I'm not going to say this is all on Jess. Mostly, yeah, but not all." I felt sticky and gross from my bath in Mary's mirror, and all I wanted to do was shower in steamy hot, fresh water until I was clean again, but there was no way I was doing that in a bathroom in an empty house. "Do you guys mind sticking around while I take a shower? I'll borrow Mom's car later to drive you home. I just . . . you know. In case I need help."

Anna nodded before going into my living room and throwing herself on the couch. I heard the TV turn on a moment later. "That's fine. But I swear, Shauna, I don't know if I want to hang out with Jess again," Anna called down the hall.

I had no answer for her, so I tottered my way to the bathroom,

Kitty at my side to keep me steady. I was about to go in, but the moment my foot crossed the threshold, my body tensed. I didn't want to take another step. That stupid brass mirror over the sink. It was nearly as big as Anna's, and all I could picture was Mary lurking inside its depths, ready to pull me back into her world.

"Guys? Can you come in with me when I . . . not when I shower, but when I go into the bathroom? I'm afraid," I admitted.

They understood. Anna got up from the couch to grab the salt shaker from the kitchen. She shook the salt at me when she trotted down the hall. Kitty stayed at my back as the three of us shuffled into the bathroom as a collective, terrified unit. My heart was in my throat when I glanced at the mirror, but it quickly sank when I saw a normal reflection. Behind me, Kitty and Anna let out their own relieved sighs.

"Here, let me," Anna said as she brushed by me to place a thin salt line beneath the mirror. She was meticulous, shaking out the grains once, twice, three times.

"Thanks, Anna. I appreciate it," I said as they headed back to the living room.

Even though we'd checked the glass, even though Anna had salted, I kept my attention fixed on the tile floor as I undressed. It felt better to avoid reflective surfaces—less chance of seeing something I didn't want to see.

I stepped over a basket of Mom's bubble bath stuff to get into the tub, sliding the shower door along its golden runners. The panels had textured, wavy glass, so I could see colored shapes through them but not details. I was fine with that—the door acted as a great, blurry barrier between me and the mirror. I turned the shower on full-throttle, anxious to burn Bloody Mary's taint from my skin. As soon as the water hit my bandages, I yelped; that much heat on my cuts was more than a little unpleasant. I bore it, though, focusing on the water swirling down the drain rather than the discomfort.

The bathroom slowly filled with pale gray steam. My face tilted toward the showerhead and I sighed, relieved, but then a mystery glob hit my forehead and slithered down my face. My eyes flew open. I reached up to touch my cheek, dismayed to find mud smearing my fingertips. The showerhead sputtered and coughed, water gurgling and struggling inside the pipes. The spout twisted in its base like a furious metallic serpent.

There was another burp from the pipes. A rank, rotten odor spilled out into the bathroom. I recoiled, my hands covering my nose and mouth, the hairs on the back of my neck bristling. I recognized this stench. It was decay. It was sour and sweet and meaty and wrong.

It was *her*. I smelled *her*.

"No. No," I moaned, whipping my head back and forth. She couldn't be here. This had to be some horrible cosmic joke, a terrible coincidence that the building's pipes backed up exactly the same day we'd summoned a ghost. Another wad of sludge spewed from the shower to splash my shoulder and front. I reached for the faucet to turn the water off.

That was when I saw her.

Mary stood on the other side of the shower door. Her image was distorted—a blur of black hair, white dress, and gray and yellow skin. How? How had she come out of the mirror past Anna's salt line? Was it because we had no handhold or candle? I could reason out how she'd gotten through the mirror earlier, how we'd failed. But how was it she was here now with no summoning, no candle, no hand-holding?

She didn't move toward me. She didn't make a sound. But I screamed at the top of my lungs, backing into the corner of the tub, banging on the wall for my friends. Panic bubbled up inside of me, a geyser of confusion that left me feeling light-headed. I heard Kitty and Anna scrambling down the hall. They were coming to help, and had I not been so terrified, I'd have appreciated exactly how brave that was.

"Open the door," Anna yelled. I could hear the doorknob twisting and rattling as they fussed with it, but it wouldn't budge.

I hadn't locked it.

They hadn't locked it.

Mary had locked it.

Kitty and Anna shoved at the door with all their weight, but the hinges wouldn't give. They squealed and bent, but the screws held tight. "It won't . . . it can't," shouted Kitty. "SHAUNA! ARE YOU OKAY?"

No, I wasn't okay. The pipes of the shower groaned in agony as the showerhead vomited thick mud. I wanted to turn the faucet off, but I was too scared to move. I whimpered and huddled down in the tub, my hands covering my face, but I kept peeking over them. I was too scared of dying *not* to peek.

Crouched as I was, I caught sight of my mom's bath supplies, including a slim tube of bath salts leaning against the basket.

Scented Epsom salts. The crystals were purple, but hopefully their color and purpose didn't matter.

Kitty and Anna were still pounding on the door, and I could hear something hard slamming against the wood like they were trying to knock it down, but it wasn't going anywhere. I was alone in this, and that meant I had to stop shrinking. I let out another sob and stood, steeling myself to open the shower door with shaking fingers.

As I touched the handle, Bloody Mary let out an earsplitting cry.

I screamed and thudded down into the tub as she pressed one of her hands to the door, smearing the pads of her fingers against the panes. I got a close-up look at the black gouge across her palm. The skin near the cut bubbled with moving lumps. My stomach churned as a beetle wormed its way out of her flesh.

I had to get to the salt before things worsened. I wrenched the door aside and dove for the basket. My chin was tucked to my chest so she couldn't slash my throat if she swiped at me. I left my back exposed despite my injuries. It was better than giving her access to my front. My fingers wrapped around the lavender-colored tube of salts. I ripped off the top, frantically flinging the crystals around the bathroom.

But Mary wasn't in the bathroom. I heard a hiss. I craned my neck toward the sound. Mary was gazing at me from inside the shower door. She'd never been freely standing in the room. The hand, the beetle, all of her was trapped inside the glass.

I fumbled my way over the edge of the tub, tossing salts at the glass door so she couldn't follow. She writhed as the salts struck the textured glass, but she never tried to poke through the door. Behind me, clumps of mud continued to sputter and spew over the tub.

The moment my bare feet touched the linoleum floor, Mary moved. She left the shower door and reappeared in the mirror above the sink. Before she'd been a blur of shapes and color in the textured glass; now she was as sharply defined as my own reflection. She glared at me, the sliver of her upper lip twitching, the flesh cracked open, oozing a trail of yellow slime down the corner of her mouth.

"Go away," I shouted, tossing another handful of bath salts at the mirror. *"Go away!"*

Mary smiled, the thin skin of her cheeks stretching tight over her skull. The veins at her temples pulsed black, as if a twisted, distorted life still fueled her body. Her dry, reptilian laughter grew louder and louder. My misery amused her. I couldn't take it anymore. I couldn't stand her being there. I couldn't stand her finding my fear so very entertaining.

I whipped around to grab the freestanding toilet paper holder from the floor. The heavy iron hit the mirror like a baseball bat, and shards of glass rained down around me.

9

As soon as the glass stopped falling, the door unlocked. Mary was appearing without a summoning, manipulating objects, haunting glass, and skipping from surface to surface. None of this were we prepared to handle. I could explain none of it.

Anna and Kitty barged in but stopped short when they saw me standing muddy and naked in the middle of the floor. I yanked a towel off of the towel bar and wrapped it around myself, shivering when it brushed against my bandages.

"Is she in here?" Anna asked, waving the shaker of table salt back and forth from the doorway. I shook my head and motioned them back into the hall so I could leap over the shattered glass to join them.

Kitty stuck her head inside to peer around the bathroom before moving. She looked from the tub to the shards on the floor. I followed her gaze, frowning at the sharp, spiky pieces of glass. One mirror down, but there were so many others. Would

I have to shatter them all? My vanity? The tall, standing mirror in my mother's bedroom? What was stopping Mary from climbing out of them right this instant?

"Kitty, move," Anna said from the hall. I leapt over the remnants of the mirror and onto the hallway carpet. Anna pressed past me with her salt to stand in the doorway, like she expected something else to go wrong. I expected something to go wrong, too. My eyes drifted down the hall. She could be anywhere. Here now.

Good God.

"Why is this happening?" Kitty asked, her voice sounding strangled.

"I don't know." I sank down onto the floor, my body smeared with mud and gunk, my stomach so tense it cramped. I dropped my head into my hands and stared through my splayed fingers, my attention fixed on the broken shards of mirror. I wished Jess had known what could happen so she could have prepared us, so we would have known to run long and run far to get away from Bloody Mary.

Then it hit me. Maybe Jess *had* known. The pictures on the wall. She'd taken the pictures down. Why would she suspect Mary could be anywhere other than a proper mirror? She'd said safety, but that was a bizarre leap to make.

"Oh, no. Come on," I whispered. "No."

I propelled myself off the floor and jogged to my room, frantically searching for my phone, never once turning my back on my covered mirror. My cell was still in my backpack, and I tugged it out and dialed. Kitty and Anna ran in after me, but I ignored them, pacing until I heard Jess's voice over a loud rap sound track from her car stereo.

"She's here, Jess. Mary was in my bathroom taunting me. How'd you know to move the pictures off Anna's wall?" I demanded.

Jess turned the radio down. I could see her expression in my head—the knitted brow, the pinch at the corners of her mouth. "Oh, my God, are you okay?"

"Why did you move the pictures, Jess?" I repeated.

She sighed. "Okay, so I...Cordelia," she blurted.

"Cordelia what?" I eased down onto my bed. Kitty came to sit beside me. Anna hovered in the bedroom doorway, glancing over her shoulder every once in a while, convinced Mary would come lurching after us from the bathroom. She gripped the salt container in her hand, her thumb skimming back and forth over its top.

"She was haunted by Mary for a long time," Jess answered. "Like, I didn't want that to happen. That wasn't what I was trying to do."

"I thought Cordelia hung up on you when you called," I said.

"She did after I told her I wanted to summon Mary, but... Look, Shauna. I didn't want anyone to get hurt, I swear. It was supposed to be a cool thing, but it went weird. Cordelia said Mary was after her. That she could see Mary in glass and shiny stuff. So that's why I took the pictures down."

"Why was she haunted for a long time?"

The silence on Jess's end grew uncomfortable. "I don't know. She just said Mary never left her alone. She followed her in mirrors and glass. For years. Mary was still following her the last time I called."

I went silent. Mary was following me in mirrors and glass, too. If Cordelia was stuck with her for years, was I? In a terrible, selfish way I hoped Mary was stuck on Kitty or Anna. But they'd gone into the living room while I'd showered. I was the one Mary had come after.

Me.

Mary was on *me.*

"I'm sorry."

"Shut up, Jess."

I sucked in a deep breath and counted to ten. I felt tears welling; I didn't want to cry. Not anymore. I'd cried enough already. Instead I clung to my anger, feeling it swell hot and bright behind my eyes. Jess had put our lives at risk because she wanted to play a stupid game. "Here's what you're going to do, Jess. Text me Cordelia Jackson's phone number. Then find out everything you can about Bloody Mary. Origins. Everything. And Jess, if you screw me over again . . ."

I didn't finish the sentence. I didn't know how to finish it. I'd what? Not talk to the person with the most information about Mary? I needed all the help I could get.

"Yeah, of course. I'm going to help, Shauna. I'll figure it out. I'll help you with anything you need," Jess said.

"Right now I need to not talk to you. If you find anything out, text me," I barked before ending the call. Anna and Kitty peered at me, questions all over their faces. My phone buzzed with a text message—Cordelia's number. I glanced at the numbers. Cordelia had information that I wasn't sure I was ready to hear.

"This woman, she was haunted by Bloody Mary for a long time. That's why Jess knew to take the pictures down. Cordelia saw Mary in glass and other shiny stuff," I explained before dialing the number. Anna and Kitty shared a look, but they stayed quiet as I waited for Cordelia to pick up. I waited. And waited. It rang six or seven times, and I was about to hang up when a deep female voice rasped a hello at me.

"Cordelia? Cordelia Jackson?"

"What?" was the flat response.

She wasn't a kind-sounding woman. Her voice was gravelly, like she'd smoked for too long or talked too little.

"H-hi," I stammered. "My name is Shauna O'Brien. I'm friends with Jess McAllister, who called you about summoning Bloody Mary."

The line went dead in my hand. Kitty reached out to pat my shoulder, and while I appreciated the sentiment, I brushed her aside. I didn't want comfort right now. I wanted answers, and this woman in Solomon's Folly was the only one who could give me any. I redialed. It didn't take Cordelia long to pick up a second time.

"Go away," she snapped.

"Mary's on me. She followed me after we summoned her. Please, help me," I said, talking as fast as I could to get it all in before she hung up.

"Are you local like your friend?" she demanded.

The question took me off guard, but I nodded in response. "Yes, I'm from Bridgewater."

Cordelia went quiet. I could hear her deep, even breathing. "Forty-seven Nickel Street in the Folly, gray house. Black windows. Until then, avoid everything shiny. *Everything.*" And she was gone again.

Part of me wanted to go see her right then, but Mom had planned a night of tacos and Sandra Bullock movies. If I bailed, she'd know something was wrong. The other problem was a ride. Mom needed her car, and relinquishing the keys required an explanation.

"Hey, can either of you drive me out to Solomon's Folly tomorrow after school? I know it's far, but I want to talk to Cordelia. It sounds like she might help me." I jotted down the address on a piece of paper by my nightstand. I could have asked Jess to take me, but I wasn't ready for her company. Apologies or not, she'd screwed me over.

"Can't. Dentist appointment at two tomorrow. I'm getting dismissed from school," Anna said. She murmured an apology before disappearing into the hall. A moment later, I heard her in the kitchen shuffling around, the door to a closet opening and then closing.

"I can," Kitty said. "No problem." Kitty didn't often drive because Jess was our chauffeur, but she did have one of her dad's cars at her disposal whenever she needed it—usually the red SUV with the sunroof.

"Thanks."

I retucked the towel and went out to see what Anna was up to. I found her standing in front of the open bathroom door with a broom and dustpan in one hand, the salt shaker in the other. She scowled at the sea of glass in front of her.

"Man, your mom's going to be pissed," she said.

"Maybe." I didn't have an excuse for the mirror, though I was leaning toward telling her it happened while I was at school—like it fell off the nail because our downstairs neighbors got too rowdy again.

Anna stopped eyeing the wreckage long enough to turn around to offer us salt. "I'll get this cleaned up if you guys will watch me in case . . . you know."

Kitty snagged the salt from her and sat on the carpet, her gaze swinging my way. "Y-yeah. I'll watch. I'm . . . Shauna, are you okay? What did Cordelia say?"

"She gave me her address and said to avoid all shiny surfaces." After seeing Mary in the shower doors, the suggestion made sense. At least she hadn't passed through to grab me, so maybe regular glass restricted her more than straight mirrors? Her possession of the showerhead was more understandable, too, since that was stainless steel, which was reflective. The doorknobs were brass, so maybe that's how she locked us in and out at Anna's place and here.

I glanced down the hall. Family pictures—shiny frames. The television in the living room—shiny screen. The windows— shiny panes. The more I looked, the bigger the problem grew. Silverware, computer screens, the stove. The microwave. The car. My cell phone. My hair clips. Anna's glasses. Anything plastic, anything glass, anything metal. Which was everything. Mary could be anywhere.

What was I going to do? I couldn't escape all of that! I was exhausted, scared, and in pain. Was I supposed to pitch a tent in the middle of the woods? Even then, wouldn't the zipper be shiny? Did she really mean *everything* shiny?

"Holy crap," I whispered. All I wanted to do was lie down on my stomach and go to sleep. I hated Mary, I hated what we'd done, I even hated Jess. I was covered in mud, I couldn't shower, and...

"Shauna?" Kitty's voice stopped me from spiraling deeper. She smiled tightly and nodded at the bathroom. "When Anna's done sweeping, if you want I'll sit in the bathroom with some salt so you can shower. I won't look, but you're all...you know. I'm sorry about the shiny thing. I'm sorry about all of it."

"Yeah, it's...I still want to punch Jess," Anna said between sweeps.

I swallowed hard and nodded, my face turned away from them so they couldn't see that I was two seconds from losing it. "Thanks, guys. Thanks for sweeping, Anna," I said. "I'll be right back." Before either of them could follow me, I went back to my room and threw myself into my computer chair, wheeling it as far away from my vanity as possible.

I looked out my window to stare at Mom's empty parking spot. She'd be home soon, and I realized I'd never warned her that we had company. She'd be pissed if I didn't tell her and she only had tacos for two. Plus, I had to borrow the car to drive Kitty and Anna home. She deserved fair warning.

I called her at work and left her a disjointed message. "Hey, Mom. Uhh. Came home from school with the girls and the bathroom mirror was broken. I'm cleaning it up now, but we'll need to get a new one. And Jess left Anna and Kitty here with no ride, so I have to borrow the car when you get home. We can do tacos after still, if that's cool. Bye." I hung up, glad my mother didn't have to work tonight.

10

Clean and rebandaged, I sank into the couch with Anna and Kitty, exhausted. The TV droned on, filling in for our silence. Words couldn't quite capture how messed up our situation was.

Mom walked in a little while later with a family-sized box of tacos and a movie. She must have gotten my message about Kitty and Anna. I hadn't asked them to stay for dinner, but by the longing looks they gave the Taco Bell box, it was clear they planned on sticking around. I didn't mind. Two more people to fight off the pop-up ghost.

"Soup's on!" Mom said, slinging her coat over the back of the chair and leaving our dinner on the table. She ducked from the kitchen to inspect the bathroom. Anna had done a great job cleaning it, so there wasn't much for her to see. "Damn. I guess we'll get another mirror this weekend."

"The glass is in the garbage," I said, abandoning the couch to grab plates from the cabinet. The girls followed me, both of them familiar enough with my apartment that Kitty went for the silverware and Anna poured us drinks.

"Soda, Mrs. O'Brien?" Anna offered.

"No, thanks. I'll grab a water," Mom said, coming out to join us. She paused by the refrigerator to get her own drink. "How's everyone doing?" Our silence spoke for us. "That good, huh?"

"Drama. Stupid girl drama," I said, piling three tacos onto my plate and loading up on hot sauce.

Mom motioned to the three of us to eat without her; she was unpacking her bag from work. "You're short a body. I take it Jessica's the girl drama?"

"Jess is channeling her demon side again," I replied.

"It'll work out. It always does," she said, sliding into the seat across from me. Her shoes flew out from under the table to thud against the opposite wall. The sound made me, Kitty, and Anna flinch. Mom rubbed her nylon-clad toes. "Today was a real bi— bear. At least we get to watch some quality TV tonight, huh? End the day the right way."

"What movie did you get?" Kitty asked, and the conversation drifted from Mom's movie to romantic comedies to what we last saw in the theaters. I tried to concentrate on the chatter instead of my looming dread, but it was hard. Especially when I picked up my chicken taco and saw Mary's face on my white dinner plate.

It was fleeting—a glimpse of black eyes and stringy hair— but it was enough to make me choke. Chicken taco flew down the wrong pipe, and I coughed and wheezed for air. Mom jumped up from her seat to whack me on the back, her hand striking my new cuts. It hurt so much, I spit guacamole at Kitty, accidentally blasting her cheek with green goop.

"Shauna, are you okay? Honey?"

I pointed at my throat and gurgled, though it wasn't a breathing problem so much as I couldn't believe what I'd just seen. In my plate. All that panic and worry about Mary being everywhere returned twofold. I dropped the remains of my taco and reached for my soda to swallow past the choking sensation.

I stopped. The glass. If Mary was in my plate, what would stop her from being in my glass?

Desperate and miserable, I went to the sink and turned on the water. I could feel my mom watching me as I splashed my face, cupping water in my palms to drink. Yes, the sink was chrome, but there was distance between the faucet and the base. I could keep my hands midway without touching anything.

Was this how it had to be from now on?

"Are you okay?" my mom repeated.

Another splash of water and I nodded. "Be fine. Just a long day. Sorry about the guac, Kitty."

"It's okay," Kitty said in a slightly disgusted tone.

"It's been a crappy day. Seems appropriate," Anna said.

Face soaked, cheeks so warm they felt like they were on fire, I retook my seat. I nudged my plate away and grabbed another taco, holding it over a napkin. In a way, I hoped Mary would pop up somewhere my mom could see. The group had agreed to keep it quiet, but if Mom had a good, hard look at Mary by no fault of mine, it'd be hard to refute my rampaging ghost claims.

It was like Kitty psychically caught my vibe, because I felt her hand brush my leg under the table. It was a small pat, but I knew what it meant, and my eyes flicked her way. We shared a look before going back to our food, much quieter now, my mom's gaze ping-ponging around the table.

"I'm not getting something," she said.

"Jess is a jerk," I said, though my voice was ragged from choking. It reminded me a little of Cordelia's voice, all grizzled and hoarse. If Cordelia looked anything like she sounded, she was one terrifying woman.

"She's always been a little difficult, but you've smoothed it out before. I'm sure this will be fine," Mom said.

I had to wonder if Mom would say that if she knew what Kitty, Anna, and I knew.

∽

"You okay over there? You're off tonight," Mom asked after we drove Kitty and Anna home.

"Yeah. Just stressed," I said.

Mom pulled the car into our parking lot right as the peepers started screaming, a telltale sign summer was around the corner. She stifled a yawn behind her hand before rooting through her purse for the house key. I saved her by producing mine from my pocket, and she took it with a grateful smile. "Movie time! Hope I don't pass out on you. Your old lady is feeling pretty old right now."

"It's okay if you do. Just don't snore."

We walked into the house side by side, Mom looping an arm through mine. We walked up the stairs like that, and strangely, it was the only time I'd felt even slightly relaxed since Mary came into my life. Mom made me feel safe despite the things I'd seen and done, and I desperately hoped whatever Mary wanted from me, she kept my mom out of it. She shouldn't be my collateral damage.

Mom opened the front door and stepped aside to let me in. Every light was off in the apartment. I expected a corpse to lunge at me from the darkness, but it was still. Then I felt a soft brush of lips across my temple. My hand swung up on instinct to knock away whatever it was. Except it was Mom. I'd just thwacked her upside the head.

"Oh. Oh, crap. Mom, I'm so sorry. I—"

"Shauna! I was just going to kiss you! What in God's name is *wrong* with you?"

She flicked on a light so I could see her death glare, and I melted into the floor. "I'm s-sorry. You startled me."

"Apparently. You're awfully jumpy tonight. Is something going on? Between this and doing the tango in your seat at dinner, you're worrying me."

"No, I'm fine. I'm sorry I hit you."

"Spill it," she demanded, arms folding over her chest.

The way she looked at me, I knew I wasn't wriggling out of it. I was so tired from the day and so annoyed with Jess and scared of Mary that I shrugged and walked toward my room. When Mom protested my leaving midconversation, I lifted my hand for her to follow. Fine. She wanted to know? I'd show her. Jess had told me we couldn't tell our parents because no one would believe us. Well, if Mom saw it, how was she going to dispute it?

I went straight for the vanity and tugged off the robe. There was no hesitation because I had a point to prove. My reflection looked back at me. Mom stood at my side, looking between me and the mirror like one of us would sprout wings. I backed onto my bed and sat, waiting for the horrible face to appear.

"Yes?" Mom pressed.

"Just give me a minute," I said.

And she did, but nothing happened. Either Mary was off mauling other unsuspecting girls or she was toying with me. *Of course* the one time I wanted her here, she played coy. I raked my fingers over my scalp.

"Jess walked away from us today. Not, like, permanently, but it's hard. She's still hanging out with Bronx because of Marc and there's drama. Kitty's upset and blah, blah. It's all super dumb. I'm not sure she's going to be our friend for much longer," I said. It was all true so I didn't feel totally awful saying it, but it didn't come close to the snarling, hissing, blood-hungry bulk of my problem.

Mom peered at me. She knew it wasn't that simple. I must have looked suitably forlorn, though, because she came to sit beside me, her hand rubbing over my thigh. "You guys have been friends for a long time. I bet she'll think about it and come crawling back."

"Sure," I said, but really, I didn't care if Jess fell off the face of the planet. Thinking her name was enough to make my jaw clench.

Mom gave me a couple minutes to brood before she stood up and offered me her hand. "Let's go. That movie was burning a hole in my bag earlier. There's nothing you can do about Jess now, so let's hang out. Maybe you'll feel better by bedtime, okay?"

I laced my fingers with hers and followed her into the living room. I didn't care about the movie, but I wasn't going to pass up an opportunity to cuddle with my mom, especially knowing what could be waiting for me on the other side of the glass.

11

Mom passed out halfway through the movie. I watched the rest of it with her head propped against my arm, my eyes pointed at the TV but not really seeing it. When the credits rolled, I gently shoved her shoulder to wake her and glanced at the clock. It was almost eleven, and I hadn't touched my homework.

Mom yawned and shuffled her way to her bedroom with a muffled, "G'night. Love you." I told her I loved her and ducked into my room. Normally, I'd close the door and kill the lights and sprawl into my pillows like an overtired toddler, but as I started to follow the routine, I thought better of it. I left it open. If something else happened, I wanted to be able to call for her. I was afraid of the monster in my closet for the first time since I was nine years old.

I tossed the bathrobe over the mirror again. For good measure, I grabbed the salt from the kitchen and lined the bottom of the mirror. My hand shook as I poured. I tried not to notice.

Behind me, my cell phone vibrated. There were two messages. The first one was from Bronx, saying I should call him. It had come in two hours ago. I didn't respond for two reasons, the first being the hour, the second being that Kitty and Bronx's dating drama was pretty much the last thing on my mind with my big fat Mary problem. I'd handle their boyfriend-girlfriend situation another day.

The other text message was from Jess. *So sorry. Go to this site.* The link was to the Solomon's Folly Historical Society. Despite my fatigue and the glare on my computer, I was curious. I swallowed past my trepidation and typed in the address. An old photograph loaded on the screen. A dozen people stood in front of a stone church. I could tell by the dress of the parishioners that this was taken a long time ago. It reminded me of the Civil War portraits I'd seen in my American history textbook.

It was an imperfect photo; the background, the church, and the left half of the group were clear. The people on the right side, though, had small water spots on them that distorted their images. It reminded me of Mary Worth's letter. Why did everything to do with her have to be so very *wet*?

I studied the picture. On the far left was a handsome man with a tall hat, a hand clasped on a walking stick, a long black jacket hanging to his knees. The way he'd tucked his other hand beneath his coat lapel suggested pride, like these were his people. I glanced down at the picture description. *From left to right, Pastor Edmond Renault, Mrs. Hannah Worth, Miss Mary Worth, Miss Constance Worth (Simpson), Mr. Thomas Adderly, Miss Elizabeth Hawthorne (Jenson), Rest Unknown.* My gaze skipped from the names to the faces. Hannah Worth was as Mary described her mother in her letter—blond and perfect in a fairy-tale princess way. Her hair was wrapped around her head in a fat golden braid, her nose was long and thin over wide lips. Her arm extended to her side to loop around the shoulders of a girl.

Mary Worth. She was holding on to Mary Worth.

I stared. The girl in the picture looked nothing like my nightmare-come-to-life. She was pretty like her mother, but darker all around, with hair that looked black or chestnut. Her eyes were big and dark against her pale skin. She was not overly thin, but not big, either. She was healthy, robust, so at odds with the skeletal ghost from the mirror. The most startling thing about her, though, was how young she looked. She was my age in this picture. How could a girl like Mary end up so monstrous?

One by one, I studied the rest of the faces. Constance resembled her mother with her flaxen hair, though she had a rounder face like her sister. She clasped Mary's hand, the gesture telegraphing their affection. Thomas Adderly was somewhat goofy-looking, with a too-serious face and slumping shoulders on a wide, heavy frame. The picture was enough to make me believe he had warts and onion breath as Mary described. As for Elizabeth, she was plain, with dark hair and dark eyes. Her cheekbones were a little too high, her face a little too angular to be traditionally pretty. Her expression was flinty, too, and cold.

I e-mailed the link to myself so I could print a copy at the school library tomorrow. A squealing noise from under my feet seized my muscles. It took a moment to recognize the sound of the toilet flushing in the downstairs apartment, the pipes shuddering in the walls.

It was going to be a long night.

I climbed into bed, my hand reaching for the lamp beside my bed table, but I couldn't bring myself to turn it off. Complete darkness scared me, so I dug my head in between my pillows and turned my back to the mirror. The thick comforter went around my shoulders, and for a moment, I imagined that blankets covering my body and my mom sleeping down the hall were enough to keep me safe.

I almost had myself convinced until I heard the scratching. It was faint and slow at first, but as the seconds ticked by, it grew more intense.

Scree.

Screeeeee.

Screeeeeeeeeee.

It sounded like the fingers of a tree branch squealing over a window pane. I tried blocking it out by huddling deeper into my mattress, the pillow bunched up around my ears to stifle the noise, but it was too shrill, too high-pitched to ignore.

Scree. Scree scree screeee. SCREEEE.

She was back. A terrible part of me had hoped she'd gone after Jess or Kitty or Anna tonight, but no, it was me again. Mary was in my room, and the only thing that separated me from her was a bathrobe and a line of Morton salt.

Scree. Scree.

THUD!

I shot up in bed, the cuts on my back screaming. My vanity trembled. My plastic bucket of makeup tumbled over, tubes of lipstick, gloss, eyeliner, foundation, and perfume scattering across the tabletop and rolling to the floor.

I picked up the salt from my bedside table and swung my legs over the bed. My eyes darted to the hall, half expecting my mother to run in and yell at me for making too much noise, but she was fast asleep, the lull of her radio drowning out Mary's return.

My fingers itched to fling salt at the vanity, but I couldn't waste such a precious resource. I slid out of bed and edged toward the mirror, but the moment I neared it, the vanity stopped rattling. I waited, expecting Mary to shriek or shake the mirror or do something else to screw with me, but she'd gone still.

I brushed the tears off my cheeks and lifted my hand toward the robe. There was no way I could sleep in this house if she was in the mirror. I counted down from three and jerked the robe aside. There was no face there, but written backward in sludgy black tar was a single word that sent me falling to the floor and sobbing.

MINE.

⚬⚬⚭

It was not a restful night. Three hours of sleep on my couch, and every thump, thud, scratch, and creak in the building sent me scrambling for the salt container. If I wasn't quick on my toes, Bloody Mary would scoop me up in her claws, the field mouse to her big, dead hawk. When Mom saw me on the couch at six the next morning, she gave me a nudge. I jumped up like she'd electrocuted me.

"You're being weird again. I don't like it. What the hell are you doing on the couch?"

"Had a nightmare," I said, knowing it was a weak answer and not caring. I shuffled to the kitchen, pretending I couldn't see her concerned scowls.

"I'm off," Mom said. "If you need me, call me. I'll leave my phone on. I'm worried about you, kiddo."

❧

I was on my way to my third class when a hand clapped on my shoulder from behind. I yelped so loudly, a hallway of heads turned my way. Bronx muttered an apology as he fell into step beside me, a stack of books tucked under his arm. "Hey, sorry to scare you. Needed to ask you something."

"Hey," I said. I didn't want to talk to Bronx, but there was no way to say that without sounding like a bridge troll, so I stepped out of the way of the crisscrossing traffic, angling my back against the wall. Bronx followed, and for a moment, I looked up and down the hall, paranoid that Kitty would see us together.

People cleared out as the bell rang again. Apparently, I was going to be late to my third class. I dropped my bag to the floor as Bronx moved to stand opposite me in the now-empty hallway, his back pressed to the windows.

The main body of our school was two floors of classrooms, the gym, the auditorium, and the cafeteria. Between the main building and the recent addition, there was a long, curving hallway, where we currently stood. One side was all windows, overlooking the football and soccer fields. The other side had two bathrooms and a computer lab.

Bronx leaned against the glass like it wasn't a big deal. I envied his calm, but then, he hadn't just spent the last day warding off ghost chicks. "I got a weird-ass message from Kitty last night. Haven't heard from her since our split, but that doesn't mean . . . you know." He stopped talking to rub the back of his neck, his eyes drifting to the floor.

"Why'd you break up with her?" I blurted. "You clearly care. So why?"

"My family's moving back to New York in June," he said. He frowned and shook his head. "My mom misses it too much. I didn't know how to tell Kitty. Long distance never works, and Kitty . . . I dunno. She'd want to try but how would we work it? We're seventeen. College is coming. I thought it was better to cut ties."

That explained it. It wasn't a particularly satisfying answer, but at least it was something. "Don't you think you should let her know your reasons? She's killing herself thinking she did something wrong," I said.

He frowned and nodded, running his hand over his hair. "Maybe you're right. Last night, she left me a message and said something about ghosts. I swear she never mentioned anything like that before. That's why I stopped you. I wanted to know if . . . you know. I wanted to know if she's okay, I guess."

I had to think about what to say. We'd made the agreement not to tell our parents, but nothing about peers. Bronx reacted exactly how Jess said he would—disbelief that we'd be so dumb as to believe in ghosts—which was understandable, but disheartening. I opened my mouth to defend Kitty, but I paused. The windows were reflecting Bronx's back. I could see his big body, the white of his T-shirt, and the black of his hair. But there was something else there, too. Black eyes staring out. Stringy hair, a crooked smile on a gaunt, graying face.

"Come here," I whispered at Bronx, waving him toward the safety of the solid wall at my back. But he didn't move when I stretched out my hand to him. Fear left me cold. I shivered from head to toe. "*Now*, Bronx!" I snapped, watching Mary tip her head up to peer at him, one of her hands lifting to paw the back of his skull.

Bronx reached for me and I tried yanking him my way, but he's a huge guy, and huge guys don't move easily. Instead, he took a few steps and then turned around to glance at what had me so transfixed. Mary lingered. She'd shifted positions so she was clear now, her palms against the glass, the pads of her fingers smushed like she'd pressed too hard. She watched us with her sunken eyes, a small stream of yellow pus oozing from her tear ducts.

"Holy shit," Bronx squealed, his voice cracking. "What the hell is that?"

"*That* is the ghost Kitty called you about, Bronx!"

Mary's staccato laughter echoed from the window. No, the

windows—it wasn't just the one pane, but all the panes in the hall. We were assailed by a chorus of cackling Mary voices. There was no one around to hear her but us. I tugged on Bronx's sleeve before sprinting toward the main building. The halls there had no windows—they were lined with lockers, and if we could just get away from the glass, we'd be safe.

I couldn't see Bronx, but I could hear his sneakers stomping and squeaking across the floor behind me. Mary's dark shadow careered through the windows to keep pace with us. She skipped from pane to pane, never losing ground no matter how hard we pumped our legs.

I sprinted around a corner, ignoring the pain in my back, my breath coming in short pants. Bronx skidded up beside me, actually running into me and nearly knocking me over. We had made it to the main stretch between the cafeteria and the front entrance to the school. It was a long, windowless corridor, lockers and closed classroom doors lining either side. My feet planted on the black-and-white-checkered tiles. I was ready to keep running if need be, but maybe we were safe here. I looked around. No mirrors, no glass, just the dull gray surface of the lockers stretching the length of the hallway. Even the paint on the walls was a drab, institutional green.

BANG! BANG! BANG! BANG!

It sounded like rapid firing, like someone had shot an Uzi in the middle of the hall. I crouched low to the ground out of instinct, my hands going over my ears as a loud, angry clanging exploded from every direction. I didn't understand what was happening. Then I saw the locks on the lockers. The shiny locks. They lifted and slammed against the metal, up and down, over and over, as if invisible hands smashed them.

Over the clamor, I heard her gravelly, dry voice.

"Mine. Mine. Mine. Mine."

12

I thought the racket would draw every human being in a mile radius of the school to gawk at the phenomenon playing out around me. The problem was the nature of the noise. It *had* sounded like gunshots. There was protocol to follow. We'd all been put through drills: lock the door, shut off the lights, hide against the wall not facing the door, keep completely silent. Mary kept clanging and banging because every teacher and every student in that high school believed someone was there with a gun.

It wasn't until Mrs. Reyes, one of the Spanish teachers, turned the corner to the hall with a cell phone to her ear that Mary's tantrum stopped. Every lock stilled, plunging the hall into uncomfortable quiet. Mrs. Reyes clearly didn't think the danger had passed, though, as she ran our way to usher us toward the nearest available door, which just so happened to be a janitor's closet. She was stone-silent as she shooed us inside, the phone stuck to her ear.

"Yes, yes, the high school," she whispered. Beside me, Bronx let out a strangled noise, and Mrs. Reyes shushed him.

I didn't know what to say. Neither did Bronx. We couldn't tell the truth, so we were stuck going along with an enormous misunderstanding. Mrs. Reyes finished her call, presumably to 911, and closed her phone. After that, we waited. And waited. And waited. We were in that closet for what felt like ages waiting for someone on the PA system to tell us we were all clear. It gave me a long time to think about what had just happened. About what Mary had just done to the school because of me.

At what point was it unsafe for me to be around people?

The answer was clear when the three of us were still in the closet an hour later, cramped, sweaty, and miserable. There was a light with a string above us, but we weren't allowed to pull it, so we were stuck in the dark. Mrs. Reyes's perfume was cloying. The sirens screamed outside while instructions were yelled out over megaphones. Sometimes I heard the grinding whir of an overhead helicopter.

This was my fault. I was the liability. I wanted to melt into a puddle of shame. I sank down onto the cold floor, my arms wrapped around my knees as I stared straight ahead. I could hear Bronx shuffling around behind me. Mrs. Reyes was coughing and sneezing, assailed by the dust in the closet.

Finally, the principal's voice piped through the overhead

speakers. "We have an all clear. I repeat, all clear. In the wake of today's event, the school will be closing early. Buses are running, parents have been informed via community outreach phone calls."

Mrs. Reyes opened the closet door. The other classrooms opened one by one. You'd think a bunch of students who'd been forced to sit silently for an hour would have a lot to say, but no one said a word. They were all too freaked out. I pulled myself to my feet and wandered back toward the hall where we'd seen Mary. I didn't want to go there, but I had to; I'd abandoned my bag there with my cell phone.

Bronx stayed with me. In fact, even when I ducked into the hall, my eyes scouring the windows for a sign of Mary, he stayed with me, his elbow touching mine. I wasn't sure if the contact was for my benefit or his. People were making their way to the parking lot, and we fell into step beside them. Outside, the school was still surrounded by police cruisers, most of them positioned so concerned bystanders couldn't block roads. There was a cluster of parents outside, too, all of them watching the doors.

I reached into my bag for my phone to call my mom, ducking away from the doors so the clamor of concerned parents reuniting with their kids wouldn't overwhelm my conversation.

"Hey, kiddo," Mom said in greeting.

"So you didn't hear?" I said back.

"Hear what?"

I explained what had happened as best I could. At least, I

explained the story of the school in lockdown after suspicious noises. She'd missed the emergency phone call because the school had our house number, not her cell number, for contact.

"I . . . wow. You must have been terrified," Mom said. "That's awful. Are you okay? You've been so stressed."

"I'm fine," I said, though my response sounded hollow even to my ears. "Freaked out, but I'm okay."

"You're sure? I have a late night, but I can leave early if you need me. Luanne owes me a shift."

"I'm okay. I'm going out with Kitty for a while, but I've got my phone. I'll call if I need anything," I said.

She grumbled under her breath and sighed. "All right. I left twenty bucks on the counter if you want a pizza. Love you. Glad you're safe."

"Love you, too, Mom." Bronx was still nearby, on the phone with his parents, too. At one point I spied Jess in the parking lot, though she hadn't seen me. Mrs. McAllister was one of the parents who'd come, and mother and daughter were standing next to Jess's car. Mrs. McAllister was fretting and stroking Jess's hair, and Jess was shooing her away like a fly. Typical Jess stuff, and for a second, I forgot I was mad at her and found a small smile.

"Shauna! What the heck?" I heard from the steps. I craned my neck and saw Kitty stumbling outside, a fistful of papers in hand, like she'd spilled her backpack and hadn't taken the time to reorganize yet. She pointed the papers at the parking lot, toward the little red SUV I liked so much. Well, normally liked—right now it looked like a shiny death machine, but so did most things.

Bronx closed his phone and looked at Kitty, frowning. "Hey."

Kitty handed me her backpack, and I held it open for her as she crammed her papers inside of it. Her eyes skipped to Bronx. She licked her lips before reaching up to pat her hair into place. It was up in a bun today, and she looked pretty enough, but being around Bronx made her self-conscious.

"He saw Mary," I said.

"Wait, he did?" She stopped primping and glanced between us. Bronx nodded as I offered an abbreviated account of what happened with the lockers.

"So the lockdown was *her*?"

"Yeah."

"I didn't believe it until I saw it, and man, that's freaky shit," Bronx said, running his hand down his face. "Got your call last night and thought you were nuts, but now...man."

Kitty scowled at him and jerked her bag out of my hands, hard enough that I stumbled a half step toward her. "Right, because our breakup is going to ruin me." It kind of *had* ruined her, but friendship solidarity said I couldn't point that out now or later or ever. At least she was sticking up for herself. She'd never do that with Jess. I supposed there wasn't much left for her to lose with Bronx, though.

"That's not what I meant. Who believes in ghosts? Really?" Bronx frowned and looked over at his car. I followed his gaze and saw Marc waiting for him. Bronx nodded at him, Marc nodded back, and Bronx shuffled a few feet forward. "I should go. But if you need help with anything, let me know. That's . . . Be careful, I guess," he said. He cast Kitty another glance, frowned, and then headed off.

"Later," I said to his back. Kitty shook her head as she turned toward her dad's car.

"I hope Mary eats him," she said.

"Kitty!"

She sighed. "Sorry. I'm just mad. Mad's better than depressed, I guess. Maybe. I don't know."

I debated telling her about his moving back to New York then, but I decided to hold off. If Kitty got hung up thinking about Bronx, we'd never get to Solomon's Folly, and I really needed to talk to Cordelia Jackson.

We climbed into the SUV and I immediately put the window down. One less shiny surface to worry about. Kitty did the same on her side, and then peeled back the sunroof. "Did you see Anna today?" she asked.

"First period," I said. "She didn't sleep well, but I guess Mary left her alone last night. She wasn't in the downstairs bathroom anymore. I just wish she'd left me alone, too, but not so much." I took out my cell phone to show Kitty the picture of the writing in the mirror. I'd snapped it before heading to the couch. I was glad I did, too, because in the morning, there was no sign of it. Mary had either wiped it off or let it disappear or . . . whatever it was ghosts did with their unsettling mirror writing.

"Holy crap. Man, I hope Cordelia has some answers for you,"

Kitty said, easing the car out of the parking lot to avoid the milling parents, students, and police.

I glanced at my phone. Half past eleven. "I really hope so, too."

⁓

Cordelia's house was easy to spot. Where other houses in her neighborhood were painted light colors with perfectly manicured lawns and attractive landscaping, Cordelia's house was a forbidding charcoal gray. The lawn was of hip-height grass, and her purple Volkswagen, rusted and with two flat tires, was parked on a moss-covered driveway. The shades were drawn and there were black squares of paper taped to the insides of the glass. The steps leading up to the screened-in porch had a sizable hole in them, like someone had fallen straight through, and there were empty wooden buckets everywhere, their insides stained maroon.

Kitty and I stared at the wreck, the sun beating down on our heads through the SUV's sunroof.

"Do you want me to go in with you?" Kitty asked.

I did, but Cordelia hadn't struck me as overly friendly. I doubted she'd take kindly to my dragging an additional stranger into her house. "Better not. She barely wanted to talk to me on the phone. I don't want to give her a reason to kick me out."

"Okay." Kitty rooted around in her backpack, looking for her phone to entertain herself while I climbed from the car. The front stairs were perilous-looking, and I leapt my way to the top step, neatly avoiding the broken boards. My fist pounded on the dilapidated screen door. There was shuffling from inside the house. A chain lock slid open. A single green eye in a sliver of pale face peeked out through the crack. I couldn't see anything beyond the hint of a woman, although I could hear the loud, static humming of a television.

"You're the haunted girl?" she asked, her voice just as crusty and grizzled as yesterday's phone call.

"Yes. I'm Shauna O'Brien."

She slammed the door shut. Confused, I knocked again, but there was no response save for a soft thudding and a muffled curse. I waited a minute, two minutes, three minutes, but nothing. Another knock and still she ignored me.

"Cordelia? Hello?" I called. Angry and scared, I headed back down the stairs, avoiding the rusted nails and deceptive bows in the wood. Halfway down the steps, the front door swung open behind me. I turned back to look. Standing in an ankle-length skirt covered in hand-sewn patches and a threadbare Gatorade T-shirt, her hair cut ragged around her ears, was Cordelia Jackson.

She was older than I expected, maybe midthirties, although her brown hair was shot through with steely gray. Her skin was pale. Pink, slicked-over scars slashed almost every piece of visible flesh. Her arms looked like they'd been forced through a paper shredder. Her face looked like she'd been mauled by a raccoon, and worst of all, she had a patch over her left eye. Three of the fingers on her left hand were missing, and two of her toes were gone, too. Either she'd fought in a war . . . or Mary happened. I didn't want to believe it was the latter; I didn't want this to be me.

"I had to go check, to see." Cordelia's voice cracked, her eye dewing and her lips trembling. She looked away from me for a moment before a small, tight smile played around her mouth. "I checked the glass and she wasn't there. For the first time in seventeen years, she's not staring back at me. My God. I'm free. I'm finally free."

13

I sat on a spindly wooden chair in the corner of Cordelia's living room. The chair legs were off-balance and wobbled whenever I shifted my weight. Fifteen feet. That was the distance Cordelia insisted be between us at all times. It was the only way she'd allow me inside her home.

"I'm sorry," she said, "but I'm not going to lose her only to get her back because I let you in."

I didn't take it personally. I was too busy taking in the condition of the house. Three steps past the door and I was besieged by a rank, coppery odor. I gagged. With the windows and doors closed, it was stuffy inside, and that made the aroma meaty and thick, like breathing slaughterhouse air. The humming I'd mistaken for a TV was actually the buzzing of flies. Everywhere. Clouds of them crawled over the black paper covering the windowpanes as if they were trying to escape. A dozen swarmed up when I sat down, and I had to keep swatting them away as they darted in front of my face. There were flypapers strung like streamers from the ceiling—curled, yellowing strips covered in shriveled black dots.

"It's the blood," Cordelia said, seeing me watch the flies. "I paint the windows with pigs' blood. No matter how many fly strips go up, they keep coming back. You'll get used to the smell."

"What? Why would you...Why pigs' blood?" I asked, my stomach churning, threatening to revolt on me.

Cordelia sank into an ancient upholstered chair across the room, next to an industrial-size sack of salt. Her fingers toyed with the burlap's fringe. She twitched then, a nervous tic in her cheek that she tried to hide behind her maimed hand. "Because it's effective." Cordelia leaned forward, staring at me intently with her one eye, her mouth pursed into a grimace. It put one of her worst scars into clear focus. The laceration bisected her thin top lip and traveled up along her cheek to curve into her nostril. "She gets better the longer she hunts you. Every scratch is a way to familiarize herself with your scent. The only thing that throws her off is to inundate her with another kind of blood. Pigs' blood is pungent. Works for inside the house. It's not like you can smear yourself in animal blood and go walking down the street, if you know what I mean. Bad enough the local butcher thinks I live off of blood sausage with all I have delivered." She cackled, a dry, reedy sound that reminded me of Mary's laugh.

"So, wait, I'm stuck with her?" I asked.

"That depends. What happened?"

I told her everything. Cordelia listened with her head tilted to the side, her eye at half-mast. Her fingers twisted in her hair before she grabbed single strands and plucked them out only to drop them on the floor beside her chair. "That's how it starts," she said. "A scratch. And losing her grip on you is why she's following you now. If you'd gone into the mirror as she intended, I'd still be haunted, but because you didn't she wants you. It's an obsession." She lifted the stub of a finger to point at her eye patch. "She took that as a trophy years ago and has been with me ever since. She hunted me and now you because we lived. The scent of your blood is the way she finds you—through any glass, any mirror, any reflective anything."

There was a groan that sounded like a dying animal. It took me a second to realize the sound came from my own mouth. My shoulders slumped and my head fell forward, my hands sliding up to cover my eyes. Bloody Mary was truly haunting me. I was her meal of choice. Not Jess or Kitty or Anna, but me.

Cordelia stood from her chair, walking through the living room to one of the tall bookcases she had lining the walls. Hardcovers and paperbacks stuffed on every shelf, additional books lying horizontally wherever there was space. "I'm not wrong, am I? She tried to pull you through a mirror and you got away," she said.

"Yes, ma'am. I mean, Cordelia," I managed, though I sounded broken. I felt broken.

"Cody. No one calls me Cordelia. Well, Becky did, but Becky's dead now." She paused, then shook her head, banishing a memory. "Something you need to understand, Shauna. Mary won't be content taking just you. She wants you alone and vulnerable. She wants to punish you for escaping her." I watched Cody pull a photo album from the shelf, her thumb skimming over the faded binding. "People like us have to make sacrifices to protect the people we care about. If you love them, leave them. Now. It's a lesson I learned too late." Her face softened, the strain of her admission making her mouth flatten into a grimace. She bent down and pushed the album across the carpet toward me. It came to a stop by my feet.

I scooped it up, my hands shaking. The idea of losing my friends because they'd suffer for the crime of knowing me scared me. I was a leper. A dirty little secret they should thrust away before they got my disease all over them. I wanted to shriek and wail and throw things at the unfairness of it all. But I needed to stay calm. I needed Cody, the only person who could help me.

I concentrated on the photo album. It was full of pictures of Cody when she was a teenager, most of them with friends or people I assumed were family members. The first few pages were normal enough; Cody's happy, smiling, unblemished face appeared in stark contrast to how she looked now.

I turned the page. There was a picture of a different girl with dark hair and a date written on the edge. Beside the date was the word *Love*.

"Her name was Jamie. She was my best friend and one of the girls who summoned Bloody Mary with me. A few weeks after Mary marked me, she took Jamie through the mirror in my parents' living room. I watched it happen. I watched her pull Jamie through. I begged, I pleaded, I even offered to go in Jamie's place, but Mary wanted my suffering. Struggling was useless— Mary is too strong. She thrust me away and took Jamie."

Trembling, Cody paused to run her hand across her brow. Even after all these years, the loss still weighed on her. "I reported it to the police, but no one believed me. I was a goth girl, and Jamie was the only openly gay kid in the school. People thought I was making it up because of how I dressed, how I acted. Jamie and I were oddballs. They tried to blame me for her disappearance, but when they ran the DNA from the scratches on my face, they realized they had no case."

"I'm sorry," I said.

Cody let out a harsh bark of laughter. "For that? Oh, please. There's a lot more to be sorry for. Becky was taken a few months after Jamie. Moira lasted the longest, but it was still less than a year after our summoning. Mary took my cousin John for the sin of coming to visit me a couple years after that. It's not just the summoning people who are in danger here. It's everyone around you."

If I had known Cody better, I would have told her how sorry I was for what she'd been through. Pity is a funny thing, though; some people want it, others don't, and Cody had proven prickly enough that I didn't risk insulting her. I delved deeper into the photo album, spotting more dates along the edges of pictures. I peered at the faces of people I didn't know, feeling despondent.

"Damn it," Cody muttered. I peeked at her over the top of the photo album. She twitched and her hand snaked out to snatch at the air. Her fingers curled over as she brought her fist close to her chest. She whispered under her breath, dark hair sliding down to cover her face.

"Pardon?" I asked.

"Fly," she said. She grinned at me. Her hand lifted and she stretched out her fingers. A smear of dead fly decorated her scarred palm. Cody pointed at the remains like this was some great feat. I didn't know what to say as she flicked the bug bits away with a raspy giggle.

She'd seemed so normal for a few minutes. Now I wasn't so convinced. Mary had done a number on this poor woman.

"I miss them, you know." She lifted her skirt to wipe away the last of the bug goo, acting for all intents and purposes like the fly incident had never happened. "Every day I wish I'd gone into exile sooner. But I thought if I could hold on, eventually someone would summon her and get hooked liked I'd been. I knew I'd be free one day. I just didn't know it would take so many years and cost my friends' lives. For what it's worth, I'm sorry it happened to you. I don't wish Mary on anyone. I warned your friend away, but she didn't want to listen."

Jess never listened, and because of it, I'd gotten haunted. The desire to curse was so overwhelming, my teeth clenched on the sides of my tongue. I wouldn't lose it here in front of Cody. She had enough to worry about without my throwing a tantrum over my best friend.

"Sounds like Jess," I spat. "That's how she is." I glanced back down at the album. When the pictures finally stopped, I let out a long sigh. I hadn't known any of the people shown, but I felt sad for them all the same. Cody, too. She'd had a life, and Mary had put that life on hold. She'd robbed Cody of what should have been her best years. At least it was over for her now.

For me, it was just beginning.

"Is there . . ." I stopped talking to take a deep breath, hearing the warbling in my voice. "Is there a way to put her away for good? A way to beat her? There has to be something I can do."

"Probably, but I'm not sure what it is. I'd guess it stems from her background." Cody pulled one of those manila envelopes with a string tie at the flap from between two thick books. She removed a piece of paper and flung it my way. I immediately recognized it as the picture on the Solomon's Folly site.

"I've seen this. It's online. That's Mary Worth."

She nodded. "Moira hit the Solomon's Folly library right after I got haunted. The original picture has water damage. If you haven't figured it out yet, Mary's tied to water. I think it has to do with the flood. That picture was recovered after the Southbridge River flooded back in 1962. The flood destroyed the Southbridge Parish—the church you see there. The town did what it could to salvage the church's older artifacts, but most of the collection was moved to storage for protection. Moira conned the librarian into letting her take a look. She was always good on her feet like that. Much better than me, anyway."

Cody settled into her seat with a notepad she'd pulled from the bookshelf. She opened it, flipped to a page, and then left it on her lap, like she'd long ago memorized what she was about to say. "Moira also uncovered a few local articles. They explained a lot—about why Mary chooses young girls to haunt, anyway."

"She'll only haunt girls? I thought she pulled your cousin John through the mirror," I said.

"She did, but she'll only haunt girls like you or me because she'll only answer a summons with four girls. Mary's father died of fever when she was a child. And Hannah Worth drowned in the Southbridge River when Mary was seventeen. Mary insisted it was murder, but she refused to name a suspect."

It looked like Cody was going to keep talking, but she jolted out of her seat and spun around, head whipping from side to side. Her hands flew down for the burlap sack of salt. She shook it around her, salt flying all willy-nilly. She mumbled and groaned. "Mary, Mary, Mary," she said over and over, the salt crystals spraying, some careening across the room to strike my legs.

I stood from my chair and braced for the ghost. My eyes scoured the room, looking for Mary's ugly face, but there was nothing shiny nearby. There was nowhere for her to hide. Cody had covered everything with masking tape or black paper.

"Where is she?" I yelled.

Cody ignored me, scurrying through the room with her salt pointed at the floor, a thick line trailing behind her.

"Mary, Mary," she said again.

"Where, Cody?!" I barked.

Cody stopped in her tracks, one foot in the living room, the other now in the kitchen. Her head swiveled toward me. She looked so empty for a moment, so fragile, but then she snorted and glanced away. Color blossomed in her cheeks like she was ashamed of her outburst.

"I thought I heard—no. No, I didn't." She lifted her salt sack to her chest, cradling it like a baby. Her cheek rubbed against the coarse burlap. "Sorry, so sorry. This happens sometimes, after so many years. You hear something or see something and you react, because if you don't react, you die. It's that simple."

I sank down into my chair, my eyes never leaving her as she returned to her seat. She fell back into the old upholstery, the salt bag pressed to her heart. She never relinquished it, not even when she leaned forward to retrieve the notepad and envelope she'd dropped in her panic.

She still looked embarrassed. I tried to smile, but it fell flat, and my attention drifted back to the picture in my hand. Hannah Worth. I traced my fingertip over her pale, plaited hair. "She was beautiful," I said.

"Yes. Yes, she was. Unfortunately it cost her, and in the long run, Mary, too." Cody let out a sigh. By the stretching silence, I knew that our meeting was over. I wasn't going to wait around for her to kick me out, and I didn't want to give her a reason to hang up on me if I had to call her back.

"Thanks for everything," I said, standing and dropping the picture of the Worths onto my seat. "I should go, though. I need to get back for dinner, but you were really helpful." Cody looked like she'd get up to show me out, but I lifted a hand and shook my head. "No, you stay over there where it's safe. You've had enough of Mary. It's cool."

I started for the door, but then she called my name again. I looked back at her. Clutched in her maimed fingers was a white envelope.

"Mary dislikes big groups of people," Cody said. "At first, anyway. The longer she hunts you, the less of a deterrent groups become. She also tends to avoid adults—especially women, especially moms. She was attached to her own mother. You might catch a glimpse of her here and there, but she won't stay. Never underestimate her. Never."

She said nothing else as she tossed the envelope at me. It struck me on the side of my knee. I bent to retrieve it, pulling out a stack of photocopied pages.

April 9, 1864

Beloved Constance,

I am so glad to hear that Boston is treating you well. I wish circumstances would have allowed for a visit before now, but Mother counsels patience. I think she tires of my exuberance. I've mentioned the possibility of leaving this horrid little village for good and moving closer to the city, but Mother insists that she prefers the quiet of the country. I think her resolve is faltering, though, especially lately. We tire of the nonsense.

The town's histrionics continue. It's gotten awful enough that Mother begged the pastor to intervene on my behalf, though his cure is possibly worse than the illness with which he afflicted me. After my morning lessons, I report to church and he has me sit in his private quarters copying scripture. I write until my hand aches. When I ask for reprieve, he strikes my knuckles with a switch.

At first, it was only an hour or two of daily tedium, but now it is four, and I can feel his eyes boring into my back all the while. He never leaves or moves. He simply stares. His attention is disconcerting. I am simply thankful that he looks upon me with loathing and not lust, as he looks upon our dear mother. I've deduced he keeps me near as a way of keeping her near. It is unnatural.

You know my disposition, Constance, and I am not one to silence my tongue under the best of circumstances, but this man's influence over the town is such that I fear I must abide his ridiculous rules or suffer dire consequence. When I refused to attend his lessons a few weeks ago—if such mindless labors can even be called lessons—Mother had difficulty selling her poultices. Mrs. Grant said "the store didn't need them." She's been buying them every week for ten years! I cannot prove that Pastor Starkcrowe swayed her, but you know how devout Mrs. Grant is. You'd think that store of hers was built by the Lord Himself.

If my suspicions are correct, the pastor punished Mother for my rebellion, which is a wicked, evil thing to do, especially with how little we claim. Halving our income is devastating. It's the sole reason I returned to him; we simply could not afford the alternative. Mother says I shouldn't assume the worst of Pastor Starkcrowe, that I have no proof of his interference, but I do find it strange that the very day I returned to his instruction, Mrs. Grant sent her son to buy Mother's goods again. It was a Wednesday, which is definitely not their usual Monday delivery. Does that not cross you as odd?

If it does not, perhaps I am the lunatic Elizabeth Hawthorne claims. I am convinced she is the force behind the wagging rumors of my mental instability. The pastor has done me few favors since his arrival, the wretch. He's slurred my character and, most recently, given me a terrible fear of the dark, something that has not plagued me since I was a child.

The first day of my return to the church, the pastor berated me for abandoning my lessons. He yelled so much that spittle struck my face, and he does not have the most pleasant breath, I assure you. The spring church festival was upon us, and Elizabeth and her awful coven were decorating the pews with flowers when I arrived. I was able to ignore their unkind whispering, but when the pastor shouted at me, they had the audacity to snicker. I glanced at them, but instead of punishing them for their rudeness, the pastor grew more incensed with me because, as he put it, I "lacked the necessary discipline to listen to holy instruction."

There was no instruction, Constance; he only shouted at me for avoiding his company a week, but before I could say as much he dragged me through the church and to the basement door.

I will not tell you that I didn't struggle, for that would be a lie, but the basement is foreboding, more a dungeon than not. It frightens me. It smells like Mother's herbs when they go to rot, and the stone walls are covered in mold. He thrust me down the stairs, and I stumbled into all sorts of strange miscellanea: a mirror, an old pew, an old bookshelf, a box of idols. I'm surprised I didn't break my neck upon the refuse. The floor had puddles of water, and there were awful beetles everywhere. Some of them even crawled on me. I doubt I'll forget the feeling of them scuttling over my skin.

"You'll be lucky to see the light of day again," he told me as he closed the door. I begged for release, thinking perhaps he lingered on the other side, but he was gone. There was laughter instead. It was Elizabeth and her odious friends. She called to me through the door, mocking me as I sat in the cold wet. It injured my pride, but I pleaded with her to let me out. She insisted she couldn't do that else she make the pastor cross. Her assurances that I would be released sooner or later were hollow and cruel.

I spent hours in the dark, my eyes fixed upon the empty mirror. Do you remember Mother's insistence that we cover the mirrors when Father took ill? Her superstitions about his dying before the glass? I thought it ridiculous at the time, but during those bleak hours, I came to understand her fears. A lightless mirror is a terrifying thing. There is no reflection, only black glass. Like an abyss. It's endless and consuming.

I haven't told Mother about what happened with the pastor. If she confronts him for his cruelty, he could contact Mrs. Grant again and we will be destitute. If she confronts the Hawthornes about Elizabeth's behavior, they bring their own complications. Mayor Hawthorne is not a nice man, and I doubt he'd believe ill of his Elizabeth.

I am sorry that my letters are so glum lately. The prospect of visiting you brightens every one of my dark days. I sometimes dream of staying in the city with you, but I am not sure I could leave Mother alone, especially with Pastor Starkcrowe's lascivious gaze upon her. Perhaps your letters will convince her that the air in Solomon's Folly grows toxic. You always were more influential than I.

Write soon, and give Edward my love. I adore you, Sister Mine.

Mary

Cody watched me leave from the porch, her hand lifted in a half wave of stubbed fingers and scarred palm. Her eye flitted over her yard, like she couldn't believe she was actually outside of her door without having to worry about Mary's assailing her from every angle. I couldn't tell if it was relief or fear on her face.

"Thank you," I called to her. Reading Mary's letter, hearing Cody's story, I felt worse than I had before I'd come. Everything looked so bleak. Seeing Cody holed up in that run-down house with those flies, that smell, the blackened windows...It was a sobering peek into my future.

"Don't forget the pigs' blood. And the salt," she called out.

"I won't," I said, approaching Kitty's car. Kitty had fallen asleep in her seat, her phone propped on her chest, face pointed at the sunroof. It wasn't until I knocked on the door that she darted up, her sunglasses flying off her nose to strike the window. Seeing that it was me and not a killer ghost come to maim her, she relaxed and unlocked the door before fumbling for her sunglasses. I started to climb in, but Cody called to me again. I paused, glancing back at the woman standing on the porch.

"One thing: tell your friend to stop calling me. I warned her."

Cody ducked back into her house. A moment later, I saw her tear a sheet of black paper off of the front window.

"So how did it go?" Kitty asked, easing the SUV out of the driveway and onto the empty street. I didn't answer her. Cody's gray house slipped out of view. Leaving felt wrong. Cody knew more about my situation than I did, and there was an illusion of safety being near her. I couldn't stay with her, of course, but a part of me desperately wished I could.

"Not good. I'm haunted, which I sort of knew, but I need to talk to Jess and Anna, tonight maybe, though I have to . . . ugh. Jess." It was more a ramble than a sentence, but Kitty nodded all the same, her hands tightening on the steering wheel.

"Did she say what we could do about Mary?"

"No, just how I got haunted. She only got rid of Mary when I got marked, which I guess is how the haunting is passed. It's messed up. She also gave me another letter from Mary to her sister. It's dark. You can read it tonight with Jess and Anna," I explained. Kitty was fine with waiting, which made me grateful I'd gone with Kitty instead of Anna or Jess. They were far less patient.

The only information I didn't share was that Cody told me

to leave my friends. I didn't want to freak Kitty out or make her think she was going to die being in the car with me. It wasn't like Kitty would leave me on the side of the road, but like the letter, it was another conversation to have with the group. It'd hurt enough to say it one time, never mind multiple times.

I hesitated before texting Jess. I knew I shouldn't talk to her. She'd endangered me. She'd heard the warnings from Cody and ignored them. The thing was, I knew Jess. She was my oldest friend and she hadn't meant to get anyone hurt—especially not me. She was reckless, but Jess had always been reckless. She screwed up a lot, but she always made good on it later. Maybe she could make good on this, too. Maybe she could help me survive the ghost.

Need to talk. Your place tonight? I typed.

Seconds later, my phone buzzed.

Bring overnight bag. Call for ride. TTYL.

I was willing to give Jess a chance, but I didn't want to be alone with her right now, either. I wanted normal people around me to buffer whatever crap she threw my way, and there'd be crap. Excuses, apologies, lies.

Kitty and Anna? I sent.

Sure.

I tossed my phone into my bag and leaned the car seat back so I was as far away from the windows as I could be. "I'm going to Jess's tonight to talk about Mary. She wants to help. You want to come?"

"Okay," Kitty said, easing the car onto the highway.

"Cool. I'll let you talk Anna into it."

Kitty groaned. "I'll talk to her. We don't need to be fighting with one another right now."

"No, we really don't."

～∞～

There were no Mary sightings in the car or in my apartment. I wasn't naive enough to believe she wasn't nearby, watching and waiting. I grabbed an overnight bag, keeping my eyes away from my vanity. It was still covered, but I knew what could be under there. Some people might be tempted to lift the robe to check, but I wasn't. I never wanted to lift the robe again.

Before I left, I snagged my salt shaker from the nightstand. Cody said to keep salt on hand at all times, and unlike Jess, I tended to listen to the people who were trying to keep me alive.

Kitty had to swing to her house for clothes, too. I waited for her in the middle of her long driveway, the salt in the cradle of my folded legs. The pavement was warm on my butt, and I tilted my head to the sun, keeping my back to the wall of shrubs. Kitty took her sweet time in the house, but I was all right with that. Outside felt safe, free from shiny surfaces.

I messaged my mom while I waited so she'd know where I was going tonight.

<3 u, staying w/Jess 2nite, I said.

Call if going out. Have fun. Love you, was her reply.

Kitty stormed outside with a duffel bag on her shoulder and a cell phone pressed to her ear. "Yes, I know Jess is a jerk, but . . . Okay. So don't come. We'll go." Kitty frowned at me and sighed, shaking her head, obviously listening to a tirade. "So come then. You're invited. Anna. Anna! Am I picking you up or not?" The closer Kitty got, the more I could hear the shouting. To her credit, she didn't look too browbeaten. Just like I was used to Jess's particular quirks, Kitty was used to Anna's. Being Anna's best friend meant stomaching a lot of vitriol.

"Okay, fine. I'll see you in twenty." Kitty hung up and motioned me to the car. I slid in beside her and resumed my laid-back position to keep my upper body away from the window glass. I wedged the salt shaker in one of the cup holders just in case. "Anna's a little mad," Kitty said.

"Oh, good. Ought to make tonight more interesting," I said.

⌘

Anna was waiting for us on her front step, her clothes wedged into a tote bag that rested between her sneakers. She slid in behind Kitty without a word. Kitty eased the car onto the road, and I kept quiet. We knew this drill. Anna burned hot when she was mad, but if you gave her a little space, she'd simmer down. Jess didn't abide that much because she was either brave, stupid, or insensitive, but Kitty and I knew to respect Anna's boundaries.

That didn't mean I couldn't be friendly, though, so I craned my neck to smile at her. Anna turned her head, nodded, and the sun flashed across her glasses. That's when I saw the two black eyes peering out at me. There were no whites, only almond shapes of emptiness. I squealed and reached for Anna's glasses. Anna saw me sailing at her face and flinched, but my hand was faster than her recoil. I grabbed the glasses and flung them onto the seat beside her, my free hand fumbling for the shaker of salt.

"In the glasses. *In* the glasses!" I shrieked. Kitty jerked on the wheel to pull the car over onto the side of the road, nearly running into a mailbox. I flew forward and bit my tongue hard enough that I tasted coppery blood. I still managed to fling a handful of salt at the glasses in hopes of exorcising the ghost.

"*Miiiiiiine.*"

The word warbled from the rear window and over to Anna's car door. The car windows started to rise despite no one touching the control buttons. I tried to push mine back down, but had to jerk my hands away at the last moment, afraid that Mary would pin me between the glass and the roof. There was a click as the locks snapped into place around us, ghostly hands forcing the mechanisms.

Mary's voice traveled from window to window as if she danced her way around the vehicle. There was an empty, hollow quality to the sound, too, like it came not from the depths of the car, but from a much larger, more cavernous chamber.

"What the hell is that?" Anna demanded, but both she and Kitty knew. They had never heard Mary's voice, but they knew. They screamed and reached for their car doors. I did the same, my hand sliding down to grip the plastic. For all that I'd had the pleasure of Mary's voice, it didn't prepare me for this. Familiarity didn't make it easier. I wanted to get out. I *needed* to get out. I gripped the handle and pulled, but nothing happened. I did it again, and again the door wouldn't unlock.

"No, NO!" Kitty shrieked as the three of us pushed on the doors like we could brute-force our way out to safety. The voice amplified before fracturing—instead of one Mary voice, there were six voices whirling around us, all staking their claim at once. I watched the glass of the car fog over, small rivulets of water coursing over the panes.

"Mine. Mine, mine, mine, mine..."

"Make it stop," Anna squealed, the words jumbling together as she threw herself flat onto the backseat, her face hidden against the upholstery, her hands clasped over her ears. I wanted to join her, but I froze when I saw Mary's gray fingertip press against the windshield like she was perched on the hood of Kitty's SUV.

"Wh-what...Is she coming? Is she..." Kitty's voice broke off in a whimper as Mary started writing in the condensation, the letters dribbling water. I expected to see the *M* of *Mine* again, but this time it was an *S*. Followed by an *H*. My hand flew to my mouth as Mary wrote out my name, the letters crooked and ungainly, the *N* backward.

The voices around us died at once, cut short as if someone pressed stop on a stereo. A moment later an ear-shredding scream pulsed from the glass, high-pitched and shrill. The car began to shake. We huddled down into the seats, screeching and pleading for Mary to stop. I wanted it to be over, for Mary to go back to wherever she came from, but she wasn't finished yet.

Her ragged, ruined hand flattened on the windshield in front of my face. I could see the skin moving, the gash in her palm burping out a pair of tiny black beetles that scurried down the car. She swept her hand to the side. The flourish erased my name, the phantom letters now replaced by a smear of black tar raining inky tears down the glass.

15

It was the school bus that did it. We were locked in a shaking car, drowning in terror, when the yellow bus pulled up to the street corner. The doors opened, unleashing a small herd of elementary school kids on the neighborhood. Mary fled as soon as they appeared.

Kitty threw open her door the moment it unlocked and bumbled into the street. I saw her whacking at her pocket. There was a wheeze just before she yanked out her inhaler, stealing a drag and falling onto her butt on the pavement. Anna crawled from the backseat, her whole body flat on the road. I dove for the sidewalk, finding a safe spot next to the trunk of an oak tree. I stared at the car unblinking, afraid that in the millisecond it took to close my eyes, the nightmare would come back.

I felt sick. I think we all did. One of the little kids stopped to peer at us, looking from Kitty to Anna to me. She was petite and blond, with big green eyes and a pink unicorn backpack that matched her jacket.

"Are you guys dying?" she asked. "If you're dying, I'll get my mom."

She couldn't have been more than nine or ten, and for her sake I forced an unconvincing smile. "No. Not dying. Just had a...an accident," I said, pointing at the car. "Just scared."

"Oh. Okay. I'm glad you're okay."

I wasn't sure how okay I was, but I wasn't going to say as much. The girl ran off to join her friends while the three of us got our collective nerve back. Anna was the first to recover. She stood from the road and wiped her pants off before turning to eye me, her cheeks flushed and stained with tears.

"Where's the salt?" she demanded.

I still had it in my hand, and I tossed it to her. Anna stepped over Kitty to fling salt over the inside of the car—in the back of the SUV, on the dashboard. She put it in the little grooves between the window glass and the rubber guard things. She put it on the seats. She rubbed it into the vents. She used every last granule on that car before stepping back and whacking her hands clean, the empty cardboard shaker abandoned on the passenger's side floor.

"W-we can't avoid driving, but we can avoid dying," she said.

Anna was right. I didn't want to get back into the car, but when I saw Anna help Kitty to her feet, I knew we had to keep going. We clustered together, Kitty's hands reaching out to either side of her so she could give me and Anna half hugs at the same time. We moved toward the car like we were walking to the gallows. When Kitty turned the engine over, we held our breaths and waited for Mary to return with her whisper games.

Nothing.

Kitty wasn't a speeder, but she got from Anna's street to Jess's house burning smears of rubber on the pavement. I held my breath for long sections of the drive, only noticing I was doing it when I'd start to feel faint. I'd breathe, then something would flash across the glass of the windows and the cycle would perpetuate. Anna refused to wear her glasses. They stayed abandoned on the seat beside her, granules of salt pooling in the curve of the lenses. She didn't touch them, not even when we got to Jess's house and she threw herself from the car.

We collected our bags and hurried up Jess's front steps, not bothering to knock. Jess's house had a kitchen, a bathroom, a big living room, and an office downstairs. All the bedrooms were upstairs. I walked through the foyer and past the stairs to look into the kitchen. Mrs. McAllister was there with Todd, handing him a paper towel full of a snack.

Seeing me, she grinned and motioned me close. "I made brownies. You should have one," she said. "Especially after that crazy day at school. I got the call and my mind jumped to the worst-case scenario. I hope they find the little bastards with the fireworks and expel them, pardon my French."

Fireworks. Right.

Mrs. McAllister cut a slab of brownie and lifted it at me as an invitation. I didn't have an appetite after the car ride, but

I liked the idea of being near Jess's mom. It felt safe. I went so far as to plunk myself down at the kitchen table beside Todd. Mrs. McAllister slid me a tall glass of milk. I murmured my thanks as I nibbled, my fingers brushing the crumbs away from my lips. Todd blabbed at me, and I nodded like I understood, but I didn't hear a single word he said. I was too busy watching Mrs. McAllister sweep back and forth across the kitchen. At that point, had she tried to go to the bathroom, I probably would have followed her.

I could hear Jess pounding down the steps. She didn't come to the kitchen right away, probably pausing to talk with Kitty and Anna, who were still in the other room. A minute later, she shuffled into the kitchen. She looked as tired as I did, and I wondered if it was fear of Bloody Mary or guilt that had kept her awake.

"Hey, how you holding up?" she asked.

Mrs. McAllister turned to look at me, her face falling into a frown. "Is everything all right, Shauna?"

"Yeah! Yeah. I'm just having a rough patch," I said, understating it by a million. "I'll be okay."

Mrs. McAllister gave me one of those tight mom smiles that said she understood even though I hadn't said a word about the problem. Our problem. *My* problem. She cut another half brownie from the pan and brought it my way, dropping it onto my paper towel. "That's when you spoil yourself with a little extra chocolate, honey. Trust me. It works." She gave my cheek a pat and then stroked my hair, reminding me of my own mom. I felt my eyes water. I was getting awfully weepy these days.

Seeing my extra brownie, Todd scowled and sat up in his chair. I watched him wipe his mouth on his arm, leaving a long chocolate smear between his wrist and elbow. "Mama, can I have more brownie?"

"No. You'll spoil your dinner."

"Won't Shauna spoil *her* dinner?" he returned.

Jess reached out to flick his ear. He batted her away like he was shooing a fly, but she ignored him and flicked his other ear, making him erupt into a series of whines.

"Come on, Shauna. I think that's our sign to retreat."

❧

Jess led us to Todd's toy room. There wasn't much in the way of real furniture, but at least there was carpet and a couple of beanbag chairs. I walked past the G.I. Joes and coloring books to get to the windows. A big bowl of salt was already on the floor, and Anna placed a salt line on the left window while I did the same to the right one. Someone had already pulled down the shades. It made me think of Cody with her black construction paper windowpanes.

"Is your brother going to barge in here?" Kitty asked Jess. Anna hadn't quite graduated to making polite conversation yet, but Kitty made the effort.

"He'd better not, if he knows what's good for him," Jess replied.

I sighed. "You realize if he goes and tells your mom we're in here, she's going to kick us out. You need to make sure he's okay with it or we'll have to move. Why not your room?"

"My closet doors are mirrors. I was being careful." Jess *fwump*ed down into the red beanbag chair before kicking off her flip-flops. "I can handle Toad if it comes to it."

Jess had zero intention of talking to her brother about using his room. How couldn't she foresee the looming disaster? No kid wanted anything until someone else had it, and that was especially going to be true when it was his older sister. This wasn't much of a Mary sanctuary if Mrs. McAllister was going to boot us out when Todd whined.

"No, Jess. We need Todd's approval. I'll be right back," I announced. I walked to the door. The doorknob's gleaming glass surface should have caught my eye, but it didn't.

I reached for the doorknob.

It reached back.

Two slimy, cold-fish fingers stabbed out from the rounded center, scraping my fingers and ripping into the skin. The jagged edges of Mary's nails jerked down, lashing at me so hard, they sliced the webbing between my thumb and forefinger.

My hand felt like I'd plunged it into a nest of fire ants. I stumbled back, blood running down my arm and onto my jeans, dripping onto the white canvas tops of my sneakers. I dug my teeth into my lip to stop myself from screaming.

Anna rushed over with the salt and flung it at the blood-smeared fingers wriggling from the knob. The moment the crystals struck dead skin, a sizzle sparked, and Mary retreated into the glass. Blood splashes ran over the curve of the doorknob and down onto the carpet. Jess found one of Todd's SpongeBob T-shirts on the floor and threw it at me. I was in too much pain to catch it, but Kitty snagged it and wrapped it around my hand, putting pressure on the wounds to stop the bleeding.

"Clean it, we've got to clean it and bandage it," Kitty said. She grabbed the doorknob without a thought for her own safety, but the salt kept Mary behind the glass. Kitty steered me out of the playroom and across the hall to the bathroom.

"Kitty, n-no, the bathroom," I said, but she ushered me to the door anyway. Anna trailed along behind while Jess ran off toward the kitchen, presumably to get more salt. Mrs. McAllister called upstairs to see if we were okay. Jess yelled something back. All I could think about was the pain.

When we got to Jess's bathroom, Anna darted in to salt the mirror. It was flush against the sink, like it was in Anna's basement, so she was able to leave a thick line along the edge. Jess ran in with a second box, and the two of them worked together to finish it.

"Okay, it's clear. Come in," whispered Anna.

Kitty started to put my hand under the faucet, but it was chrome silver. I jerked back, afraid to get too close. Kitty understood, filling the sink with hot water for me. The faucet was still right there, but at least there was enough distance between it and the bottom of the basin that I could avoid any more finger jabs. I dipped my hand into the warm, steamy water, gasping and slumping at the fire racing up my arms. I watched through tear-swollen eyes as the water turned a red-swirled pink.

"God, we need to . . . do something. This, the car. I don't know. Do the 'I believe in you' thing again or something," Anna said. "We need to brainstorm."

SLAM.

One moment the mirror had our reflections, the next Bloody Mary was there, her face smashing against her side of the glass. Bones crunched, like she'd broken something in her own face, but that didn't stop her from bashing her head against the glass again and soiling it with her thick, crusting fluids.

I yanked my hand from the sink and the four of us huddled against the bathroom wall.

"G-get your mom," I rasped at Jess. "GET YOUR MOM!"

Jess looked confused, but she didn't ask for an explanation. She darted from the room to shout for her mother, asking her to come upstairs. Kitty and Anna and I remained, staring at Bloody Mary, who grinned and licked at the smears she'd left on the glass. She stopped and looked straight at me, her head tilting to the side. It forced the muscles in her neck to go taut, the stretch of skin bursting a small gray pustule along her collarbone. A flurry of black beetles poured down her dress. I could almost hear the click-clicking of their jaws.

Kitty gagged and Anna whimpered, but I was frozen, pinned by Mary's black-as-midnight eyes.

Mary stretched up and down as if her body were elastic. One minute she was tall and impossibly thin, the next low and squat. Repeatedly she pushed her palm to the glass to see if it'd give, but the salt kept her contained.

Then she lifted her hand and splayed her fingers. The tips were covered in my blood. Mary raised them to her nostril holes. I realized with sickening dread that she was *smelling* me. She was sniffing my blood.

"Oh, God," I murmured. Mary smiled, showing us a row of yellow-gray stump teeth. Slowly and deliberately, she popped a finger into her mouth, sucking it clean. Her tongue ran along her knuckle and underneath her nail to capture every last drop of my blood. She lapped at her palm and then slurped the tip of her finger before moving on to the next finger, her eyes fluttering in perverse rapture.

"Why? Why is she doing that?" Anna asked.

Mrs. McAllister rushed into the bathroom and came straight for me. She reached for my hand and hissed when she saw the blood swirls curling over my wrist and forearm. I glanced past her leaning blond head at the mirror; it was empty. The moment Jess's mother arrived, Mary fled. I wanted to cling to Mrs. McAllister and never let go, like a little kid on the first day of school.

"Oh, hon. How did you manage this one?" she asked, pulling me toward the sink. She put my hand back under the faucet, turning the water on cold as she rummaged through the drawers of the vanity for bandages and Neosporin. I wasn't thrilled to be so close to the chrome, but having Jess's mom there was as close to safe as I was going to get.

"I broke a glass," Jess said from the hall. "It's my fault."

Mrs. McAllister cast a sharp look at Jess before dabbing ointment on the shredded flesh between my thumb and pointer finger. It hurt enough that I cringed. "Easy, girlie. If this doesn't stop bleeding, you might need the hospital for a stitch or two. Keep an eye on it. Do you want me to call your mom?"

"No. It's okay. If it doesn't stop bleeding, I'll call her myself."

She nodded and layered some gauze on the injury before wrapping me in medical tape.

"Did you clean up the glass?" Mrs. McAllister asked.

"Yeah. It's fine. Sorry, Shauna," Jess said, stepping aside as her mother ducked back into the hall.

"Good. I'll come see you in an hourish, Shauna. We'll check how you're doing, okay?"

I followed her into the hall, eager to put the mirror behind me. "Sure, thanks. Oh, hey, Mrs. M? We're working on a project tonight and need extra room. Is it okay if we use Todd's playroom? If he needs stuff, it's cool. We can go somewhere else," I said.

She nodded. "Sure. I'll tell him to grab a couple toys for the night and scram."

Jess opened the door wide so I could sidestep the knob and settle back down on the floor. I felt stiff and old; my throbbing hand made my back spasm, too, like my body decided my hand needed sympathy pain.

"What the hell is going on?" Anna demanded, following me inside. She still had the salt with her, clutched to her chest as she peered from me to Jess and back again. "This is crazy. What is going *on*?"

I looked between my friends. Seeing their weary, terrified expressions, I knew it was time to talk.

16

The car haunting had Jess on edge. I watched her drift to the window to peel back the shade, looking out at the cars in the driveway like they were monsters lying in wait.

With all of us together, I detailed what I knew about Cody's haunting, how Mary was passed to me from a blood tag, and how Cody's friends and cousin died. I warned them that they were in danger, but none of them made any motion to leave. I should have told them this was it, that I had to go away after tonight, but I wasn't ready yet. It was selfish, but I was too scared to go it alone. Maybe one day soon I'd have the will to insist they go, but today wasn't that day.

Finally, I described Cody's fly-ridden house and the pigs' blood. Jess snatched the second letter from my hands, insisting on reading it aloud and refusing to relinquish it when she was done, her fingers smoothing over the paper and flattening the curled edges.

"Everything okay?" I asked.

She laid the letter flat on the carpet. "Don't you think this is sad? Like, what's said here? He abused her. No wonder she ended up becoming a crazy bitch." I could see the inherent tragedy developing in Mary's letter, but I had a hard time assigning pity to her. She was trying to kill me. One day, she'd try to kill every person in this room. Feeling sorry for a would-be murderer was stretching it.

"I'm not sure," I admitted.

Anna wasn't so diplomatic. "I don't. Bad stuff happens to everyone in life. That doesn't mean you have to turn into a jerk. Not to the people who don't deserve it. Those guys?" Anna pointed at the letter with a snort. "The pastor, that Elizabeth girl? Fine, haunt them. But what did we do to her?"

Jess was about to reply, but Kitty cut her off. "I don't think that's how ghosts work. Not in the movies, anyway. Think about it. They die and then something disturbs their resting place or someone breaks their stuff and they come back. I just don't think they can see right or wrong anymore."

Kitty made me think about Mary's rising. The mirror. The darkness. The bugs. Mary must have died somewhere around the church, I thought. Maybe she died *in* the church. Pastor Starkcrowe had threatened to lock her downstairs indefinitely.

"Hey, anyone got a laptop?" I asked.

"Yeah, give me a second." Jess got up to head to her room. Before she touched the doorknob, she bunched her shirt into a wad to form a makeshift glove. It sucked that we'd been reduced to such maneuvers, but there was nothing to do about it. Adapt or die.

Jess reemerged with her computer. I eyed it, checking for shine, but it was constructed of brushed silver and matte plastic. I felt relatively safe having it in the room. I motioned for Jess to fire it up. The screen had a reflection, so I kept my distance by pressing my back to the wall on the opposite side of the room.

"What are we looking for?" Kitty asked.

"You said that thing about the ghost being disturbed, and you're right. That's how it works in books and movies. Maybe something happened to her body. Cody mentioned that there was a flood in the sixties. If Mary's remains were in the church and something disturbed them, maybe that caused her to start haunting people."

"The legend did start in the sixties," Jess said. I remembered her texting that to me the other day. Anna must not have gotten the same information. She looked surprised Jess would know that fact off the top of her head, but before she could ask about it, Jess offered an explanation. "I did some research. Mary Worth died in 1864, but the legend of Bloody Mary didn't start until the sixties. There was a hundred-year gap."

Anna scowled. "Seriously? You knew all these things about Mary Worth and you still thought summoning her was a good idea? Wow. Great plan, Jess. Well done. Ten out of ten." The sarcasm was palpable. I glanced at Anna, then over to Jess, hoping for a peaceful resolution, but neither of them noticed me.

They were fixed on each other. Anna was squinting, a combination of no-glasses and annoyance. Jess looked furious. Her eye twitched and her ears were the color of a cherry tomato.

Finally, Jess broke the silence. "I said it before, I'll say it again: I screwed up. I know it. We all know it. But being sorry doesn't fix this. So here's how it is, Anna. We play nice until Shauna's Mary-free, and then you get the hell away from me. Or if that doesn't work, leave now. I'm here to help. If you're not going to help, go home." Jess never raised her voice, but she didn't have to. There was enough fire in her tone that I cringed. I understood what she was saying in spite of it, though. The Mary problem was bigger than our personal gripes. If we wanted to solve this mystery, we needed to work together.

I was about to ease the tension, but Jess cut me off with a muttered, "Of course, then you'd have to get back into a car to go home, and we know how that goes right now, don't we?"

It was mean; Anna hadn't been the only one in that car. It'd certainly scared me to death, and thinking about it again was enough to make my heart skip a beat. Kitty shrunk down into her beanbag chair, drawing her knees to her chest and hugging them. The lower part of her face was hidden behind her crossed arms, and her eyes jumped from shadow to shadow.

Anna started throwing her stuff back into her tote bag with a dry, humorless laugh. "You're *such* a bitch sometimes. If that's your attitude, fine. I'll call my mom and go home. I can help Shauna from there."

"Whatever," Jess said, thrusting the computer aside.

"Wait," I said to Anna. "Wait. You know what, Jess? I get what you're saying about putting Mary first, and I appreciate that. I really do. But you keep saying you're sorry, but you've never actually apologized to us. And that matters. This is scary stuff. And while it'd be more convenient if Anna stopped copping attitude"—I braced, expecting Anna to snarl at me for that, but she remained quiet, her hands wedging her clothes back into her overstuffed bag—"it's her right to be mad. We were all scared out of our minds in the car—she looked like she was on the hood. She shook it and... whatever. Either apologize *to* us instead of *at* us or I'll figure out this stuff at my place."

Jess looked like I'd struck her. Her eyes bored through my skull. Anna's lips were pinched in a flat line; she expected Jess to start screaming. Kitty snagged the computer, avoiding the fight. I had no idea what she was doing hunkered down behind the screen, but her fingers were loud on the keyboard.

Jess let out a shrill whistle like a teakettle boiling over. I stiffened, ready for a tantrum, but something dissuaded her. There was a soft sigh followed by a groan. She dropped to the floor beside me with a hard thud. "Fine. Fine, I get it. Yeah. I guess I... I am sorry. I'm sorry you're all scared. I'm scared, too. I'm scared for Shauna and myself and you guys, so for what it's worth, I'm sorry. I do really want to help Shauna now."

Anna rolled her head back to peer at the ceiling. She took a few long breaths to clear her head and nodded. "Fine. Let's just figure out what Shauna needs. She's the priority." She shoved her tote bag aside and slid down next to Kitty, leaning into her side.

"Thanks, guys," I murmured.

"Hey, come here," Kitty said. "I found Mary's church on the historical society site."

It was a black-and-white picture of an old church with a tall steeple. A brunette woman stood before its double doors smiling, holding a rake and wearing overalls. The caption read, *Adeline Dietrich, Southbridge Parish, 1961, two months before the flood.* We'd seen a snippet of the church in the Mary Worth picture, but not the whole deal. It was a beast of a building, with large cathedral windows and two side chambers that sprouted off the main body like arms. The stone looked dark, almost black, but it was hard to tell the true color by the picture alone.

Jess reached out to tap the screen. "Oh, holy crap. I know where that is," she said. "It's right next to my grandparents' place near the river. It might have flooded, but most of the structure is still standing. Maybe we should check it out?"

The idea was interesting, though I did remember what Cody had said about Moira's library research. "We could. I'm not sure what we'd find. Isn't most of the stuff in storage?"

"Yes, but if the pastor locked Mary in the basement like he threatened... I doubt they'd move a body. There would be some reference if they found the bones, right?" Anna asked.

I nodded. "That'd be noteworthy, yes, but there's no information beyond the caption."

"Or maybe the body's still there," Kitty whispered. I looked at her. We all looked at her, and then we all looked back at the picture. If that was the case, we had some hunting to do.

⁓

Jess wanted to spend Friday night climbing around the church. She had the patience of a toddler. Anna was the one who told her we needed a Mary break, that I'd just been stabbed by dead-girl fingernails. I wasn't convinced it'd get better than this—I'd seen how Cody looked. But a night's reprieve sounded nice.

Instead of racing to the church, we researched over pizza. There wasn't a lot of progress, though. Anything we found about Bloody Mary related to variations on the summoning—how people claimed to summon her, the different names associated with her legend. By the time midnight came, we were tired and frustrated and too cheese-inflated to move.

Jess sighed and flopped back to stare at the ceiling. "We should have gone to the church. We need a better lead."

"Maybe tomorrow?" I asked.

Kitty frowned. "I can't. My dad's dragging me to visit my grandparents during the day, and I have plans tomorrow night. You guys can go without me if you want."

"I've got a family cookout tomorrow during the day," Anna said.

"So let's go at night," Jess said.

I didn't love that idea. If Mary was there in some guise, did we really want to face her in the dark? We were at enough of a disadvantage in the daylight. "Are we sure that's a good idea? What if she lives there?" I asked.

Jess shook her head. "She'd be cutting up everyone in Solomon's Folly if she lived there. Why would she bother with the mirrors if she didn't have to? Besides, we're better off going at night. Less reflection if there's less light. The car's less of an issue that way, too. Plus I doubt the locals want people climbing all over their historical buildings. This gives us a little cover."

"I hate to admit it, but she's got a point," Anna said. "And I can go tomorrow night, but I don't think we should leave Shauna alone between now and then. We've gotten lucky so far—the kids showing up with the car, Mrs. McAllister with the bathroom. But if we leave her on her own, it could get ugly. We should take shifts this weekend."

"I can help on Sunday during the day," Kitty offered.

Jess nodded. "Cool. I can take tomorrow day, so Anna's off the hook with the cookout. But tomorrow night when she gets home, let's hit the church and see if we can find anything. Sound good, Shauna?"

None of it sounded good. I was happy for the company, of course, but the idea of crawling through a deserted church at night with a monster haunting me wasn't high on my list of Awesome Things to Do. I was running out of options, though. We'd already tapped the Internet and Cody. We needed more.

"Sure," I said hesitantly. By Anna's less-than-enthusiastic expression, she was in accord. Jess was the only one energized by the possibility, but then, she'd been Mary-obsessed since we started.

Which reminded me.

"Hey, I meant to ask you earlier. Why do you keep calling Cody?"

Jess dropped her head, blinked, then shrugged. Her fingers returned to the second Mary letter. She reached behind her back to retrieve her red notebook and jammed the pages inside the top cover.

"Trying to find out if we can put her away for good," she said. "I have questions. I want to help you."

"Well, stop. I don't want to alienate the only other person in the world who survived Mary Worth." Jess started to say something, but stopped herself, her brow crinkling and her teeth digging into her lower lip. I knew that look. Jess had a secret. We were too far into this Mary thing for her to pull punches now. "What?" I pressed, and she squirmed beside me like a worm on a bait hook.

"There's one other girl who survived Mary. Well, not a girl anymore, but, like, you know," she said. "Elsa Samburg. She was haunted in the seventies. She's still around, but Cody's more accessible."

"How do you know that?" Anna demanded.

Jess ran her hand over her mouth nervously. "Aunt Dell mentioned her in passing. It's not like Elsa would be much help. I don't know how we could talk to her."

"Why not?" I asked.

Jess looked away from me, her eyes fixing on the blood-stained SpongeBob T-shirt on the floor. "She's in a mental hospital. She lost her mind."

17

The Elsa Samburg news surprised me, but it shouldn't have. I'd seen Cody. And I'd had Mary on me for only a few days and I was already questioning my sanity. Mary was perfect paranoia fodder. What I found more alarming was Jess dropping another "Oh, by the way" on us. There were too many of them. If she'd had all this information, why had she ever suggested we summon Mary?

Recklessness, yes. Selfishness, yes. Her worst traits all tied up into one huge, horrible idea that was going to get me killed.

Jess's motives were on my mind as we huddled into a pile to sleep. We were like puppies—no one was comfortable being alone, so we curled together around our pillows. I could feel Anna's leg against mine and Kitty's elbow grazing my arm. Jess stayed out of her room and slept with us on the floor, too. She was so close, I could hear the soft cadence of her breaths.

Sleep eluded me. Part of it was the footsteps in the hall as Jess's family shuffled around the house before settling down for the night. Part of it was the wind through the trees. Part of it was the howling of a neighborhood cat and the barking of a dog. All of it conspired to keep me awake as long as possible. My last conscious moment was the thought that, yes, Mary could send anyone over the edge.

Mrs. McAllister woke us at nine the next morning with a dozen doughnuts and orange juice. It was way early to be up on a Saturday, but she stepped over our prone bodies to set the food in the middle of the room, like we were a pack of wolves. I pushed myself up to snag breakfast. Anna and Kitty joined me while Jess snored. After we ate, Kitty poked Jess's shoulder, narrowly avoiding Jess's morning flails.

"Hey, I'm taking Anna home," Kitty said. "I'll talk to you guys later. Good luck at the church."

Jess grumbled and nodded, her hands sliding down her face to rub the sleep away.

◦◦◦

We needed to move out of Todd's space for the day. Jess came out to the hall with the salt clutched in her hands. "Sit here," she said. I slumped down onto the floor while she went to anti-ghost her room. She crossed from her bedroom to the linen closet a few times, using sheets to cover the closet's sliding glass doors. I could hear her moving furniture around before she poked her head out and motioned me in.

The room looked safe enough. The windows were salted. The

mirrors were covered or turned toward the walls. She'd even taken her pictures down so there wouldn't be anything staring at us from the frames. I stepped over a heap of dirty clothes on the floor and flung myself onto the bed. The carnival pony was there and I hugged it to my chest, my chin resting on its fuzzy pink mane. Jess eyed me and smirked, sinking down into her computer chair, the monitor on her desktop covered by a sweatshirt so there was no reflection.

"I'm glad I've got you to myself. I had an idea I wanted to run by you without the extra ears." She paused to think, tilting her head to the side. "It's not a nice idea, but I have to throw it out there. I don't want you stuck. I won't lose you. I refuse."

She sounded so fierce, I found myself smiling. Jess was an idiot, but there was something to be said for unrelenting loyalty. "Okay?"

She pulled her feet up onto the seat of her chair, her toes sticking out over the edge. She'd painted her nails a bright, cheery teal. "I was thinking we could get someone to take the tag from you. Someone who deserves it, though, so we don't feel bad."

"WHAT?!" I hadn't meant to yell, but I was too shocked *not* to yell. "No!" I shouted. "No! I'd never... not to anyone else. How would I live with myself? Jesus, Jess. Use your brain."

Jess reached out to pinch me, hard, on the bicep. I smacked at her and rubbed the sore spot with my bandaged hand. "I *am* using my brain. If the choice is living with yourself or too dead to live with anything, I'm picking living with yourself every time. Guilt goes away. Being dead doesn't," she said.

I shook my head. It wasn't an option. I'd rather chisel away at Mary Worth's legacy to uncover her secrets than pass the problem to someone else. There had to be a reason for all of this, and when we found that reason, we'd have a solution. I had to believe something from Mary's past was the linchpin to this whole terrifying mess. We just hadn't found it yet.

"Well," I croaked, my voice cracking from strain, "I didn't think there was anything in the world that'd make me want to go to this church tonight. But congratulations, you've managed it."

Jess sighed, resting her chin on her knee. Her eyes skimmed to her sheet-covered window. "Don't be stupid, Shauna. You want to live. I want you to live. I'm not going to let you die."

∽

Anna returned after dinner, when the sun was past the horizon and the skies were more gray than gold. Her glasses were off, so either she'd put in contacts or preferred temporary blindness to having her eyes poked out by ghost fingers. I talked to my mother briefly, assuring her I'd be home later tonight. She said be in by midnight, but she wouldn't walk in until after two— she tended bar at McReady's until closing, so I wasn't worried about missing curfew.

I texted Kitty to be sure she didn't want to be in on this madness. She sent me a message back, saying *Out with Bronx,* followed by a smiley emoticon.

"Kitty's talking to Bronx," I said as we waited for the last light to disappear. I wanted to avoid the deathmobile as long as possible. "I'm wondering if he texted her after the Mary thing at school yesterday. Either way, I'm hoping good things come of it."

"Same," Anna said. "Except I'm mad she didn't tell me about it herself. I wonder if she thought I'd try to talk her out of going out with him again?"

I shrugged. "Who knows? But if she thought you'd fight her on it, probably. You know she doesn't do confrontation."

"I, for one, thank God they're talking," Jess said. "Maybe if he sticks it in her she'll stop being such a huge drain. One more guilt trip and I was going to feed her to a crocodile."

Anna reached out to whack Jess's forearm, her face scrunched up like she smelled something foul. "That's so crude. Did you have to put it that way?"

Jess's smile was unrepentant.

We piled into the car at nine, this time with Anna in the front passenger seat and me sitting center in the back, my legs straddling the bump between the two foot wells. I slouched down, a box of salt in my lap. Anna had devised an ingenious method to prevent us from being Mary mauled: clear packaging tape. She drizzled salt crystals over the sticky part before laying strips across the glass on a diagonal. It wasn't a solid line, but at least we knew the granules were enough to keep Mary from pushing through.

Jess got us to Solomon's Folly before ten. There was something different about the town after dark. During the day, the Folly was any other small New England town with its picket fences and quaint storefronts, but at night, it took a turn. The narrow streets had no lights. The drive was one tiny, dark, curving road into the next. Fog spread over the land in a thick paste, casting a dank pallor over the sprawling fields and farmland. The trees were clawed behemoths looming over the roads, a canopy of foliage blocking the moon and any vestiges of its light.

"Good God, this place is creepy," Anna said. We passed a gas station on the main stretch, a neon OPEN sign blinking in the window. The lights above the gas pumps were lightbulbs on strings, each swinging with the breeze.

Jess said nothing as we turned onto a stretch of dirt road that made the car shimmy. She guided us away from civilization and toward . . . I didn't know what. Nothingness. We were in the middle of nowhere, our car bouncing over the divots in the gravel beneath us.

The road narrowed until it was only suitable for a single car. It sloped downward, too, though it was too dark to see what it sloped toward. Jess killed the engine and plunged us into perfect darkness. She fumbled around in the front seat until a circle of light blasted her in the eyes. A Maglite. She handed me and Anna flashlights as well, each a fraction of the size of her own. Jess threw open her door, and Anna followed suit. I climbed out next with a flashlight in one hand, a salt box in the other. Neither gave me any comfort.

Jess aimed her flashlight down on the ground. I heard rushing water and the call of a night bird. Anna paused to swing her flashlight toward the river. The water was black and angry, the banks steep. The trees nearby were all dead, their branches dry and emaciated—like Mary's spindly, bony arms. I shuddered and stepped to Anna's side. She trembled beside me.

We stood that way awhile, peering at the river, until a light turned on across the water. I jumped in surprise. There was so much darkness here that a flash of light was startling; it was a sun against a blackened canvas. It took me a second to realize it was a porch light. There was a house on the opposite bank, and though I didn't like the idea of being seen tromping around the old church, it was good to know we weren't far from the outside world.

"We should go," I said. Anna nodded and turned her flashlight away so we wouldn't be spotted. A screen door slammed across the way. It may have been too late for secrecy.

Jess's footsteps were fading in the distance. We scrambled to catch up, Anna stumbling in a hole hidden in the knee-high grass. I looped my arm around her waist to hold her upright. Once she was steady, she continued to cling to me, the salt box wedged in between our bodies. Jess walked deeper into the night, her path keeping us parallel to the river. The walk went on and on, taking us uncomfortably far from the car. Finally, Jess stopped. My eyes adjusted to the light as I took in the enormous black lump of a building twenty feet in front of us.

Churches are supposed to be pointy things that stretch to the sky, but this church had long ago lost its steeple and portions of its roof. It looked like a dome now or, with the rooms extending from the sides and the shadowy trees surrounding them, a hulking wood tick feeding from the ground. Jess swung the Maglite up to the entrance where double doors once stood. There was an open archway inviting the unsuspecting into its maw. That's how I saw the church—a monstrous, living creature that wanted to swallow us alive.

"Oh, this can't be a good idea," Anna said.

Jess walked on. "It's necessary."

Jess approached the front of the church and pressed her hand flat against the stones. She pulled back and rubbed her fingers together as she craned her head back. "It feels wet. Like, slimy-wet. Be careful. Don't fall."

"Be care..." Anna's voice died as Jess ducked inside the passageway, taking the light of her big flashlight with her. Anna and I shared a moment of solidarity standing there together—until we heard the rustling overhead. The trees lacked the foliage to make any sound. I swung my flashlight up just in time to catch them. Bats.

"Oh, holy crap. Let's get the hell out of here," I said.

Catching a glimpse of flying furballs, Anna grabbed my hand and dragged me toward the church. For better or worse, we were going in.

18

"How did you ever find this place?" I asked into the dark. I could barely see, but I could hear Jess fumbling around nearby. She cursed as something skittered across the stone floor. It struck the wall next to me with a loud clack.

Anna swung her flashlight in a wide circle. The main room of the church was smaller than I'd expected. The congregation must have only had about a dozen pews for worshippers. At the altar, there were two arching holes where windows used to be, but the panes were devoid of glass. A tree branch had grown in through one of the gaps, its ends spearing through the roof. Slivers of moonlight cast silver shadows across the black walls.

"We're near my grandparents' house. It's a ways up the river. I'd come out here as a kid with my cousin to play," Jess said.

I eased farther inside, following the sound of Jess's voice past piles of rubble. There was a smell I couldn't identify— almost like cleaning solution. My sneakers crunched through leaves and debris. I slipped. It wasn't just the moisture that sent me colliding into the walls. There was a layer of muck smeared across the floor stones, too. Bracing, I swung my flashlight down to examine the murky, lumpy texture on the floor. I wasn't sure I wanted to know what it was.

Anna reached out to steady me, her hand gripping my elbow. I saw Jess duck through an open doorway to our right.

"What are you looking for?" I called out.

"Mary talked about a basement doorway. I'm trying to find it. There's nothing in here but grit and broken ceiling, though. A few bookcases."

"Didn't she say Elizabeth watched her get locked inside? She was decorating the pews when he dragged Mary off. This main room is where the pews would be. The door's got to be somewhere in here," Anna replied.

Anna was right. I turned my flashlight to sweep the area. The back wall beneath the windows was solid—there was no door to be found. I edged farther to the left inside the main room. There was a door opposite the one Jess had crept through that I guessed to be the entryway to the second side room. An old bureau was pushed flush to the wall. The bureau was wide enough and tall enough that something could be hidden behind it. I eased my way across the cold, slimy stones, taking Anna with me.

"Hey, Jess. Come here!" I called out. Anna and I shuffled together, our feet moving like we were skating. As we neared the corner, the smell intensified. Now I recognized it as ammonia. Why ammonia here? Was it from the dresser? The dark wood *was* covered in a pale green mold, and there were distortions and lumps riddling the surface.

"Now what?" Anna asked.

"We move the dresser, I guess," I said.

I held the flashlight in my mouth and put the salt on top of the bureau so I could get a grip. The bureau was layered in decay. I tried to push it away from the wall. It wouldn't budge. Anna went to the opposite side to help, and the two of us managed to wriggle it a half a foot forward. Once Jess joined us, we maneuvered the bureau far enough out to see behind it. A narrow door was wedged in the corner.

"It's real," Jess whispered. She reached out to touch the planks of the door, reverent when she slid her fingers over the rough wooden surface. There was an old-fashioned iron latch in place of a proper doorknob. Jess reached for it. A faint grinding noise rattled the air as she pressed the button tab at the top. The door wouldn't open. The latch was rusted shut or the lock had been jammed.

"Here, hold this," I said to Anna, handing her my flashlight. She angled both beams at the door as I reached for the lock. My feet slid across the floor, but I found some purchase by wedging my leg against the wall. Jess and I fussed with the latch. The tab finally gave, a mechanism inside squealing in protest as we bullied its gears after so many years of disuse.

"On three," Jess said. She counted and the two of us pressed and pulled, forcing the latch to open. The good news was, it worked. The door swung toward us, sending us skidding. Jess stumbled back and landed on the floor.

The bad news was more bats. *So* many bats that hadn't left for their evening feeding. A chorus of high-pitched squeals rang out, and then the flutter of a thousand wings beat the air as the bats blasted up from the dark. I dove for the floor and Anna huddled on her haunches, the flashlights dropping and skittering away. My hands sailed up to protect my head as bats skimmed across my hair with their wings and feet. I cowered lower, my only defense against the aerial assault.

The explosion of bats was over as fast as it had begun, the last of them squeaking off into the night. Anna fumbled around to collect the flashlights. Jess, however, whimpered behind me.

"Oh, *God*, nasty. Nasty," she groaned. I glanced over at her to see what was wrong. Jess still had her Maglite and was pointing it at the sludge on her fingers. The sludge we'd been sliding in all this time. The sludge I now realized was bat guano. Not only was the basement full of the creatures, but they must have been living in the remaining eaves of the church as well, which explained the ammonia smell.

Disgusting.

"Don't think about it," I said. I reached out to help her to her feet. She clasped my sleeve and smeared me in some of the muck. I struggled to take my own advice. She skidded into my side and we stepped toward the top of the steps to peer through the door, our free hands clasped together, fingers laced in apprehension and fear.

Stairs leading down into an unfathomable dark—stairs with no railing and no walls to support a would-be visitor. This had to be the place. My pulse pounded. Jess edged forward but stopped herself at the threshold. The stairs were steep and narrow, and there was a glistening sheen on the stone that indicated a long, slippery trip if she misstepped. She swung the Maglite around the room to get a better look. It was maybe fifteen feet long by twenty feet wide. Water covered most of the floor, though I could see dry spots at the corners of the room. Directly across from the stairs, there were crates stacked against the far wall, most of them covered by drop cloths in various states of decay.

The ammonia smell was thick and concentrated in the basement. Jess pointed to a crumbling break in the wall along the ceiling, a gap no bigger than a bowling ball, with a tiny bit of moonlight shining through. The bat entrance.

"I'm going down," I said. I knew I had to do it. Jess was right; this was necessary. Daylight and shovels would suit me better, but I was willing to risk the darkness to search for answers.

Jess swung the flashlight my way, blasting me in the eyes. I lifted my hand to block the light, and she jerked it away with a deep breath.

"You sure? It's ... Not sure how safe it is," Jess said.

"Are *you* actually asking about safety? Who are you and what have you done with Jess?" Anna asked from behind us. Jess grunted; I tittered a little.

I was careful where I put my sneaker. Jess held out her hand to steady me. For a moment, I thought she'd descend into the basement too, but she stayed at the top to anchor me as long as she could. Four steps. Five steps. The stone was slick, but my going slowly and Jess's hold kept me upright with minimal slippage.

When I was halfway to the bottom, Jess followed, easing her way down while Anna took position in the doorway, her dual flashlights illuminating the path into the recesses. We were like a chain gang, with one of us near the bottom, one hovering midstairs, and one at the top. I extended my toe to check the water's depth. The floor beneath felt solid, though I felt a tire-size dip caved into the middle, like the stones were sinking into the ground. If I avoided that portion, I thought I could stand without too much problem.

I tugged away from Jess and took the last step. The slope was harder to avoid than I'd presumed. I was standing in cold, black water up to my ankles. I forced myself to concentrate on the crates ahead of me.

"You okay?" Jess asked as I sloshed toward the crates. If Mary's body was down here, it wasn't in the crates, but I was curious what *was* inside them. The first drop cloth disintegrated upon touch, some of the fibers sticking to my fingers. A chunk of cloth fell into the water by my feet. I shivered and brushed off my hands before rooting through a crate.

"A little light over here?" I called to Jess. She lifted the Maglite enough that I could see a stack of books inside the crate, though the covers were too decayed to touch. I eased my way over to another crate and peeked over the edge. This one was half-collapsed, its contents oozing onto the floor. What remained inside was rotten, but among all that moldy, uniden-tifiable sludge, I spotted something shiny.

I remembered the mirror from Mary's letter and wondered if this might be it—if that tiny glint from within the crate was a missing piece to the puzzle that was Mary Worth. I carefully slid it out and lifted it up. A part of me wanted it to be a clue, but another part wondered what I'd do with it if it were. But looking at it in the dim light, disappointment quieted my fears. It wasn't a mirror, just glass.

Something scurried across my hand. I glanced down and saw a black beetle—the same beetle I'd seen worming its way out of Mary's skin. Black, shiny carapace, too many legs. I felt it skitter over my arm and I flicked it away, shuddering. Didn't bats eat bugs? Yet this one somehow flourished down here in the dark. It was another thing to add to my Do Not Think About list.

I returned to the crate of books. I picked it up and moved it aside to look at one of the middle crates. The topmost layer would likely be damaged from the bats above, and the bottom layer would likely be drenched by water. The best place to find something useful was somewhere in the middle.

This crate was not as wet as the others, though the stack of papers inside was still impossible to read. Next to the stack was a small metal box. I pulled it out, taking a moment to brush the slushy remnants of old papers away from its top. The front had a loop for a miniature padlock, but there was no lock there anymore. Maybe there never was one.

"Point the light right on me?" I called up the steps.

Anna aimed both flashlights in my direction as I tugged

open the lid of the metal box. It squealed, its hinges hungry
for oil. Inside was a stack of black-and-white photographs that
were surprisingly undamaged. For a moment I tensed, thinking
I'd discovered more pictures of Mary, but the images were too
modern. I did, though, recognize the person in most of them. It
was the Dietrich woman from the church picture. She was smiling and posing for shots, sometimes in groups, sometimes on
her own. She was no more than twenty or thirty in most of the
pictures. For a moment, I stared at her. There was something
oddly familiar about her smile.

Before I could place the smile, something quick and small
scuttled across my arm. I dropped the pictures back into the
crate just as I felt another beetle crawling up my calf. More
crept on me, tickling me with their thread-thin legs. I returned
the crate and reached into my sleeve, grabbing on to a hard
shell attached to a set of violent, hairy legs. I flung it across
the basement.

"Uuuuugh. Bugs," I cried, hiking my pants up and itching
where I'd felt one scour my ankle. The beetle had climbed up
to my knee. I reached for it, right as I felt another one wiggle
its way across the back of my neck. And another one graze my
cheek to run down my front, into my shirt and under my bra.
"Jesus!"

"Are you okay?" Anna asked.

"Yeah. No. Maybe—I...Beetles. Like, the black ones that
come with Mary. I bet she's here. Maybe under my feet. There's
a dip in the stone, so maybe she's buried—" My voice cut off
on a squeal as another bug crawled down my back and another

across my hip. I wanted to get out of here. I turned back for the stairs, but I couldn't move because of the *hands* that tore from the water, anchoring my legs in place.

The jagged edges of Mary's fingernails punctured through my thin socks, jabbing at my skin. I tried to kick her away—to walk toward Jess who was reaching for me, screaming instructions I couldn't understand in my panic—but those hands jerked on me and I fell forward. My arms stretched out, stopping me from smashing my face against the cold steps. I landed hard and wailed, my forearms and knees throbbing in pain from the impact. My legs were in the puddle from the knees down, and her iron grip moved from my ankles to my calves.

"Take my hand. TAKE MY HAND," Jess shouted.

"The salt. Anna, get the salt!" I yelled, my fingers clenching on Jess's forearm. Jess locked her grip on me and pulled up while Mary pulled back. I swiveled my head around, scanning the water's surface from the light of Jess's Maglite. Mary exploded up in a spray of rancid black rain. She was covered in wet leaves and strings of dead vines, her torso above the water while the rest of her remained hidden below. Strands of hair were plastered to her lumpy scalp, her dress glued to a skeletal frame.

Mary let out a wheezy chitter of laughter as her hands locked around my knees. She jerked me back and away from Jess. I sailed through the air and landed in the water, splashing the walls as my body made contact with the floor. The air was forced from my lungs, another stab of pain shredding its way through my already-bruised arms.

We were stupid. Stupid to be there. Stupid to be unprepared for the worst. Mary snarled and I felt her fingernails raking over my legs. She was trying to cut me through my jeans. She let out a furious squeal as I felt her fingernails rip into my sides. Instant anguish, those little razors digging into my stomach and twisting. I squirmed and tried to crawl away, but Mary clutched a hand into my hair. I felt cold, wormlike fingers slithering along the back of my scalp before she took a fistful of my curls and pressed my face into the water.

My nose hit the floor stones. White fireworks burst behind my eyes. I heard Jess screaming my name, I heard Anna shouting. I held my breath. I held it so long, my lungs ached. Just as I was about to open my mouth and let the flood in, Mary screeched behind me, her hands falling away. I tore my face up with a bellow, furiously gasping for air, as Mary snarled and thrashed behind me.

"Shauna! Come to me. Come on," Jess hollered. I opened my eyes, squinting against the water drops running down my face. I crawled toward Jess's voice. My vision swam, but I was able to make out two sets of shoes on the steps—Anna had come down too, and when I lifted my gaze, I saw she was rapidly firing salt at Mary.

Jess tugged me to the stairs. I cleared the first two steps without slipping, but Mary lunged at me again, her fingers tangling in the hem of my T-shirt. I kicked out at her, my heel striking her arm with a loud snap. She let go with a rattling snarl. The three of us made the perilous climb upstairs, Anna tossing salt the entire way. It was enough to keep Mary away, though each time I looked back at her, a little more of Mary had spilled out of that black puddle on the floor.

"I'm almost out of salt. It's almost empty. We have to go," Anna croaked. Jess reached for my wrist, grabbing it and dragging me through the church and toward the front doors. I looked back to make sure we weren't abandoning Anna. She stayed a few steps behind to rifle the rest of the salt, but when Mary crawled out of the basement, dragging herself up by her hands, Anna tore past us to get to the car. I couldn't blame her—Mary erect was fearsome. She was more spider than ghoul right now, one of her elbows bent in instead of out, her feet flat to the ground so she scurried instead of walked. Her back was arched too low. Her head dangled at an unnatural angle while her white serpent tongue thrust out from between her lips, licking our scent in the air.

Jess and I ran, the Maglite swinging back and forth with Jess's frenzied gait. I hurt all over. My chest ached from gasping. I was dizzy with fear, but I kept pace with Jess even as Mary snorted and groaned at us from behind. We crested the front steps of the church and stumbled into the grass, Anna only a few feet ahead of us.

Four steps out of the doorway, two enormous lights blasted us in the face. We stopped short, stuck between the apparition and the disorienting lights ahead of us. Then it registered—those were headlights. It was a car. A car with flashing blue lights on the roof.

19

"All right, kids. Rein it in. You're not supposed to be out here," a disembodied female voice said from behind the car. "This is Ms. Dietrich's private property."

I put my hands up and walked toward the car, trying to look inconspicuous. I wanted to get away from the church and be near the person with the gun as quickly as possible. I couldn't hear snarling behind me anymore, but I didn't trust the dark. The dark had too many secrets.

"Hi! Hi, we saw ... something, but it was ..." Before Anna got too far into an explanation, she noticed me edging away from her and followed. I saw the policewoman's outline and then I saw the policewoman herself. Tall, thick through the shoulders, a little heavy; she was older than my mom, with short black hair peppered with gray and a pair of glasses on her face. She had her hand on her hip, but not near her weapon. I let my hands drop to my sides.

"Ms. Dietrich called me out when she saw you drive up. What are you girls doing out here?" she demanded.

Jess trotted up next to us. She was pale, her eyes a little bigger than they ought to be, but she faked being okay better than me and Anna. Anna looked green, her arms wrapped around her middle as if to hold her insides inside. The wind had picked up, whipping the grass around our feet into a frenzy. My wet clothes clung to my skin. I shivered, my teeth loudly chattering. "We were playing Truth or Dare," Jess explained. "Go into the church at night."

"Got ya. Well, how about you show me a license and registration so you can Truth or Dare your way back home?" the cop said.

⌒⌒

The officer drove us back to the car, remarking not once, not twice, but three times about how bad we smelled. Anna had shared our bat encounter. The cop grunted, regretting inviting us into her cruiser. This was the type of stench that lingered.

At the car, Jess handed her paperwork to the officer. My eyes swung back in the direction of the church. Mary was there somewhere. Or maybe she wasn't. It was hard to tell which thought was more terrifying. She'd either slithered back through the water and into her glass world or she was here, in this world. Maybe she was hunting me. Maybe she was tearing up Ms. Dietrich. I felt sick from the smell and the fresh gouges in my sides. My arms ached. My legs itched from the memory of beetles dancing over my skin.

The cop tapped Jess's license. "Are you related to—"

"Gus McAllister. He's my grandfather," Jess interrupted.

The officer nodded and handed the ID back. "All right, here's the deal. You're going to get in that car with your friends and you're going to drive straight home. Massachusetts law still has a curfew for teenagers, and if you want the privilege of driving, you honor it." The officer turned to point at me and Anna like we were Jess's shameful secrets. "And no more trespassing, girls. That church isn't a playground. Someone could have gotten hurt."

She didn't know the half of it. "Thank you, officer," I said.

∽

The silence was oppressive during the ride home. When Jess got us back to the section of the highway that had things like streetlights and modern buildings, she turned on the radio. Anna reached out and snapped it off. Jess glared at Anna. I caught a glimpse of Anna's furious expression through the passing lights.

"Just take me home. I'll get my stuff from you tomorrow," I said, my voice ragged from screaming. My throat felt like I'd gargled with dust.

"Are you staying with her tonight, then?" Jess asked Anna. Anna hissed a confirmation back. Jess shrugged off Anna's anger, but I knew Jess was bothered—her shoulders were tense and her jaw clenched.

I was wet and scared. The salted tape was securely on the

windows, but I wanted more. I wanted every ward we could muster to keep Mary away, and right then, we had nothing else.

"Do you think she's . . . Is she free? Did we free her?" I asked, my voice warbling.

Anna groaned, a feral whine that sounded more animal than human. Jess shook her head.

"No. I've never heard of that happening," Jess said.

"But you don't know for sure," I added.

"Well, I'm taking an educated guess. Mary went away the moment the policewoman showed up. So she probably disappeared or—"

"But if she disappeared, does that mean she blinks out like you flipped a switch? Or does she physically have to go back to the place she passed through?" I asked.

Jess hesitated and then sighed, defeated. "I don't know. Maybe Cordelia would, but I don't know."

Silence filled the car as Jess pulled into my driveway to drop off me and Anna. Jess lifted her hand in a half wave; I returned the gesture. Anna ignored it. I put my key into my house lock, doing my best to overlook the flickering lightbulb in the building's hallway. I'd never noticed the light or heard its low-grade hum before, but I noticed a lot of things lately that I hadn't a week ago. Perpetually searching for a ghost had heightened my senses, like a rabbit living among wolves.

"Can I borrow some clean clothes? After a bath? It seems safer," Anna said. "You first, of course, but . . . please?"

"Yeah. Absolutely."

We took turns bathing. I stayed alert, waiting for Mary to stare back at me through the water, but we were alone. Had we unleashed the devil upon Solomon's Folly?

"I have to call Cody," I said. "I know it's late, but in case Mary's out. She should know."

"Yeah, you do. I was just thinking the same thing," Anna replied.

I finished my bath. The warm water on my battered body felt wonderful. Well, it felt wonderful everywhere that wasn't my arms, my hand, my shoulders, or my sides. Mary hadn't gotten my gut too badly, but there were scrapes and scratches there. Less than a week in and I looked like I'd been maimed by a blender. I was the scraggly neighborhood cat that got into too many fights.

"Hey, so, I don't know how to bring this up, so I'm just going to come out with it," Anna said, peering at the wall, her eyebrows low over her eyes, her mouth tight. "I'm not sure I can make the Jess friendship work. I know she apologized, but each time she reveals something she knew, each time something bad happens with Mary, I can't deal with it. She threw us into a *seriously* dangerous situation. I'm terrified all the time—for me, for you. If we're doing stuff to help you, I'll be there. I don't want to lose you as a friend, but I need to stay away from Jess awhile."

Anna had the right to feel angry and scared. I wasn't going to try to talk her out of it. Not again, anyway. Just like Kitty's situation with Bronx—the stuff I'd found important a week ago no longer seemed like such a big deal. Right then, getting out of the bathtub without another wound took most of my concentration.

I wrapped a towel around my sore body and drained the tub so Anna could take her turn. While the water ran, I called Cody, but she didn't pick up the phone. I left a voice mail and warned her about the church and Mary. For Cody's sake, for the sake of my conscience, I had to hope Bloody Mary was back behind the glass.

20

Anna slept in my bed with me. Or, well, she *stayed* in my bed with me. Sleep didn't come easily for either of us. I looked at the clock at least once every hour. I felt Anna moving next to me, sometimes hugging one of my pillows to her chest, sometimes rolling close to me. Human contact was one of the few things that gave us comfort. I had to adjust her arm once or twice because it grazed the gashes in my side.

Mom's Sunday schedule was kinder than the rest of the week—she only had the day shift at McReady's, so she'd be gone from eleven until six. Mom chattered through our pancake breakfast, only commenting three or four times on how tired and unresponsive Anna and I were. Perkiness was impossible.

"All right, well, I'm off. Don't do anything too crazy without me. And Shauna, make sure you take out the trash today. There's something really stinky in it," she said, brushing her lips across my temple before heading for the door. "I'll see you soon, Anna. Have a good day!"

"Bye, Mrs. O'Brien," Anna called after her. My mother's footsteps pounded down the building stairs.

It was a quiet few hours. I checked the news to see if there'd been a murder spree in Solomon's Folly. Nothing. Jess texted to check on me, and I sent her a small, inconsequential update. I didn't mention what Anna had said; I figured I'd let the two of them sort out their friendship. I also didn't bother changing out of my pajamas. For that matter, Anna didn't bother changing out of my pajamas, either.

Anna's parents collected her a little earlier than Kitty's scheduled arrival. I was alone, hugging my supply of salt. I'd covered most of the shiny surfaces in my room, including socks on the doorknobs and paper bags over the windows. Glass bottles were bagged, pictures were all removed and tucked into the closet.

Kitty arrived just after twelve. I came out of my room in the same checkered pj pants and tank top from last night to discover Kitty wielding a large pizza in one hand and holding Bronx's hand with the other.

Bronx waved at me, looking around the apartment. He'd never been here before, and I always got a little self-conscious when people visited for the first time. It wasn't really a show-case, but he smiled and motioned at the floor-to-ceiling windows. "Those are cool. They remind me of church windows."

"That's because it used to be a church way back when," I said.

"Ah, cool," he said.

"Sorry we're late. Figured we'd pick up some stuff on the way," Kitty said. She put the pizza down on the coffee table and then dropped her pocketbook on the armchair. It was a huge leather bag—the type that weird girls carry small dogs in. Kitty didn't have anything living inside her bag. Just salt. Lots and lots of salt. She brought out three canisters and lined them up on top of the entertainment unit.

"How are you holding up? How was last night?" Kitty asked. I waited for both of them to sit before picking my spot on the floor next to the table, purposefully keeping my back to the television. Kitty and Bronx claimed the couch, Bronx eagerly diving into the pizza. "Bronx and I were talking. This Bloody Mary thing is so unreal. We've got to figure out a solution soon. I've covered all *my* mirrors and I'm not the one haunted. I can't get her out of my head."

Bronx nodded. "Yeah, I think I'm a tough dude, but after that insanity Friday in school, I just . . . yeah. This is messed up."

"Thanks, guys. Last night was . . . I don't know if it's the worst that it's been, but it was right up there." I proceeded to explain all the details, from the drive to the abandoned church, the haunted basement, and the cop who kicked us off of Ms. Dietrich's property. Kitty forgot to chew through the telling, the slice of pizza suspended halfway to her mouth. Bronx managed to continue eating despite his stunned expression.

"Holy crap," Kitty said, putting the slice down to wipe her face with her shirtsleeve. Realizing Bronx was there, she cast him a quasi-guilty look before picking up a napkin and repeating the gesture.

"The worst part is we learned nothing," I continued. "Zero. We could go back today, but it wasn't safe the first time; it won't be safe the second time even with daylight. I wish Cody would call me back. I'm worried about her."

"I'm sure Cody's fine," Kitty said. Her hollow reassurance did little to boost my confidence.

"You did learn something, you know," Bronx said a moment later. "If that church is on private property, maybe you can trace who owned it—you've got the current owner's name. My dad's big into tracking family ancestry. He's up to three hundred years ago in Greece now with our family history. There's a lot of information on the Web. The town hall would also help. They track everything, man—births, deaths, land purchases. You could maybe tie something back to Mary that way."

I nodded along as Bronx spoke. It was worth a try. I wasn't sure what I'd find, but compared to the big pile of zero viable solutions I had, it was another lead. A better idea than Jess's solution to find a new victim.

It was also a better idea than going back to the church.

"Why not?" I said. "Mary might be buried in the church. Or might have been. If so, maybe the person who owned the church knew something about her death. Or maybe Ms. Dietrich owned the church when it flooded and could tell us if any remains were disturbed. I'm grasping at straws here."

"Ugh. Yeah, but good luck talking to her if she's the one who called the cops on you," Kitty said.

I shrugged. "It was dark, and we were far enough across the river that it would have been hard to see us. I don't have to tell her I was the one trespassing. Either way. Thanks, you two. I might try to research more before I go back to the basement. Although I'm not sure I've got the guts to go back now. There's more to see in the daylight, I know, but it was so..." I couldn't finish the sentence. Thinking about Mary tearing up out of the water, the bugs, the bats. I shuddered.

Bronx forced a smile for my sake and slid the pizza box my way. I took a slice, hoping it was enough to distract me from the memory of last night. And the night before that. And the day before that. Kitty reached out to thread her fingers through his black hair. He batted her away, but she kept going at his bangs and giggling. He smirked at her, and when she wouldn't stop fussing, he put his pizza back into the box to tug her into his lap. She squealed as he half turned her so her legs were dangling over the side of the couch, her sandals falling to the floor with thuds. I watched her offer him a bite from her own slice. He unhinged his jaw to devour half of it in one go.

"Wow. Hungry much, you hog?" Kitty asked. Bronx tossed his head back to laugh.

"I'm an athlete. We have big appetites," he said. Apparently she bought into it because she fed him the rest of her slice before grabbing herself another. When he lunged forward to try to steal that, too, she bopped him on the nose with one of her acrylic nails.

This was more like the Kitty I knew. The morose girl we'd been shouldering for the last month lacked this sunshine. Maybe it was kind of dumb that it took a boy to get her back on track, but I wasn't going to complain. She was happy. I needed a little happy around me.

"Glad you two are better," I said. Both of them turned to smile at me, then at each other, and I suddenly felt like an outsider in my own house. They were doing that mind-meld couple thing people who'd been dating awhile did, and it gave me a third-wheel complex. I got up to get myself a drink, but paused to grab one of Kitty's canisters of salt before heading into the kitchen. The moment my back was turned, I heard what sounded like a lip-smacking kiss. I smirked as I approached the fridge. Brushed steel surface or not, I had to drink. Fortunately, Mary wasn't inside the shine.

I grumbled, unsure of how to express dread and relief at the same time.

I tugged open the door and grabbed an iced tea. Right as I latched on to the can, a loud bellowing rang out from the parking lot. It took me a second to identify the siren sound as an obnoxious, whirring car alarm. Bronx gently shoved Kitty aside before heading for the windows. He rummaged through his pocket to pull out his car keys, his thumb hitting a button on the plastic alarm thing.

"If someone bumped my dad's car, he'll kill me. I'm going to go check it out," he announced, turning around to head to the front door. Except Bronx never got the chance.

Spindly arms of yellow bone and gray flesh burst out from the windowpanes and wrapped around his torso. Bronx's eyes bulged, a high-pitched squeal ripping from his throat. The biggest, strongest guy I knew was yanked off his feet like he weighed nothing. He hovered there a second, thrashing and kicking against the windows. The arms jerked him back. Hard. The windows exploded as Bronx was thrust outside, hurtling through the air, body spiraling to the ground amid a rain of sparkling glass.

∽

I had no idea how she'd done it. So far, Mary had struck out through the glass or pulled things into the glass when the surface had softened. This time, Bronx hit something solid. The only explanation I could come up with was maybe it'd been jelly until he collided and she chose to let the surface harden. By then, the force of her pull was enough to send him sailing. Which meant she'd done it this way on purpose. Mary wanted Bronx to fall.

I stared at the empty space Bronx had just occupied. Kitty's screams echoed around the room, heart-wrenching and shrill. I never made a sound, not even when I raced to the window to see what I could do to help. Yes, Mary could still be near, but I had my salt. I hadn't dropped it, and I opened the top and sprayed it around as I neared the man-size gap, waving it back and forth like a fire extinguisher.

My imagination had already painted the world red, Bronx landing on his head and smashing his brains across the pavement. I forced myself to look. Bronx was sprawled on the ground below, but there was very little blood. He'd landed in such a way that his upper half was cushioned by shrubs. The problem was his legs. They were bent at odd angles, and one of his feet pointed in the opposite direction it was supposed to go.

She'd crippled him. Bloody Mary had crippled Bronx simply because he was near me, in my house. I pressed the back of my hand to my mouth so I wouldn't cry out, hot tears streaming down my cheeks. I felt horrible. I barely knew Bronx, but my ghost had managed to hurt him all the same. I wanted to throw up, to scream and tear down the walls around me, but Bronx needed me calm, not bugging out and shrieking in panic like Kitty. It was my fault he was down there. It was my fault that I hadn't insisted my friends leave when Cody told me to let them go.

This was *my fault.*

It was then that I heard him. It was faint, but I could hear him calling for us. He needed my help, not my self-recriminations. I made for the door, grabbing Kitty's arm and dragging her behind me as I ran for the steps. "Call 911," I said, but she was too busy screaming to hear me. I stopped on the second flight to shake her hard enough to rattle her teeth, my tear-stained eyes boring into hers. "*Kitty, he's alive.* Call 911 now!" I yelled at her.

She whimpered and fumbled in her pocket for her phone, following me as I raced for the building's foyer. I heard her talking a second later, her voice cracking when she had to tell the operator the nature of her emergency. I nearly ripped the front door off its hinges as I ran outside, vaulting over trash barrels and thrusting bags of recycling aside to get to Bronx.

He turned his head to look at me, face pale, eyes glassy.

"What was that? The arms. Was that her? Was it *her*?"

"Yes," I said, crouching beside him. Bronx grabbed for my hand, squeezing my fingers so hard, I was afraid he'd shatter them. "Kitty called the ambulance. They're on their way."

"My legs hurt. Real bad. They hurt, Shauna."

"I know. I'm so, so sorry." I considered telling him it was good he felt pain, that we were lucky he wasn't numb from the waist down or dead, but I was pretty sure he didn't want to hear that. Bronx gave my hand another squeeze and I winced. Kitty caught up with us, tears streaming down her cheeks and dribbling off her chin.

"Oh, Bronx. Baby," she said, collapsing onto her knees beside him. She reached for his other hand and slid her fingers over his. He turned his face to stare at her. She managed a watery smile, but then his body convulsed, his spine arching up off the pavement as he let out a wet gurgle and a roar. Kitty climbed on top of him then, sprawling her body over his as she wept hysterically.

"Kitty, be careful. He's fragile. Just be careful, okay?" I whispered. Anything else I could have said was cut off by the siren of an approaching ambulance.

21

Kitty hugged me and climbed into the ambulance with Bronx. I watched the lights disappear around the street bend before going upstairs. I hadn't noticed the glass on the pavement before, but now, when I wasn't hyped up on terror and adrenaline, I saw how lucky I was that I hadn't ripped my heels to shreds running outside to get to Bronx. I glanced up at my apartment and peered at the shattered opening in the wall. From here, it looked like a jagged wound in the building's side.

I called my mother to tell her what happened, repeating myself several times through tears and hysterics. She told me she was leaving work now and to stay put. I hurried inside to wait for her. She was going to kill me. It was an accident, yes, but one I couldn't explain. She'd asked me how it happened on the phone, and I just kept saying I didn't know over and over again. But I did know. I just didn't know how to make her believe me.

Mom flew into the apartment twenty minutes later. I was curled on the couch around a box of salt, sobbing. I heard the door slam. I lifted my face to her, my eyes so bleary with tears I could barely see. I was able to catch Mom's expression, though. Fury. But seeing me crumpled and limp and weepy, she softened and rushed to my side. She sank into the cushion next to me, stroking my hair. I hadn't cried like this since I was a little kid, but I didn't care. There was no shame. I cried for Bronx. I cried because of what happened last night. I cried because I was afraid I was going to get everyone killed. I cried because I was going to die.

It took a while for me to regain control. My mother crooned to me all the while and, when she was convinced I didn't have a tear left to shed, repeated her questions from earlier. I went with the simplest explanation I could conjure: he was leaning against the windows and they broke. It was an old building, it was plausible, which was probably why she didn't drill me too much. "No, Mom, no one was horsing around. And no, Mom, no one pushed him." It was good enough for her.

"Why don't you go lie down?" she said, her lips skimming across my forehead. "I have to make some calls, clean up around here. We'll check on your friend later, okay?"

"Yeah. Okay. Thanks." If she thought it was weird that I was hugging a box of salt like a teddy bear, she was good enough not to say so. My thoughts were on fire, hopping from one terrible Mary thing to the next. Lying on my bed, I replayed the events of the last week over and over and reduced myself to a quivering, sniffly mess. My temples pounded from all the crying, but I reached for my cell to call Cody again anyway. This time she answered. It wasn't the relief it would have been an hour ago; I knew Mary was on me now, back in the glass where she belonged. I knew because I'd watched her fling a kid out a window.

"Hi, Cody," I said, hiccupping at the end and gritting my teeth. "Hi. Sorry to bother you again."

"No, no. Hi, Shauna. I called you back a little while ago and you didn't answer. Is everything okay?"

"No. No, everything isn't okay." I told her all the same things I'd told Kitty and Bronx earlier about the church, but now there was an epilogue to the story, and I told her that, too. I heard her suck in air on the other end of the line before she groaned, like I'd gut-punched her.

"You need to get away. I told you this, and I don't say things because I like to hear myself talk. For their sake as much as yours, get rid of your friends. I lived with that guilt, that survivor's guilt, and it's awful. You need to split off now before it gets worse."

"I know, I know," I said. I'd known it before, too, but now that someone had really, truly gotten hurt, I couldn't procrastinate any longer. As much as this Mary thing was going to suck solo, it'd suck much, much worse if I dragged my friends down with me.

I took a deep breath and nodded like Cody could see me. "I'll do it. Today, after I hang up with you. But even without them, I just want...I need to figure this out. To beat Mary. I want to beat her so badly. And if she's in that basement, if her body's there, maybe there's a way. I can't lose that hope."

There was a long pause on Cody's end of the line before she said, "I understand that. I never lost hope, either. It was harder at the end, but it was still there. If you want, I'll go with you when you go back to the church. I know the situation you're in, and I'll help. The floor wasn't like that when we went years ago, but if it is now, maybe there really is something under there." She paused to take a deep breath before adding, "And when we go, we go during the day, we go with salt. But after you get situated, after you get a plan in action, we'll go together."

To volunteer to help me was brave after so many years of being haunted. But it made sense, too. Mary had tortured Cody for almost twenty years. Anyone would want the opportunity for closure, to even that score. "Thanks, Cody. Thanks a lot."

"You're welcome. If you need anything else in between, let me know. And thank you for warning me about last night. As far as I know, Mary always goes back to the mirror. It calls to her. I've never heard of her staying on this side, but I'm not sure if that's good or bad."

To be honest, neither did I.

⤜⤏

I promised I'd cut ties with everyone right after the call, but that was a lie. I did craft an e-mail I could send to all three of them, but then I spent a few hours rereading it while I mustered the will to send it. It wasn't poetic or drawn out. It was the bare essentials:

Hey. I'm sorry everything is so messed up. Mary
threw Bronx out a window. Between last night and
today, it's clear it's no longer safe to hang out. I
love you, I appreciate your help, but you have to
stay away.—S

So simple and yet so final. The draft blinked at me, taunting
me to send it, but I couldn't push the button yet. When Mom
came in to get me for dinner, I told myself I'd send it after I'd
eaten. Mom had been busy while I'd been sequestered in my
room. She'd boarded over the hole in the wall with flattened
moving boxes and thick tape to keep out drafts and bugs.

After a salad, I went back to my room and drifted between
half sleep and staring at the ceiling. What I didn't do was press
Send on the message. Not until right before midnight—Kitty
had just sent me a text that said Bronx was going in for emergency surgery on his spine.

She said he might not walk again. Bronx's bright promise of
a football career was gone because Mary wanted to punish *me*.
I couldn't do that to other people. I had to protect my friends.
I sent it. Jess would try to call to yell at me for being so dumb,
so I shut off the phone. I kept the light on when I climbed under
the blankets. Mom visited one last time, spending a lot more
time fussing over me than usual. I liked the attention, the feel
of her hands toying with my hair. It made me feel loved, which
was something I needed right then. Being haunted by Bloody
Mary was proving to be pretty isolating.

"I love you, Mom," I said.

"I love you, too, Shauna," she returned before leaning down to give me a good-night kiss. I hugged her tight, then she wandered off back to her room, closing my door in her wake.

⌒⌒⌒

I stayed home from school the next day, telling my mom I was sick. I should have informed Jess, too. Her car horn blasted at quarter of seven. I hadn't answered my phone, so she came for me in person. When I didn't emerge from the building, Jess blasted the horn again, and then a third time, probably pissing off all my neighbors. There was no way I was going to venture downstairs to tell her that I was staying in, so I turned on my phone to text her. There were many messages from Jess and Anna, and a couple from Kitty. I ignored them all to tell Jess to go to school without me. Her response was, *no fuk u.*

"Oh, come on, Jess. Don't fight me on this," I said, about to send another response, but I heard the slam of the downstairs door followed by feet on the steps. A minute later, she pounded on my front door, laying siege, her fist a battering ram behind every knock.

"Cut the crap, Shauna. Open up." When I ignored her, she did it again. And again. And again. "Shauna, open the goddamned door!"

Realizing she wasn't going to leave until someone called the cops on her, I got out of bed and stormed down the hall, my salt tucked under my arm like a security blanket. I yanked open the door and glared at her. She gave me a critical once-over and frowned. Admittedly, I looked terrible: my teeth weren't brushed, and neither was my hair. I wouldn't normally let anyone see me like this, but my care factor about my appearance was nonexistent.

"Get dressed," she said. "You're not doing this."

"Doing what?"

Jess was not amused by the question. She shouldered past me into the apartment, sending me staggering back in the process. She gave me her best death glare before tromping to my room and waving her hand around. "Let's go. Dressed. Now. I'm not letting you ditch me. Us. We got into this together, we're getting out of it together."

I closed the door and glowered at her back as she disappeared around the corner to rifle through my bureau. "I'm doing this for your safety. Look at what happened to Bronx," I protested.

"It sucks, but we're in this together until the end. Here." She came out of my room to throw jeans and a T-shirt at me. When I let them fall straight to the floor, she pushed them toward me with her sandal. "Come on, Shauna. You can't hide. Our odds of figuring this out are way better as a team. You've got to keep your shit together. Now *get dressed.*"

I stooped for the clothes and eyeballed her. "Why are you doing this? I'm trying to protect you."

"Let me worry about myself. I know the risks; so do Kitty and Anna. If they bail, they bail, but I'm not going anywhere. You need a bra and panties. Go." She circled around to herd me into my bedroom. I tried to push back, my feet skidding over the carpet, but Jess was strong thanks to years of playing sports. I wasn't going to win this fight.

"I'm doing this for you!" I finally snapped, but Jess gave me a sharp look before her arms folded over her chest. Her legs braced like she was settling in for a long, nasty battle.

"No, *I'm* doing this for *you*. Go. Now."

I stopped fighting. Deep down, I didn't want to. Yes, I had heard Cody, but what I wanted most in the world was a friend, and I had one standing in the hallway threatening to kick my ass if I tried to ditch her. It was bossy and ballsy and stupid, but that was Jess's way. And right then? I was glad for it.

22

I stared at the windows of my classroom, expecting to see something wicked inside the panes. I was sorting life into two categories now: time between Mary attacks and actual Mary attacks. My teacher was reduced to background noise as I counted the number of glass beakers lining the corner storage station.

Kitty texted mid-class to say Bronx got through surgery, but they wouldn't know his prognosis for a while. I took that to mean she wasn't in school today, and that made sense. You didn't recover from watching your boyfriend take a three-story nosedive overnight.

I was shuffling my way to my second class when Anna caught up to me in the hall. I didn't see her coming, and she greeted me by resting her hand against the flat of my back. I let out a screech and dropped my books. Other students in the hall turned to stare at me. Anna apologized for startling me as she stooped to help me pick up my stuff.

"You ignored my texts last night," she said, stacking my papers into a neat pile.

"I turned my phone off. I meant it, though. You really should stay away. She's always around now."

Anna stuffed my homework at me before gathering my books. I watched her do it, not helping in the slightest, though I wasn't sure why. I think my brain was just that gone. "Yeah, well, deal with it. I'm sticking around. It's not your fault you're haunted."

"You sound like Jess. I tried to stay home this morning, but she dragged me here by my hair." I winced. Comparing Anna to the person she'd sworn to avoid forever was probably a bad plan.

Surprisingly, she smiled a little and nodded, like somehow, this had bettered her opinion of Jess. "Well, that's the first smart thing she's done in a week. What kind of friends would we be if we ditched you?"

"Smart ones?" I returned.

She fell into step beside me as I meandered toward my next class. Other kids were running to make the bell, but I couldn't be bothered. Anna seemed content to keep pace with me.

"Maybe, but either way I . . . Look." She stopped talking and walking at the same time, her brows pinching together with strain. There was gravity to whatever it was she wanted to say to me. She shuffled her feet, looked down, and then back up. It was still weird to see her without her glasses on, but I'd get used to it sooner or later. "After you messaged me last night, I got really worried, especially when you didn't text me back. Jess was in the same boat, and she called me. We talked. Forget everything I said yesterday. *You're* more important. I was listening to Jess talk last night, bugging out about what's happening to you and insisting we have to help you, and I realized I need to be more like that, you know? More focused on what's going to get us through this. So that's what I'm going to do. With Jess, because she really does care." She smiled a little ruefully, lifting her narrow shoulders in a shrug before adding, "I get mad too easily. But I'm going to try to chill."

"You do. But we like you anyway," I said.

She snickered and turned back toward the hall. Her hand came out to graze my arm, fingertips tracing over the black bruise near my wrist from when Mary tripped me into the church's stone steps. It was a gentle touch, not hurtful in the least, but it set her to scowling. "We'll figure it out, Shauna. Just don't leave us. And I promise, we won't leave you. At least, I won't. I'll always have your back."

⌘

Jess didn't sit with me at lunch. I saw her in the cafeteria; she saw me, too, then put her tray at another table anyway. Anna slid in opposite me and we both watched as a few of Jess's softball friends sat with her: Laurie Carmichael with her spiky black hair and high-pitched shrieker voice, Becca Miller with the biggest attitude problem this side of the Mississippi, and Tonya Washington, who was actually funny.

"They have a softball game later. Jess mentioned it last night," Anna offered. I nodded, but the timing struck me as odd. Just this morning, Jess had insisted we stick together,

195

but by lunch she'd already screwed off? When she glanced my way, almost like she felt the weight of my stare, she frowned and looked away.

Was Jess mad at me? Maybe. Maybe she was pissed I'd tried to ditch her. She wasn't normally sensitive, but this whole experience had certainly changed me for the worse. It wasn't so hard to believe it'd changed her, too.

Anna and I ate in silence. Halfway through lunch I realized that I had to go to the restroom. Every bathroom in the school had mirrors and steel doors and steel everything. I wanted to hold out until the end of the day, but after five minutes of squirming, I let out an exasperated sigh. Anna lifted her head to blink at me.

"I have to pee. And I'm afraid it'll . . . you know. With Mary."

Anna put up a finger to indicate I should sit tight before she headed over to Jess's table. She bent down, whispering something into Jess's ear. Jess nodded, excused herself from her friends, and jogged out of the cafeteria. Anna came back to collect me, offering me her hand like she was the mom and I was the kid and this was totally normal. I grabbed my book bag and took her hand without a second's hesitation.

"I left some packing tape in Jess's car Saturday," Anna said. "She's going to get it and meet us in the locker room. It's the closest bathroom to the parking lot."

We sped along, still holding hands. When we got to the gym, Anna let go of me to scout out the locker room. She emerged a minute later and we waited for Jess, who showed up with the roll of tape in one hand and a fresh box of salt in the other.

"Hey," Jess said in greeting. "We good to go?"

"Yeah," Anna said. "The locker room is empty."

They ushered me inside and told me to sit on a bench next to the lockers while they prepped the other side of the room. I tried to wait patiently, but the combination of a full bladder and nerves meant I fidgeted and scooted across the wood.

The high school locker room is shaped like a *T*. On the left-hand side of the long portion, the top of the *T*, are about a dozen shower stalls with skimpy white shower curtains strung up for privacy. The right side holds all the lockers and the door that leads into the main school building. Between the showers and the lockers is a floor-to-ceiling mirror almost eight feet wide. Next to it is the door that opens out to the soccer field. The bottom part of the *T* connects to the gym at the end, with a supply closet on the left side and three bathroom stalls on the right.

Anna worked on the big mirror near the showers using the box of salt I had in my bag. Jess took the bathroom mirrors and used her own stuff. I watched Anna cut off strips of tape and make a big *X* across the glass before laying a line of salt on the floor. I could hear Jess working in the other room, and when she finished, she came out to claim the tape from Anna, probably to treat the smaller mirrors over the sinks in the same fashion.

I waited as patiently as I could for them to finish. Every few seconds I'd eyeball the padlocks on the lockers around me, expecting them to explode in a creepy ruckus, but they stayed dormant. After what seemed like days, Jess came and directed me toward the toilets.

"That's as good as it's going to get," she said. It wasn't much consolation, but there wasn't much else we could do to make it safe. I scurried away from the lockers, my hands already fiddling with my pants as I took the corner. Jess had salted pretty much everything in the bathroom, including taping the chrome stall door for me, and I mumbled my thanks as I closed the door. I could see Anna's and Jess's sneakers outside, both of them waiting around to protect me in case things got weird.

I finished as quickly as possible, managing a grateful smile for them as I approached the sink. My hand darted out to turn on the water, but then reared back like something inside it might bite. Nothing happened. It was just a boring old sink with boring old water. I washed my hands and grabbed a paper towel, feeling a little better that we'd made it unscathed through something so simple and yet so complicated as taking me to the bathroom.

"So much work for such a stupid thing," I said to them, and they both laughed, though it wasn't so much a humor thing as it was exhausted resignation.

"Should we clear the tape?" Anna asked Jess.

"I guess. Let's get Shauna out of here first and then we'll strip it down."

Anna nodded and led me out like she'd become my personal Seeing Eye dog. I gave the lockers a furtive glance as we passed them on the way to the exit. I placed my hand on the long silver bar to the door and pushed. There was no click to indicate that it released. I pressed the bar again and again. Nothing happened.

I looked at Anna. She blanched and reached out to shove the door with me. It was useless.

My eyes pounded in their sockets like they might propel out of my skull. Not now. Not again. "Jess! Check the door to the gym!" I called. Anna slammed her body against the door as I darted through the locker room to get to the door leading to the soccer field. A chorus of groans from the shower section stopped me short. I knew that sound. I'd heard it in my own bathroom right before the mud and gunk. This time, though, instead of one shower under duress, it was twelve. The pipes shrieked in strained agony as the showerheads quaked and rumbled inside the fiberglass shower walls.

"She's coming," I whispered, my voice drowned out by a series of earsplitting whines. "She's here."

23

Clang. Clang. Clang. Clang.

The pipes screeched with a rhythmic banging, like someone was pounding on them from the inside with a hammer. Yellow clouds rose from the metal shower drains, the ghostly fog pouring over the tiles and wafting across the floor. The showerheads gave a collective squeal as hot, black water blasted into the stalls.

"Let's go!" Anna said, rushing past me to throw herself against the soccer field door. The padlocks on the lockers behind us sparked to life, rattling and slamming like they had in the hall last week. Jess was making a thudding noise around the corner. Anna started kicking the door.

"Shit. Shit. What did she do?" Anna shoved at the door one last time as if this time it would magically open. But I knew it wouldn't. She knew it wouldn't, too. The bar wouldn't work because it was aluminum covered in chrome. Shiny things were Mary's domain.

"What's ... Why ..." Anna brushed past me, inching toward the showers. I followed her gaze, watching the geysers of black sludge shooting up from the drains. Water flowed from above and below now, creating an unnatural, fetid bog that oozed its way across the floor. The first tendrils of encroaching water curled around Anna's tennis shoe before splintering off into the checkerboard grooves of grout in the floor. It wasn't until the runoff was a few feet away from me that I recognized the danger: the salt line underneath the big mirror. The water was only a few feet away from the salt line.

"The line. She's going for the line. She's going to dissolve it," I said. There was a crisscross of salt across the glass's surface, yes, but without the salt line on the ground, was it enough? I glanced at the taped mirror. At first, I couldn't tell if the condensation on the glass was on our side or Mary's. Then Mary appeared through the moist gray haze to slam against the mirror. She hissed at the salted tape upon contact before neatly sidestepping to one of the wedges of open glass where the tape didn't reach.

Mary's eyes fixed on me, her fingertips dragging down the flat surface. She was so close, I could hear her rasping and rattling, like she was trying to breathe through phlegm. Anna dashed for the gym door, shoving the box of salt at me as she passed. I heard her talking to Jess, but I couldn't make out what they were saying. The sound of bodies banging against metal resumed. They were trying to force the door open. I stared at the mirror with my heart lodged in my throat, my feet itching to *run, run, run.* But to where? Bloody Mary was still trapped in the mirror behind the salt line, but soon, much too soon, the water would wash it away.

I stood there, frozen, as the water slithered across the floor. In the past, when I'd watched horror movies because I thought being scared was fun, I always got angry at the characters whose hands shook so badly they dropped the car keys when the monster was chasing them. It felt unbelievable. If someone wanted to survive, she would keep it together long enough to get away. Now, standing in the locker room like a frightened lamb, I understood. Fear shut my body down, like it had done to Jess the first time Mary came through Anna's mirror.

Jess and Anna ran up from behind me, Jess straddling the bench next to the bathroom so she could salt a fresh section of tape. I watched her work, wanting to tell her it was too late, but the words got stuck in my throat. I was too scared to talk. My mouth opened and closed, but no sound came. It wasn't until Anna clapped a hand on my shoulder that I found my voice again.

"There's no time, Jess. Look," I said.

"Bullshit. No ti—" Jess wanted to argue, but then she saw the water creeping steadily along. Her eyes flicked to the mirror. Mary bobbed her head and smeared her face against the surface, her nostril slits flaring.

"No, no, no, no. NO." Jess grabbed her salty tape and scrambled back.

"We're stuck," Anna announced, her voice dripping misery.

"No shit, we're stuck." Jess barreled her way toward the gym supply closet and rifled through it. Kickballs, softball gloves, and safety equipment flew out the door. A moment later, she made an *aha* noise followed by a loud metallic clang. She came out with an umpire mask covering her face and an arm of baseball bats. "Come here. Take one. If she gets near..."

I didn't know what effect swinging a bat at a ghost would have, but Anna and I took our bats anyway. The extra bats dropped to the floor, the water now deep enough that they splashed when they hit. Jess wrapped her bat with her tape strip, the salt facing out. Clever. I wish we'd thought of it sooner.

As we armed ourselves, the water crested the salt line and dissolved our defense. Mary's hands poked through the glass where Anna's tape didn't touch. It was that easy for her. The mistake we'd made was leaving a section of glass big enough for her to pass through. Circles rippled across the mirror's surface, the quadrant of glass quivering as it turned to gel. Her wrists came next, then elbows and arms, followed by her head. When her foot crossed from her world into ours, splashing down in the black drain water, she let out a gurgling chuckle.

I'd seen Mary in Anna's bathroom when she tried to climb from the mirror. I'd seen her scuttling up the steps of the Southbridge Parish. But I'd never been close enough to get an unadulterated look at her. Her upper body was how she appeared in the mirror: her head was balding, her black eyes never blinked. Her rubbery half lips sported tiny pus blisters. Her neck was too thin over her clavicles, skin graying with patches of green and purple. Her arms were winter branches, bare and knobby and too pointy.

What I'd never properly seen was her lower half. Her once-white dress was brown from too much time crawling through muck, the hem of the skirt tattered and torn and ankle-length. It was hiked up to her knee on the left side, exposing the bones of her leg. The skin had worn so thin, her tibia and fibula were visible, the nerves and muscle long since rotted away. Her left foot was swollen and blue-tinged, like a moldy sponge that had absorbed too much water. Her right leg was whole, but a gash along her calf released a steady stream of onyx beetles into the water on the floor, like her fleshy bits only served as a festering ground for insects.

There was no hint left of the girl from the photograph. Instead, there was five feet of ghoul. If Mary and Jess stood side by side, Mary would barely crest Jess's chin. She was so tiny, and yet I knew what she was capable of doing with that body. Death had given her a strength that her frail frame had not. I took a step back from her, my breath coming in short, panicked pants as Mary stretched her arms to her sides, test-ing her freedom.

"Stay together. Try to stay together," Jess said, snagging her box of salt from the bench and backing toward the show-ers. I followed because I didn't have any better ideas. Part of me wanted to hide. It was a childish instinct to assume the monster couldn't see you because you couldn't see it. But that wasn't how this worked. Mary would find us anywhere.

"Matter of time," I murmured, my hand squeezing around

my pitiful arsenal of salt and a softball bat. Jess glared at me from behind her umpire mask. I turned my head around to see what Anna was doing, but she wasn't there. She'd ignored Jess and gone her own way, toward the bathroom. It was just Jess and me in the shower section, the showerheads above blasting scalding water, the drains below spewing frigid black sludge. Half of my body sweated, the other half was riddled with goose pimples.

I heard Mary's labored breathing around the corner. Her feet shuffled along as she cooed and trilled, sounding far too pleasant. *Splash, splash, splash.* Her footsteps neared, then the sounds stopped. Jess and I looked at each other, wondering what could possibly interest Mary enough that she'd pause her hunt.

"Are you two all right?" Anna asked from the toilet stalls. Her voice drew Mary like a siren's song. The ghost let out a hiss and barreled away from us to find Anna. All I could picture was Mary shredding Anna apart.

She wasn't going to hurt my friend.

I ran out of the shower room, screeching at the top of my lungs. Mary trundled toward the bathroom, her arms swinging wildly to either side. Her fist tangled in a shower curtain, and she yanked it down before kicking the plastic away with a snarl.

"MARY! COME ON. IT'S ME. COME ON!" My voice cracked halfway through, but I continued to shout, waiting for the dripping dead thing to turn around and look at me.

She spun, her eyes wide. Her head tilted back as she sniffed the air, the growl that escaped her throat pregnant with menace. A beetle climbed from her right nostril to scurry across her cheek before disappearing into the neckline of her dress.

"That's it. Come get me. You want me, not her. Come on." I readied the salt and bat. I expected her to dive at me, but she moved forward slowly, like she wanted to savor the moment. *"Mine,"* she rasped. I shook the salt box at her, trying to keep a distance between us, but she lurched my way with grim determination. I'd had every intention of facing my fate when I'd come around this corner, but as she closed in, my feet moved back. My survival instinct had kicked in, telling me to run.

Mary was a few feet away now. I had to choose: bat or salt? I picked the bat, the salt splashing down to the floor by my feet when I dropped it. I swung the bat, hoping to maintain a gap between me and Mary, but she grabbed the end and jerked. The bat flew from my hand. Mary peered at it for a second, like she didn't know what it did, before tossing it behind her.

I picked up the box of salt. The bottom had gotten wet, but I ripped off the top and grabbed some of the dry salt. I was about to fling my first handful when a blur of motion drew my attention. Running at us with her bat raised above her head was Anna. When Mary stopped at the cross section of the locker room *T*, Anna had a straight shot at her and she took full advantage, her weapon poised and ready.

Before Mary could react, Anna slammed the aluminum bat down in an arc. It crashed into Mary's shoulder with a sickening crack. Mary wailed and staggered, almost dropping to a knee. I took my opportunity to throw the salt. It struck her on the left side of her face. Mary slapped and clawed in agony. One of her fingers squished into her eye, and a stream of viscous black goo oozed down her cheek and over her chin. She thrashed like she was on fire, her feet sliding across the wet floor as she retreated. We had a small advantage, and we had to take it if we wanted to live.

More salt. I threw as much as I could as fast as I could, some of it damp and clumpy from the box's dip in the water. Mary blindly lashed out with her claws, but Anna brought the bat around again. There was a snap as Mary's wrist took the brunt, her hand crunching and skewing off at an odd angle. By then, the locker room was almost completely full of steam. I could barely see Anna wielding the bat next to me, but every one of her swings gave me a brief glimpse of her face. Her lips were pursed in concentration, her face splattered with a spray of Mary's tar-blood. Around us, the padlocks rattled and the shower pipes groaned.

"Jess, come on. She's moving back. We need you!" I called, but Jess never came. I didn't know where she was or what she was doing. I was too busy trying to shove Mary back to check on Jess. I advanced on the ghost. She retreated toward the mirror, unable to go left for fear of getting hit with the baseball bat, unable to go right for fear of another fistful of my salt. For a moment, I thought we had beaten her, that we'd all live through this fight. I thought Bloody Mary would be forced into the mirror and we'd lock her away with the salt from my stash.

The next time that Anna swung the bat, Mary charged. Anna gasped. The steam swirled up, blocking my sight. Anna's bat rattled to the floor. Anna cried out in a muffled scream. I didn't think, I reacted. I ran at Mary and Anna with my salt, hoping to save my friend, but Mary reached out for me and . . .

thrust me away. She sent me sprawling onto my butt in the water with a single push to my chest, the salt box splashing away to my side.

The motion of my body sailing back dispersed the haze for a second. I glimpsed Mary dragging Anna toward the mirror. Mary had Anna by the hair, her moldering hand wrapped tight in Anna's long tresses. Anna thrashed and screamed, but it was no use. She was hooked tight. Anna was pulled to Mary's body—as close as I'd been when Mary had captured me with her nails during the second summoning.

"SHE'S GOT ANNA. HURRY. SHE'S GOT ANNA!" I screamed to Jess. I crawled across the ground and managed to grip Anna's ankles with my hands. I pulled on her, trying to stop Mary's progress, but the ghost was so unnaturally strong that I was pulled through the water as though I were weightless.

"No!" I howled, my voice breaking when Mary stepped over the bottom ledge of the mirror. She was going back to her world and taking Anna with her. I tightened my grasp, but it made no difference. Mary gave another hard tug, and I watched through a wall of tears as Anna was pulled over the ledge and into the mirror's surface. Anna's screams cut short as liquid glass rushed into her mouth.

"JESS, HELP!" I shouted, still pulling on Anna's feet.

Jess was suddenly there. Her bat dropped by her feet before she opened her box of salt and began tossing handfuls at the mirror. I thought it was a good idea at first, that she was forcing the ghost into retreat and we'd pull Anna to safety, but the moment the crystals touched the glass, the surface began to harden. If she continued, it'd get too thick for us to pull Anna out.

"No. *No!* Stop! It's going solid! You're using too much! Help me pull!" But Jess ignored me, firing the salt instead. As the last of Anna passed through the undulating glass, my hands went with her. I remembered the cold jellylike feel of the water from when Mary had dragged me through. This was thicker, more rigid. Salt clusters were drying on the surface. The glass was crystallizing. If I didn't pull my hands back soon, the surface would go hard and I'd either be stuck between the worlds forever or lose my hands.

"No. Please, no..." I wept, but there was nothing I could do. The pressure around my forearms became unbearable. I was forced to let Anna go. I wrenched my hands from the glass seconds before it hardened. Fog rose up inside the mirror far thicker than the steam in the bathroom. A second later, a long arc of crimson splashed across the glass followed by another. And another. Rivers of blood rained down on the wrong side.

Anna's blood.

24

It didn't seem real. When the showers stopped spewing, when the black water sank back into the drains, when the fog cleared from the room, I kept thinking that Anna would come back. Except that wasn't the reality. The reality was that Anna was gone. Forever.

I sat a few feet from the mirror without flinching, catatonic. My guts ached, my eyes burned. Mary could have hauled me inside the glass right then and I would have been too stupefied to do anything about it. But she didn't come. She left me there to snivel, my pants wet, my knees hugged to my chest.

Jess stood beside me crying softly. She put her hand on my shoulder, but I pushed her away. If she'd listened to me, if she'd pulled Anna instead of salting the mirror, Anna might have had a chance. But Jess never listened to anyone. She did what she thought was best—her ideas trumped all ideas—and now Anna Sasaki was dead.

In the end, I ran. It wasn't brave or noble. It probably wasn't the right thing to do, but after what felt like hours of sitting on that wet locker room floor, I climbed to my feet, grabbed my bag, and ran. Jess called my name, but I kept moving. I ran from the locker room. I ran from the school. I ran until my legs ached. I ran until they stopped aching and I felt like I could run forever. My apartment was miles from the school, but I ran all the way there without pause.

By the time I hit my parking lot an hour later, I was covered in sweat. My clothes and body had fused together; my hair was matted to my skull. My lungs hurt. I didn't care. Stopping was the worst thing I could have done. While I'd been punishing my body, I wasn't thinking about Anna, but the moment I climbed the stairs, the moment my key slipped into the lock of my door, I started bawling.

I dove into my bed. I buried my face in my pillow and screamed myself raw. When my throat felt like I'd swallowed a porcupine, I stopped to tear off my damp, sweaty clothes. I rolled into a ball beneath the covers. I stayed that way until the calls started. It was Jess, furiously blowing up my phone before resorting to sending texts that I refused to read. I shut it off. I didn't want to hear from her. If I had my way, I'd never look at her again. All the sorrow and rage I felt at losing Anna was directed at Jess. She'd put Bloody Mary before common sense—before our safety. Anna had been right to be mad at her. In the end, Anna was the only one of us who had had any sense.

⚬⚭⚬

It took them a day and a half to realize Anna was gone. Her parents called the night of her disappearance to ask if I knew where she was, but I told them I hadn't seen Anna since school lunch. I went to bed after that, sleep my only reprieve. Even then, I was plagued by dreams of Anna, of Mary. It wasn't much of an escape. I woke to tears running down my cheeks.

Tuesday morning, I told Mom I still didn't feel well. She took my temperature and despite the lack of fever, she let me stay home again. I rarely asked. I left my room only to use the bathroom, the box of salt never leaving my side. Mary never showed. I immediately went back to bed—not hungry, not thirsty, not feeling alive at all.

Mom was supposed to work a double, but at suppertime, there were feet pounding up the apartment steps and then the slamming of the front door.

"Shauna? Are you here?" I heard from the other room.

"In bed," I said. "Headache."

Her purse hit the floor. She ran to my room, her keys jingling inside her pocket. She thrust the door open to peer at me, her eyes huge. I sat up a little to look at her, the blanket tucked to my chest, and she crossed the room in three strides to hug me. It was sweet at first, affectionate, but then it grew stronger, more a clutch than an embrace.

"Why didn't you pick up your phone?" she barked at me.

I blinked, cringing as she gave me another hard squeeze. "My phone was off. Sorry."

"Oh. Oh, honey." She sank down on the mattress beside me and put her palms on my cheeks, her thumbs stroking my cheekbones. Her eyes narrowed. I probably looked awful. I'd been crying so much, my face felt hot and there were splotchy hives all over my upper chest. "So you heard, then. All right, at least you know. Luanne at work pointed out the AMBER Alert, and when you didn't pick up the phone, I just... I came straight home. I'm so glad to see you, but don't shut your phone off again. Don't, please," she said, and she pulled me back into her arms, forcing my face into the crook of her neck.

There was an alert on Anna. For a moment, I worried that the police would come pounding on my door, demanding answers, but that would mean they'd have to know Jess and I were the last people with her. And how would they find that out? Someone may have seen us leaving the cafeteria, but we were always together. That wouldn't raise any suspicions. No one had been around the locker room when it went down, either. The halls were empty because of lunch.

I couldn't worry about it. Even if the police came sniffing around, they wouldn't find anything except salty water. Jess had torn the tape from the mirrors before she bailed. There was nothing incriminating to find. Anna wasn't just dead, she was gone. Permanently. I clung to Mom and burst into more sobs. She stroked my hair, her lips grazing my temple.

"It'll be okay. Anna is fine," she crooned. I wanted to scream at her that, no, Anna wasn't fine, that she'd been killed in front of me.

Mom made me tea and brought me toast that I wouldn't eat. Her phone rang in the other room and she left to answer it. She returned a minute later, her fingers toying with the buttons on

her coat. "That was Luanne. Some local folks are going looking for Anna—clues or...well. You get it. Did you want to go?"

"No, thanks," I said. I didn't want to see all those people. I
didn't want to answer the questions I knew were coming. I had
the answers, but no one would believe me. I didn't trust myself
not to scream them in someone's face. It was much safer to stay
at home and grieve, and if not grieve, then to sleep forever so I
didn't have to feel anything.

Mom looked surprised. "Really? I thought...She's your
friend. Why not?" It should have occurred to me she'd ask
that, and I should have had an answer prepared, but I didn't.
I glanced at the wall and shrugged. She reached out to lift my
chin with her finger so I was forced to look at her. "Shauna?"

"I'm afraid of what we might find," I blurted. "If she's dead
and mangled and...you know." It was weak, I knew it was
weak, but it was the best I could come up with on the spot.

I was afraid she'd see right through it. She frowned, but
after a moment, she pulled away from me and sighed. "Okay.
I suppose I can understand that. That'd be hard. Well, harder.
It's just...I don't know if I should go. One of us should, I think,
but I don't want to leave you alone."

"No, it's okay. I'm okay, and if you do find something, you
should call me. I just can't, not right now. I want to sleep."

She watched me for a long while before shaking her head.
"No, I don't think I will. Go to sleep. I'll be right outside if you
need me."

I was just about to drift off when a knock struck our front
door. I rolled out of bed to poke my head into the hall. Standing

in the apartment doorway in his service blues was a police officer. My pulse pounded in my ears. I forced myself to approach, my arms wrapping around my chest so he couldn't see that I wasn't wearing a bra.

He was nice, all things considered. He asked me when I'd seen Anna last, and I told him in the bathroom after lunch. Had I heard from her on the phone after that? No. Did I have any reasons to suspect she'd run away? No. Had she been spending time with anyone unusual? No. It took five minutes for him to question me. He left me a name and a contact number before wishing Mom and me a good night.

When the door closed behind him, Mom peered at me from her seat on the couch.

"Are you okay?" she asked.

"No."

⌒⌒⌒

Mom woke me Wednesday with news that school had been canceled while the investigation continued. I rolled over and went back to sleep. When I came out of my bedroom at nine, Mom was on the phone, standing next to the refrigerator. She had called in to work. Her too-loud phone conversation also informed me that search parties had scoured for Anna throughout the night, and scent dogs had been brought in to find her, but so far there'd been no trace.

Nor would there be, but I was one of only two people who knew that. Maybe three, if Jess had told Kitty. Who I hadn't even called yet. I ran my fingers over my face and groaned.

"Are you okay?" Mom asked, her hand moving to cover the receiver on the phone.

I shrugged. She offered me a box of cereal for breakfast, but I waved her off. I wasn't hungry. I wasn't anything except numb.

"Right. I'll call you back in a bit, Luanne," she said, flipping her phone closed and sliding it into her pocket. She motioned me to a chair, and I sat in it because I had no idea what to do with myself. I drifted through the apartment like a ghost. "She asked if we wanted to join this morning's search. They're moving out from the school to the Hockomock Swamp."

"You go. I'll be fine," I said.

"You don't look fine, but I guess that's to be expected." She shook her head. "But I'd like to help with the search. All I can think is what if it had been you? The Sasakis must be beside themselves. But I don't want to leave you alone if you're not all right."

"I can handle being alone."

"If you're sure." She sounded hesitant, like she needed my reassurance that I wasn't going to disappear on her if she left for a few hours.

"I'm sure," I said. Logically, I knew I should want her to stay. I should want hugs and love and every ounce of maternal care that I could get. But I was too emotionally stunted to give a damn what she did. I was a hollow robot going through the motions of being human.

Mom got back on the phone, and I craned my head to eyeball the bathroom, weighing the risks of a quick shower. I really couldn't put it off much longer. I retrieved the box of salt from my bureau and prepped the bathroom as efficiently as possible, even shaking a few granules on top of the shower lever and showerhead to keep the water from turning muddy. I used face-cloths as anchors, too, so the crystals couldn't slide off.

I'd adjusted the shower temperature when I spotted Mary watching me from the frosted panels. It was that same hazy, mirage-like image it'd been the first time, like she was on the other side waiting for me. Instead of freaking out, I skipped the conditioner and got my ass out of there as quickly as possible. I didn't care that she watched me. There was no fear.

This should have been victory. For the first time, I'd mastered my terror over the ghost on my tail, but there was no joy there, only resignation. Mary watched me because she'd always watch me. It was what my life had become.

As I left the bathroom, a towel on my head and one around my body, Mom was heading for the door dressed in jeans, a long-sleeved T-shirt, and work boots. She looked like she was going to a construction site. I understood why—the Hockomock Swamp was overgrown and dense. I'd been in there for a biol-ogy field trip once, and it'd been a punishing, wet experience.

"Hey, Luanne's waiting for me downstairs. The car's in the driveway if you need it, but if you go out, text me? I don't want to come home to an empty house. I think I'd have a meltdown."

I nodded. She blew me a kiss and turned to leave, but stopped before stepping over the threshold. She looked at me over her shoulder, her fingers drumming on the back of the couch. "You're sure about my going? If you want me to stay—"

"Go, Mom. I'm fine. I'm here."

She cast me another long look before rushing over to hug

me, her lips grazing the towel on top of my head. "All right, all right. Humor your old lady. She's worried about you." I hugged her back, and she took that to mean she really could go, that I wasn't going to erupt or die because she abandoned me for a few hours. She stroked a hand over my bare shoulder and ran for the door to meet her friend.

With Mom gone, I knew I had to call Kitty. I didn't want to, but I had to. I grabbed my phone from the nightstand. Waiting for me were a dozen missed calls and a series of texts from Jess, each one angrier and angrier. I scrolled through, deleting most of them until I got to the second-to-last one. It leant me pause, and I found my upper lip curling like a rabid dog about to bite.

Working to get u unhaunted and ur ignoring me. Don't b a bitch.

The insinuation that I didn't care about my well-being was a nasty grenade for her to lob. I texted her back with a simple, *Go away.* Before she could blitz me with more messages, I dialed Kitty's number. A half a ring in, Kitty picked up with a pathetic whimper.

"Sh-Shauna, I ca— I can't. I can't. Bronx and n-n-now Anna." Before she could complete the thought, she was crying, and I was close to joining her. I breathed hard, full draws in through the nose and out through the mouth to keep my calm. It helped a little; only a few tears leaked from the corners of my eyes to dribble down my cheeks.

"I know. I'm sorry I didn't call. I was so messed up. My mom just left to join a search party, and I want to say something to her but I can't," I said.

"What can you say? No one would believe.... God. I can't believe she's gone. She's been my b-best friend since we were six. Six!"

The next half hour was spent doing what I could to comfort her, but words weren't sufficient. Nothing I could say would help. Kitty was entitled to her grief. So was I, for that matter. I wrapped up the call when my voice started cracking every other word.

"I love you, Kitty. I'm so sorry. I tried to save her. I did everything I could. I'm sorry," I said.

"I know. I know you did. Th-thank you. I love you, too." She sniffled and croaked out a good-bye before hanging up. I cradled my cell to my chest, feeling worse than I had when I'd called, but that was no surprise—Kitty sounded awful. We both carried the burden of Anna's death, but hers was heavier. Anna and Kitty were more sisters than not. Now one sister was gone.

I rolled onto my hip to face the wall. It took a few minutes of slow, deep breathing to get my wits about me. I'd cry again today, it was inevitable, but I had one more thing I needed to do before I let myself wallow. I had to talk to Cody.

She barked a hello a moment later.

"Hi. It's me," I said.

"I'm sorry," she said. "I saw the news."

I whimpered and dug my teeth into the sides of my tongue. That simple statement rocked me to the core. She could have chided me because I hadn't forced Anna out of my life like she'd told me to do twice already, but she didn't. There was nothing except sympathy in her tone. In a weird, twisted way, I almost wished she'd yelled at me instead. The anger would have given me something to cleave to.

"Thank you. I just wanted to let you know, and I told Jess off and I . . . Maybe next week we'll hit the church? I need a few days," I said.

Cody sucked in a deep breath. "Yes. We'll go when you're ready. In the meanwhile, I think that's for the best. To keep Jess away. She called me this morning and I . . . There's something not right there. Take care of yourself and keep her at arm's length."

"What'd she do now?" I asked. I could hear the hesitation in Cody's voice, debating whether or not she should tell me. It was strange; she was such a straight shooter that I never figured she'd hedge on anything, but something Jess had said bothered her. Jess had somehow managed to flap the unflappable. "Cody?"

"Right, I'm sorry." Cody grumbled beneath her breath. "She was asking about the tag—how I got haunted, the circumstances of it. But it wasn't so much what she was asking as how she was asking it that bothered me. Which is why I didn't want to say anything because it's hard to convey appropriately. . . . You know what it was? Your friend sounded excited and intense, and for a minute, just a minute . . ." Cody paused to suck in a deep breath before blowing it out into the receiver. It nearly deafened me, but not so much that I couldn't hear her when she said, ". . . for a minute I really didn't know whose side she was on. Ours or Mary's."

25

I was done crying. I was still miserable, but thinking about Jess, I was also *angry*. And anger was fuel. I could channel it and concentrate on the matter at hand—getting unhaunted. What did I know? Jess had been too invested in Mary since the beginning. I'd chalked it up to enthusiasm for something new and cool, and though it seemed like forever ago now, I felt excited about Mary in the beginning, too.

The problem was that Jess knew things we didn't and had all along. She dropped information when we absolutely needed it, but she had never been forthright with it. I sensed she had a piece of the Mary puzzle that I was missing, but how was I supposed to get it from her? Even if we were talking, I couldn't assume she'd be straight with me. She'd been lying by omission all along. It was frustrating, doubly so because I had so very little to go on. There was the church, yes, and I would revisit that hellhole soon enough, but what else could I do from home?

I abandoned my bed and turned on my laptop, keeping the salt on hand in case Mary tried anything cute with the screen. The search engine popped up and I stared at it awhile, wondering where I should begin. The only new development was the Dietrich lady who'd been in all those pictures at the church. I followed Bronx's advice and signed up for an ancestry Web site.

At first, it didn't look like much. Adeline Dietrich was born in Solomon's Folly in 1940. Her mother's maiden name was Abigail Brown, and she had married Richard Dietrich. Adeline had one sister named Ruth. Following the Brown line, Abigail was the child of Michael Brown, who was the only child of Mary Simpson Brown, who was the child of...

I stopped reading and stared. Mary Simpson Brown was the child of Constance and Edward Simpson, and Constance's maiden name was Worth. I clicked on Constance's sister, and there it was, Mary's name, with the dates of 1847–1864. Adeline Dietrich was related to Mary Worth. Frantically, I jotted it all down on a piece of paper so I could show it to Cody when I saw her. I wasn't sure how Mary's family tree would help us, but maybe the clue to putting the ghost away for good existed somewhere in the names on this page.

I pored over the tree once more to ensure I hadn't misread anything. This time, instead of only paying attention to the mothers and fathers, I branched off to look at siblings, too. There were a few who had died young in the late 1800s and early 1900s, and a few others who'd died childless. The tree didn't extend all that far, most of it contained to Massachusetts and Solomon's Folly in particular. By the time I got back to

Ruth Dietrich, Adeline's sister, I was ready to be finished, but I clicked on Ruth's name all the same. When the screen popped up, I had to rub my eyes once, twice, three times, because I couldn't believe what was in front of me.

Ruth Dietrich maintained her maiden name as her legal name, but she had married in 1962. Why she'd kept her name wasn't interesting to me. What was interesting was who she'd married. Augustus McAllister. He and Ruth had one child together. Stuart McAllister. Jess's *dad*.

"Holy shit," I whispered. I clicked on Stuart, and sure enough, listed beneath him and his wife, Allison Jamison McAllister, were their two children—Jessica and Todd. Augustus McAllister was the colander-wearing Grandpa Gus, and Jess's Aunt Dell must have been a nickname for Aunt Adeline. In the church, I'd said there was something familiar about those pictures of Adeline. What was familiar was that she *looked like Jess*.

I didn't have the complete puzzle, but I did have one more answer. This wasn't about some stupid ghost hunt for Jess. This wasn't a game. This was about her legacy, and her legacy was that she, Jess McAllister, was a blood relative of Mary Worth.

∽

I didn't know what to do with the information. On one hand, I wanted to confront Jess. On the other, that'd require talking to her. I tried calling Kitty back, but she wasn't picking up her phone. She'd mentioned going to the hospital to see Bronx when we'd talked earlier, and they didn't allow her to have her phone on in there. I left her a text to call me later.

After Kitty, my thumb went to Anna's speed dial digit. She was always the next one on the rotation, the third in the series of friends, but now she was gone. She'd never be here again. I climbed back into bed and hugged my pillow, squeezed my eyes closed, and huddled underneath my blankets. The vague excitement I'd felt over the Jess discovery was swallowed by helplessness and despair.

I'd said I wouldn't wallow all day, but that's exactly what I did, right up until my mother came home two hours later. I drifted in and out of sleep, my waking minutes plagued by thoughts of Jess, Mary, and Anna. I didn't wake up when Mom walked into my room at suppertime, but I almost hit the roof when she leaned over my bed to run her fingers across my forehead. She startled me so much, I almost jumped out of my skin.

"*What?*" I shouted, shooting up in bed so fast, I smashed my skull against the wall behind me. It hurt, and I wrapped my arms around my head. Mom reached out to pull me to her, forcing my face into her midsection. She smelled like sweat and outdoors stuff—pine needles and sap and mud. She smelled like the Hockomock Swamp.

"They called off the search for now," she said quietly. "Are you okay? Your head?"

"Yeah. Yeah, I'm okay," I lied for what felt like the millionth time. Mom's fingers stroked the back of my neck before traveling up to my newest wound. She probed it a little, and I shrank away from the touch, but the pain was already abating.

"Good. It sounds like they're going out looking again

tomorrow. I have to go back to work, but if you want to stay home from school, you can."

I shook my head. "No, I don't want to be here alone." And I didn't. For all that I'd fallen into a casual ambivalence about Mary during my shower, I wasn't stupid enough to court an early demise by staying in a house full of shiny stuff alone any longer than necessary. I'd been lucky so far, but luck wouldn't last. I was overdue for another ghostly visit.

⟁

I was silent all the way to Mom's work the next morning. Before relinquishing the car to me for the day, she made me restate my promise to call her the moment I walked into the apartment. I swore I would, and she held both of my cheeks while she kissed me, telling me twice how much she loved me.

I pulled the car out of her work parking lot and drove exactly one street down before pulling over. Packing tape and a lot of salt later, I had the car warded enough that I didn't have to fear for my life.

I didn't expect school to be so full. I figured more parents would keep their kids at home considering the potential kidnapper in our midst. Police were stationed outside of the main entrances, and there was a news van parked along the street. I walked in through the parking lot doors and made a beeline for my locker, but before I could reach it, there was a hard tug on my wrist from behind.

"I have to talk to you," Jess said.

I yanked my hand away and kept walking.

"Stop. Seriously, we need to talk. I've got something going on af—"

"Shut up. SHUT UP!" I hollered, whipping my head around to glare at her. People stopped to stare at us, some whispering behind their hands. I leaned toward Jess, my lips inches away from her ear. "I know, Jess. I know why you dragged us into this. I know why you're so hung up on Mary. I hope it was worth Bronx's legs. I hope seeing your great-aunt was worth Anna, you bitch."

She looked like I'd struck her. There should have been some satisfaction in her stunned silence, but there was only hurt and anger. Everyone had lost so much while Jess stood there without a single blond hair out of place.

I jogged away from her to get to my locker, slamming my books inside and grabbing the ones I'd need for the day. She didn't follow me, but halfway down the hall I heard her voice rising above the morning din.

"I'm going to help you, Shauna! You're my best friend."

She probably meant that as a promise, but under the current circumstances, it sounded a lot like a threat. I headed for my first class, my eyes averted so I didn't have to look at anyone, so I didn't have to see any dead-girl faces staring at me from glass windows, doorknobs, or anywhere else. They'd waxed the tile floor last night, too, so I couldn't look down. I had to stare at the books clutched in my arms and hope I'd find my way.

Shiny above, shiny below, Mary was everywhere and nowhere all at once.

I threw myself into my desk right as my phone vibrated inside my bag. It was probably Jess, but on the off chance it was my mom, I stole a peek. It was neither. Kitty texted me to tell me to call her after school, that her parents had let her stay home an extra day. I wanted to send her a message explaining Jess's tie to Mary, but it was too complicated, too messy for a text. I sent her an abbreviated *Kay* with an emoticon heart.

The school day didn't have much to do with school. The teachers didn't bother teaching so much as letting my class-mates talk among themselves. At one point, our guidance coun-selor came in to discuss resources available to anxious students. It was a pretty glum affair, and I trudged to lunch feeling like I should have stayed home after all. But anything was better than the depression jockey on my back.

It was strange to sit in the cafeteria alone. With few excep-tions, my quartet of friends had been together for years, and yet there I was in the corner by myself. Kitty was home, Anna was dead, and Jess... well, Jess was across the room sitting with her softball cronies. I didn't want to look at her, mostly because I didn't want to give her any indication that there was a way to fix us, but toward the end of lunch, I glanced her way anyway. I couldn't help it; I wanted to see if she was as sad as I was. That's when I saw the red notebook. Red notebooks weren't a noteworthy thing in general, but Jess hadn't owned one before the Mary stuff. Either this was coincidence, or she had her summoning notes on the table in front of her.

Jess nodded at Becca, Laurie, and Tonya. She opened up the cover and her hands danced all over the place, her expression animated. This was her "I have a really good idea" sales pitch. I knew it because I'd fallen prey to that very same charisma when I'd agreed to summon a ghost in Anna's basement. If that's what she was doing now, if she was getting herself a fresh batch of idiots...

"You wouldn't," I whispered. Except she would. I knew she would. While Becca and Laurie dipped their heads forward to take a better look, Tonya stood up and waved Jess off, shaking her head. Jess called her back, but Tonya kept on walking, taking her lunch tray to another table to sit with other friends. Jess scowled after her for a moment, then turned back to the remaining two. I had a sinking feeling watching the three of them huddled together, a smile spreading across Jess's face.

I had to warn the girls. I was obligated. But by the time I abandoned my seat and gave chase down the hall, they were gone. I saw Becca after the next class, but before I could grab her attention, she headed inside the science lab and her teacher shut the door. After school, I stood by the buses—Laurie bused in and out every day—but she never showed up. When the bulk of the students were loaded and the doors closed, I ran toward the parking lot.

My sneakers skidded through the grit just as Jess drove away with one body in her passenger seat, another in the back.

26

I called Jess, feeling obligated to warn her off of any terrible ideas before they became terrible actualities. She didn't answer because she was a horrible bitch. A *driven* horrible bitch, which was even worse.

Mom said go straight home, but Mom didn't know what I knew. I drove to Jess's house, willing Jess's car to be in the driveway when I got there, but it wasn't. I ran to her front door and knocked. Mrs. McAllister answered with a dishrag in her hands. By the lift of her brows, it was clear she was surprised to see me. It made me sad to see her face; I probably wouldn't see much of it in the future. Ditching Jess meant ditching her awesome family. Related to Bloody Mary or not, the McAllisters had been kind to me.

"Hey, kiddo. Good to see you. I'm so sorry about Anna."

Before I could do anything about it, I was pulled into another mommy hug. I indulged for a moment, my jaw clenching so I wouldn't cry on Mrs. McAllister's shirt. Sympathy was nice, but it tended to leave me a soggy mess, and I didn't need that right now. I gently disengaged, my eyes glassy and swollen with unshed tears.

"Thanks. Is Jess on her way here? I need to talk to her," I said.

She reached out to stroke my forehead much like my own mom had done just this morning. And last night. And the afternoon before that. It seemed to be a go-to mom comfort gesture. "She's on her way to Kitty's. Maybe you can catch her there."

My blood ran cold. Jess had two people in her car when she left school. She'd tried for another with Tonya, but Tonya had walked away. If Jess was on her way to Kitty's, that would make four girls, and with four girls . . .

"Thanks, Mrs. M!" I said, sprinting for the car. I heard her call my name, but I threw myself in and peeled out of the driveway, one hand on the steering wheel and the other on my phone. I dialed Kitty, waiting for her to pick up, but I got dumped into her voice mail. I kept dialing and she kept not answering. I sent a text; there was no answer. I didn't know for sure if Jess was summoning Mary again, but between the notebook, the girls, and her earlier promise to help me, the pieces fit together.

I whipped around a corner hard enough that two tires lifted off the road. Kitty was a pushover. She would agree to anything Jess wanted. Well, maybe not a pushover—Jess was just good at getting her way. She'd bully and bully until people relented, myself included. If Jess threw Kitty a line about saving me, Kitty would want to help. I wished she'd tell Jess NO for once, but that was impossible. Kitty was too nice for her own good.

I tore up Kitty's super-long driveway, nearly hitting her shrub wall at least four times before parking. My eyes strayed to the rearview mirror. I half expected it to have a tongue or fingers or some other dead body part lolling out of it, but Mary was nowhere to be found. I almost wished she were, because then I'd know she wasn't inside Kitty's house.

I rushed inside, not bothering to knock. Kitty did all of her hosting downstairs in the media room, so I beelined for the basement door. I reached for the knob just as screams blasted up from the other side of the door. There was the thud of feet on stairs before the door swung open and whacked me in the face. I doubled over as it struck my nose, my hands covering the stabbing ache. Becca and Laurie burst from the dense blackness of the basement, both of them panicked and terrified and frantic to escape. They shoved past me and scrambled for the front door, screaming at the top of their lungs the entire way.

Rot smell wafted up from the darkness, the unmistakable tang of too sweet, too sour, and too wet. *Bloody Mary was here.*

"God. GOD!" I lunged for the light switch and ran down the stairs.

The back wall of the media room had a big decorative mirror hanging over the leather couch, which was probably why Jess chose it to summon Mary. It was plenty big enough for Mary to pass through. The couch was pulled away from the wall, and there was a salt box on the floor beneath the mirror. The lines were fully formed; there were no breaks that I could see.

Somehow, though, Mary had found a way through the wards. Maybe they'd dropped the handhold. Maybe they'd forgotten the candle.

Half the bottles from the bar were smashed, and the stools were thrown askew. A few of them were broken into pieces, long shards of wood littering the booze-drenched ground. The pool table was tipped on its side in the corner of the room, its felt top shredded by Mary's claws. The couch was gutted, the springs from the cushions exposed and menacingly sharp.

There was no one in the room. I couldn't see Jess or Kitty, and although I had heard Mary's laugh and smelled her distinctive stink, I couldn't see her, either. I panicked that I was too late. Maybe Mary had dragged them both into the mirror. My stomach knotted at the thought, but then with crunching, squelching steps, Mary trundled out of the adjacent laundry room. I actually felt a little relieved to see her. She wouldn't be here if Jess and Kitty were on the other side of the glass. She'd be too busy bleeding them like she'd bled Anna.

"Kitty! What happened? Where are you?" I called out, praying she was somewhere safe. My voice caught Mary's attention and she craned her head my way, casting me a jack-o'-lantern grin with her crooked, broken teeth. There was a crack at the corner of her lip where the pustules had been the last time I saw her. They'd erupted, and now her smile extended up too far, into her cheek like someone had taken a razor to the edge of her mouth. The flaps of skin hung too loose, explaining the wet, wheezing sound Mary made every few seconds.

"Run! You need to run! The salt's not working!" It was Kitty, her voice squeaking out from behind the upended pool table. It was smart to use it as a barrier against Mary, but it wouldn't last. Mary was far too strong for a little thing like a pool table to stop her.

"Get out of here, Shauna!" Jess commanded from the same position. "Just go. I've got this under control."

"No, you don't," I said. I made my way to the closest broken stool, my fingers wrapping around a snapped leg. The end was jagged and sharp. Under normal circumstances it would make a fine weapon, except Mary was anything but normal. I watched her walk over a sea of broken glass to get to me, some of the pointy bits wedging into the soles of her feet. It didn't slow her down, not even when each foot left a perfect footprint of sludge-blood in the carpet.

I wasn't going to lose Kitty to Mary, too. I circled the ghost and moved toward the pool table, keeping Mary in my sights at all times. I walked backward, navigating the floor debris as best I could, only stumbling once or twice in my circuit.

"*Leave,* Shauna," Jess repeated.

"You're not getting Kitty killed, too. What'd she tell you to get you to summon her again, Kitty? That you could help me? Well, you can by taking the ghost. It's a shitty deal," I said, my eyes pinned on Mary, the stool leg raised in case she grabbed for me. She was only about six feet away now. I continued to retreat, past the pool table and toward the carcass of the sofa. Mary was content to follow, as if she knew that there was nowhere I could go.

I heard Kitty whimper my name right before the pool table

flew away from the wall. It could have been Kitty trying to escape; it could have been Jess flinging Kitty in Bloody Mary's direction. Either way, Mary's attention snapped away from me. She charged the pool table, her skeletal hands gripping the side and heaving it over her head as she screeched. Jess and Kitty dove away from her, Jess going left toward me while Kitty rolled right, crunching over broken glass, as the table crashed into the wall.

I slid behind the couch. Mary sniffed the air, her eyes flitting from Kitty to Jess to me, as if she didn't know which target would prove the most succulent. When she turned toward Kitty, I let out a shrill whistle and slammed the stool leg against the couch.

"Over here, you dead bitch! Come on, it's me you want!" I tried to taunt her into coming for me by making a clamor, but Mary cast a grin over her shoulder and spun back to Kitty, her hands swiping. Kitty made a break for the bar, pieces of bottle glass breaking beneath her shoes. Mary liked the chase; she followed Kitty, shriek-laughing and lunging in a twisted game.

I moved out from behind the couch, starting toward Mary with the stool leg at the ready, when I felt an arm wrap around my waist from behind. I was wrenched back and slammed into a tall, warm form. Jess. Her free hand grabbed for the stool leg in an attempt to wrestle it away from me. I gripped it tighter, but Jess grunted and kicked her knee into the back of mine. We tumbled forward as one unit, narrowly missing the exposed springs of the couch, my elbows slamming down into the glass and splintered wood.

"No. Leave it alone," Jess growled, giving the stool leg another jerk. "Just let Mary grab her and we'll see if—*oomph*." She snarled as I elbowed her in the gut, shifting her position so she could better sprawl on top of me to pin me. Her left hand buried itself in my hair, her right sliding under my chin and gripping hard. "*Knock it off. If Mary cuts her, she gets her scent. It'll buy you time. We can save Kitty later.*"

"ARE YOU INSANE?" I screamed. "*You can't trade one friend to Mary for another.*" I bucked like a bronco, but Jess had me secure. She flexed the hand in my hair and pulled my head back before tearing the stool leg from my grasp. It landed a few feet away. I heard crashes from the bar and glanced up in time to see Kitty hurling the remaining liquor bottles at Mary's head. Mary just laughed and leapt toward her, nearly catching her by the sleeve.

"I'm doing this to save you! Stop being such a pain in the ass!" Jess shouted, loud enough that my ears rang. She yanked on my hair, making my scalp tingle with the force. No matter how much I writhed and kicked, I couldn't shake her, she wouldn't let go, and I grunted my frustration, the heel of my sneaker smacking her in the shin.

"Come on, Jess! I don't want this. Let me go. Let Kitty go, for God's sake. *Let me go!*"

"Shut up, Shauna. This is temporary. Just so she doesn't kill you before we can solve it. Kitty will be fine. I promise. I promise she'll be fine. We'll figure it out!"

"No, Jess! No. GET OFF OF ME! GET OFF!"

I screamed myself raw, twisting and turning. Mary got

closer and closer to catching Kitty with every swipe. She edged her way around the bar with a series of rasps and chitters, her lips twisting up to reveal mold-riddled gums and yellow fangs. Another dry rustle of laughter and she tottered toward Kitty, her talons extended to rend flesh from bone. Kitty whimpered and dove across the bar, trying to vault to the other side, but Mary grabbed for her leg, her hand twisting in the hem of Kitty's jeans. Mary jerked back, and Kitty sailed down the polished wood.

Kitty gave a plaintive wail, and I knew this was it. If I didn't do something, Kitty would either be cursed, maimed like Bronx, or killed. I couldn't let any of those things happen. I had to lure Mary our way, but how? Without the bar stool, the only things I had within arm's reach were glass shards from a broken champagne bottle, but they weren't big enough to inflict much damage.

But then, maybe I didn't need to do a lot of damage.

Blood. Bloody Mary loved *blood*. After the doorknob exchange, she'd slurped it off of her fingers like it was her favorite candy. If I wanted to make Mary give up Kitty, I had to give her an incentive. I reached for the nearest shard of glass and slammed it into the back of Jess's hand.

"You bitch. YOU BITCH!" Jess howled, rolling off me to cradle her injured hand to her chest. Blood welled up thick and fast, ribbons of it running down her wrist, dripping over her lap. It was possible it wouldn't be enough, that Mary only wanted my blood, but if that was the case, I'd jab myself in the palm to make her come this way. I had no qualms about offering Jess in my stead first, though. She deserved a little pain.

The effect was immediate. Mary swiveled toward us, catching the scent. She tossed Kitty aside like an abandoned toy to charge me and Jess, a rattling wheeze erupting from her lips with every step. She stopped just in front of me, so close I could see glass poking out of the meaty parts of her feet and through her rotting toenails. A rain of swamp water droplets splashed down over my head as she leaned over me to grab Jess. I dove for the bar stool leg, Jess screaming in terror behind me. Glass tangled in my shirt, tearing the fabric and scratching my skin, but I didn't stop crawling until I had the weapon in my hand.

Mary pulled Jess close. Jess shrieked and flailed, but Mary's grip was ironclad. I pushed myself to my feet and edged away, watching them. For all that I hated Jess, I couldn't watch her get maimed or dragged into the mirror. I stumbled toward the back of the couch and spotted a Tupperware container full of salt on the floor. I picked it up and got a handful, throwing it at Mary. I waited for her flesh to burn, but the granules just hit her and fell to the floor. She lifted Jess's hand to slurp the open wound, swallowing every drop of blood with a delighted groan.

"Oh, God. Oh, God. Get it off. *Get her off of me.* SHAUNA, HELP!" Jess looked at me, her eyes wide and pleading. I tried another handful of salt from the container, and again it did nothing. I began to tremble, my teeth chattering like I'd been dunked in ice water. We had so few advantages against Mary, and now one of the staples was failing us.

"It's sugar," Jess said. "Get Kitty's stash. Hurry. She... Hurry!" Mary was rubbing her face against Jess's injury now, like a cat marking its territory. It took my brain a moment to absorb what Jess had done. Sugar instead of salt. She'd laid false lines in front of the mirror so Mary could come out and grab one of the girls. It wasn't that Mary had grown immune to the stuff, it was that *I didn't have the right stuff to hurt her.*

For a second, I almost let Bloody Mary have Jess for all the pain and hurt Jess had caused, but I couldn't be that person. *I couldn't be Jess.* I looked over at Kitty, who had retrieved the box of salt from the floor. She tossed it to me, and I tore off the top to get a good handful before flinging it Mary's way.

The salt struck Mary in the side of her neck, oily smoke wafting from her skin. She let out a furious howl and jerked away. I'd thought the pain would send her scampering back toward the mirror, but as Jess shimmied away from her, trying to escape, Mary snatched at her blond hair, wadding it in her fist. Mary's other hand pulled back before she swiped it down, her claws raking Jess's shoulder blades. Jess screamed. She was marked as I'd been marked. Those razor nails had claimed her with five bloody tracks.

Jess wept for pity, but the ghost paid no mind. Mary snickered as she leaned in to drag her white, blood-smeared tongue up over Jess's cheek, leaving a glistening snail trail of spittle across Jess's face. Jess looked like she wanted to shrivel up and die, but she couldn't—Mary held her too tightly. She'd become Mary's prize of the day.

"Help me. Help me," Jess rasped as Mary started walking her toward the mirror.

I tossed the salt to Kitty so I could better grip my stool leg. "Don't use it until I tell you to," I ordered. I circled Mary. She tittered at me, her eye narrowing as she dragged the struggling Jess across the room. I thought about hitting her with it like a baseball bat, but it wasn't thick enough to do any real damage. It was pointy, though. I eyed Mary's body to pick my spot. She must have read my thoughts, as she swung Jess around in front of her, using Jess's body as a shield.

"Don't move, Jess," I whispered. Jess stopped struggling and went deadweight, causing Mary to stumble forward. I lifted the spike over my head and ran at her, aiming for her eye. There was a wet sucking noise, a squish, and Mary's scream echoed through the basement, loud enough to shake the foundations of the house. She relinquished her hold on Jess to grab her own face, groping at the wood impaled in her eye socket.

"NOW, KITTY, NOW!" I screeched, grabbing a stunned Jess and pulling her out of harm's way. Kitty swept in with her salt, throwing handful after handful to force Mary to retreat. There was a last, ear-blasting bellow before Mary turned for the mirror and dove into its quivering depths.

27

Kitty flung salt at the mirror until it turned solid. Mary was back where she belonged, on the right side of the glass. We fell silent; the only sound filling the room was Jess's weeping. I looked over at where she lay in a crumpled heap. Her hand was still bleeding, and there were claw marks in her back, just as there had been in mine. If what Cody said was true, my tag had been replaced by the promise of a better, fresher victim.

I grabbed the salt from Kitty and walked into the adjacent bathroom. I didn't lay a line. Instead I approached the mirror over the sink and waited. I was nervous—Mary was surely pissed at me after what I'd done to her face—but she didn't come at me, not even when I put my hand against the glass in invitation. It was a normal, boring reflection staring back at me now.

"Hey, Shauna, she's out here still. She's trying to get out and she looks really mad. I think she's coming back for you!" Kitty yelled.

"No," I said, reemerging from the bathroom and glaring at Jess's huddled form. Pitiful as she was, I felt only anger. Cold, hard anger that she could be so selfish and stupid. "She's here for Jess."

While I'd been in the bathroom, Mary had pulled the spike from her face. There was a huge hole where her eye used to be. My stomach lurched when beetles crawled from the orifice to fly off into the smoky haze surrounding her.

Jess looked at the mirror and then at me. Her hand reached for me, fingers wrapping around my ankle to give it a squeeze. Her blue eyes were rimmed red, her skin paler than usual. Tears and snot covered her face. "Help me. Please. I was only doing it for you. I wouldn't lose you to her. You're like my sister."

"Shut up," I said. "Just shut up and go home, Jess."

"But—"

"Shut up and go home," I repeated, my look hard.

Jess got to her feet, her fingers skimming over the cut in the back of her hand. Two bright spots of color flamed on her cheeks as she turned to address Kitty. "I'm sorry. I wanted her to go for Becca or Laurie, but they . . . I'm sorry. I wouldn't have let Mary have you, either. It just . . . I'm sorry. Please. I can't lose everything. Not now. Not if she's . . ." Jess craned her neck back at the mirror, shuddering when she saw Mary's face pressed to the solid glass, her hands clawing at the surface like she could dig her way through. "Not if she's going to hurt me. I was trying to help. I swear."

I braced for Kitty to do the nice-girl thing and forgive her. I figured she'd take one look at Jess and then try to talk me into relenting. Kitty shook her head and pointed at the stairs. "Go," she said quietly. "Go home, Jess."

"But, Kitty—"

"Leave. Please."

Kitty's rejection sent Jess into a rage. Her face went so red it was almost purple, the veins in her temples and neck cording. Her hands balled into fists, the tension making the cut on the back of her hand ooze fresh blood onto the carpet. "Fine. FINE! I don't need you. I'll figure it out. On my own, if I have to. I'll do it on my own."

She stomped toward the steps, climbing them two at a time to get away from us. The moment she was out of sight, Mary disappeared from the mirror at our side, intent on following her newest victim. Jess's sobbing drifted down the stairs right before the house door slammed. A car engine revved a moment later, tires squealing across pavement as Jess pulled out of Kitty's driveway.

"This is weird to say," Kitty said, squatting so she wouldn't shred her pants with the glass. "But I feel like we're not done. Like we need to figure out how to get rid of Mary forever. If not for Jess, then for the people around her."

"Or the next group of girls who don't know what they're getting into," I agreed. It wasn't a happy thought, but a necessary one, and I sighed. I sank down next to Kitty to lean into her side. She slung an arm over my shoulders and we hugged. And then we cried. It wasn't just for Anna and Bronx and all the fear and misery of the past week; it was relief, too, that the nightmare was over for now. At least for tonight, I could sleep in my bed and not wonder what was on the other side of the mirror looking out at me.

I lifted my head to glance around the room, looking for a paper towel or a napkin somewhere among the debris. The room was a wreck. I climbed to my feet and started picking through the carnage, doing my best to avoid glass and wood and everything else that wanted to impale me. "Your dad is going to kill you," I said. "I'm sorry."

"Yeah, he is. I don't even know what to say to him, but... ugh. It's the least of my problems, I suppose." Kitty went upstairs to grab some trash bags, the broom, and a vacuum. We went to work cleaning after that, removing as much of the debris as we could. The couch and bar stools were ruined as well as all the alcohol. The pool table was shredded, and the carpet next to it sported Mary's tarry-blood footprints.

It wasn't until I pushed the couch back into place beneath the mirror that I found the red notebook. Jess must have brought it in with her when the girls were summoning Mary. I sat on the single remaining cushion and tossed the cover open. Kitty came to stand beside me, her hand on my shoulder as I leafed through. All of Jess's notes were there about the summoning rules, and the two letters we'd already seen, but there was an addition since the last time I'd peeked at the pages.

A picture. This wasn't a photocopy, but a real picture from a long time ago. It was Mary Worth standing alone in front of the Southbridge Parish. It was hard to believe this was the same girl from the group shot we'd seen. Her eyes were large and intense beneath her dark brows. She'd lost too much weight, the round fullness of her cheeks replaced by harsh angles. Her dark hair was tangled and unkempt, and there was a smear of dirt along her chin. She wore a white dress, but it was in poor condition, the bust covered in a series of splotchy stains.

"She looks so mad," Kitty whispered. I agreed. Mary did look furious. Her head was tilted down so she could look at the cameraman from beneath her eyebrows. Her hands were balled into fists by her sides. She was full of a fury she could barely contain.

"Jess is related to her, you know," I said. "Mary's her great-aunt times five or something."

Kitty's mouth dropped open. "She . . . Wait, what?"

"Yeah. That's why she's been so crazy about this. That's why she probably has this picture in the first place. Mary's her relative." I flipped the picture over. *Mary Augustine Worth, February 16, 1847–October 28, 1864* was written on the back.

"That's unreal. It explains so much, though."

"Explains, yes, but doesn't excuse," I said.

Kitty took the picture from me to get a better look, then shuddered and handed it back, her finger tapping against Mary's glowering face. "I can see the start of the ghost there," she said. "I can see the resemblance. Not in the last picture, but this one, yes."

So could I. I stuffed the photo back into the notebook and closed it. An envelope tumbled out of the back, landing at my feet. It was thick, like it'd been overstuffed. I picked it up and lifted the flap. Inside was a stack of coarse yellow papers time had worn thin at the edges. It was written in Mary's hand, but unlike the other letters, this was an original.

I glanced at the date on the first page, the ink faded but still legible. *October 27, 1864,* it said. The day before her death. Which meant clutched between my fingers, in sweeping, formal script, were Bloody Mary Worth's last written words.

October 27, 1864

Constance,

I understand why you cannot come, and while it is difficult for me to be joyful about anything these days, this baby is a blessing. Your offer to send Edward in your stead is sweet, but you are too close to delivery, dear sister, and I would not risk you or that precious child for anything in the world. Once I have a fine niece or nephew, you can sweep me away from this slice of Hell. Until then, take care of yourself and your baby.

The pastor would not relent on Mother's funeral, but he is ever incapable of decency. The stain upon her character persists despite my protests, and as such, she was not allowed to be buried with "decent Christians." I advised the constable that Pastor Starkcrowe was seen walking with Mother before her disappearance, but the constable is assured of the pastor's innocence. He, too, believes Mother cast herself into the river. You can guess my opinions on the matter. Pastor Starkcrowe is a lecher of a man far too comfortable with his cruelties. I only wish others would see him for who he is.

I mourn our mother every minute of every hour. She was far too good for this world—too kind to live amongst such injustice. She deserved better than an unmarked grave outside of town. I visit her remains daily to ensure no animals desecrate her. The rocks are piled high. I will care for her to the best of my ability while I toil in Solomon's Folly.

To answer your question, yes, there have been more incidents. I grow accustomed to the dark, though with winter coming, it will be colder and more unkind. I plan to tuck blankets in the cellar in preparation. Boots, too, for when the water rises, and perhaps a candle and flint. It is strange the things you can tolerate given enough exposure. The basement with its beetles and bats does not terrify me as it once did.

No, what plagues me most lately is my capacity for anger. Before I was sent to "repent" yesterday, the pastor struck me across the mouth with the back of his hand. He flayed me from cheek to lip. It did not move him to pity. He dragged me to the basement despite my bloodstained dress.

Elizabeth bore witness to our exchange. She had the audacity to taunt me through the door again. I didn't answer her provocations, but I cannot claim this as an attestation to character. I was simply too enraged to speak. My hatred for the pastor, for Elizabeth Hawthorne, and for every girl like her has grown bone-deep and all-consuming. I despise that our mother was so wronged and suffered the final indignity of a non-Christian burial. I despise that God is an absentee shepherd who has forsaken me and those I love.

I am a creature born of injustice and fury.

I must finish my writing now, as the pastor has rationed my lantern oil. He was assigned my guardianship in the wake of Mother's death. Every night he locks me in my room so I cannot escape, but I do not mind. The door between us grants the illusion of separation. It keeps him out as effectively as it keeps me in.

Perhaps tonight I will sleep. Last night, my cheek ached and Elizabeth's taunts were too fresh in my mind. They still echo *through my head, that singsong lilt of hers making it all the more obscene. I would scratch my ears from my skull if it would make the memory of it go away, but I think it would stay with me regardless.*

Some things are simply too cruel to abide.

Bloody Mary.

Bloody Mary.

BLOODY MARY.

Acknowledgments

A lot of wonderful people helped get this into print.
Thank you, Christian Trimmer, for bringing me into the
Hyperion fold. What a fantastic book family. Thank you, Tracey
Keevan, for taking my little piece of coal and polishing it to a
fine gleam. Thank you, T. S. Ferguson, who was the first edi-
tor to tell me, "Modernize this." It got me on the right path.
The fact that you became my friend along the way is amazing.
Thank you, Crystal, Lauren N., Renée, Brian, Nikki,
Christi, Claire, Melinda, Laurie, Lara, and Reuben, for lending
me your eyes. Thank you, WFR crew, for putting up with con-
stant cut-and-pastes. Thank you, Scott Storrier, Matthew Finn,
and Marty Gleason, for always listening. Thank you, Becky
Kroll, Chandra Rooney, Evie Nelson, and Sarah Johnson, for
tearing me apart to make me better. I wouldn't trade your cruelties (or friendship) for anything in the world.

Thank you, Miriam Kriss, for picking up a book from the
slush pile X years ago and saying, "I like them." I am forever in
your debt for making this particular dream a reality.

Thank you, Greg Roy and Eric Tribou, for spending

countless hours dead-eyed while I droned on about books. You are my second family and I love you.

Thank you, Lauren Roy, my sister from another mister and best friend. I have no idea which deity I pleased to get you in my life, but I'm thankful every day that you're around. You are a spectacular person and make me better by association.

Thank you, David Finn, for tolerating me day in and day out. You've believed in me, my books, and this strange life we share. That means more than I'll ever let on. I hope you're paying attention because this line is for you: you're a superhero.

Thank you to my family, who've been so supportive. I love you all. Mike and Mike—you're two of the most wonderful dads a girl could ask for. Drew Cole, I'm so lucky you came into my life when you did and helped me grow into a quasi-normal human. And Mom—whenever someone says something good about me or my work, I want you to claim a piece for yourself. I would not be the person I am without your steel, your love, and your rapier wit.

And last but not least, thank you, Dot, for tapping away in that front room for so many years. Yours are some big shoes to fill.

DON'T MISS THE SEQUEL TO
MARY: THE SUMMONING

UNLEASHED

Sister Mine,

Below, I have listed my dastardly deeds since you abandoned me for Boston. "But Mary," you say. "I did not abandon you so much as find a handsome gentleman to kiss me breathless for eternity." The result is the same, Constance. I have brought a reign of terror to Solomon's Folly. I will not be sated until I have tainted everything you love with my terribleness.

1. I have claimed your room as my own. The pink sashes are gone because pink is an affront to all that is good in the world. I have replaced it with a shade of green you would abhor. I do this as both a declaration of war and because green is a far superior color.
2. I have taken over your gardening duties. This is not to help Mother but to destroy your handiwork. Plants wither in fear at the sight of my boots. I am not blessed with your green thumb but, as Mother says, a black thumb, and I shall use it to wreak havoc upon your peonies.
3. I have taken your place on the church choir. The psalms you hold so dear are now sung so off pitch, dogs bay thinking me their pack mistress. Our sweet mother has asked if perhaps I would like to do a Sunday reading in lieu of the hymnals, but I remain stalwart.

(To her chagrin, I might add. When I expressed that I preferred the music, she looked much like your peonies—wilted and sad.)

4. Despite your instruction that the shawl you knitted me last winter should not be worn with my shapeless blue frock, I have done just that. I disavow fashion! I want those who look upon me to know repulsion and fear. Your innocent lace is a weapon in my hands.

5. I have taken over your duties with the Spencer girls, and I believe they find me the superior nanny. What better way to vex you than to fatten up the children you love with so much shortbread, they explode. Whilst Mrs. Spencer will undoubtedly take offense to my practices, the children will love me best, and that is all that matters.

   (I caught Agatha with two meaty fists in the shortbread pan. The child had eaten half the contents in the three minutes I took to attend her sister's nappies. I would have been impressed if I was not so horribly afraid she'd get sick.)

6. Mr. Biscuits is a traitor. Your poorly named dog has all but forgotten you. He sleeps at the foot of my bed every night making terrible sounds and equally as terrible smells. Every morning he looks upon me like I am the sun in his furry little world. This is likely because I am the one to feed him the scraps, but let's pretend he is drawn to my shining disposition.

7. Not only did I not go to the summer dance, I told Thomas Adderly that I would rather wash my hair than attend. I did not do this simply because Thomas is overly ardent and annoying. No, it was to defy your terrible sisterly advice! For shame, Constance! For shame!

(Honestly, the boy is dull, and I've seen better teeth in horse mouths. There's also the Elizabeth Hawthorne problem. Her preference for dull, horse-teethed gentlemen causes me far too much grief. While attending a dance may have been nice, the company was lacking and the repercussions weren't worthwhile.)

8. Last, but by no means least, I cancel my trek to Boston. Fie upon you and your fancy home! I shall remain in Solomon's Folly until my skin is withered and my teeth fall out!

(I am suffering a summer cold that has wetted my lungs, and Mother says I must wait to travel. While I do not like postponing, my sickness has kept me abed the last few days. I will write you when I am less apt to play the part of Pestilence. I hope to reschedule soon.)

I hope this letter finds you miserable (blissfully happy) and that Joseph snores in his sleep. (That would be awful. Mr. Biscuits is bad enough. A full-grown man must be thrice as disruptive.)

Write soon, my beloved harpy.

Your sister,

Mary

The darkness has a face.

Gray skin stretched over a craggy skull, black veins pulsing at the temples and cheeks. It has no nose, no lips—only voids crusted with liquid decay. Broken teeth jut up from the gums like yellow stalagmites. A white, wormlike tongue wags to taste the air. Tufts of hair top half-rotted ears, leaves and debris tangled in the elbow-length strands.

The darkness has a voice. Sometimes it's wet, like pipes choking through a clog. Other times it's dry and slithery, like snake scales gliding over rock. It depends on whether she's laughing. Mary likes to laugh, but only if she's bled someone. That's when the raspiest rattles echo from her throat.

Nothing is normal after a haunting. School, friends, boys... who cares? How can you worry about the mundane when you've seen the extraordinary? When one of your best friends was killed by a ghost before your eyes?

I still can't look in a mirror, because I see her. Mary. She's tattooed on my brain. Vines swathing her thin frame, clinging to a ragged dress with a copper-splattered bodice. Talons tipping the spindly fingers, the edges as sharp as razors. One leg swollen with water and ready to burst, the other nothing but bone. Beetles everywhere, living inside a walking corpse, scurrying beneath the skin until they gnaw their way out.

The thought of her is enough to send me fleeing to my mother's side. Last week, I caught a glimpse of my reflection in a picture frame and hit the floor as if I were in an air raid. Mom doesn't understand my twitchiness. Worse, I can't explain it. She would never believe me. I hadn't believed Jess when she'd first told me about it, either.

Jess. She got us into this mess. Bloody Mary Worth was her obsession and we were stupid enough to follow. When Jess positioned us in that bathroom, when she checked her compass points and placed the candle and salt line, we didn't think anything would happen. It was just a game. Then a ghostly hand pressed against the glass. We should have ended it there, but one more summon, Jess said. Just one. I relented. No, I encouraged my friends to go along with it because I was curious.

Now I'm scarred, Jess is haunted, and Anna's dead. Regret weighs on me from the moment I wake in the morning until I drift into my dreams. I want to walk away, to let Mary be Jess's problem, but I have a debt to repay. To Anna. To other girls who'd play the game. Jess will pawn the ghost onto someone sooner or later. Mary will continue torturing girls from the mirror.

I have to do something about it.
The question is... what?

⁓

The letter from Mary to Constance Worth Simpson should have made me laugh. It should have warmed me to the authoress from a century and a half ago. I'd have thought her clever and charming. I'd have said something like, "I'd be her friend."

But this letter had been stuffed inside of Jess McAllister's notebook, wedged between two pages of handwritten notes about Bloody Mary. Despite the tone, it was no joke, as proven by the three other letters present. They cataloged Mary's plight from start to end—a smart, funny teenager deteriorating along with her circumstances. A cruel pastor robbing her of her mother, and in turn her humor. Anger filled the gaps, but eventually that was taken, too, when she was murdered at seventeen years old.

The ghost of the legend wasn't born evil. She was made that way. Two cups tragedy, one tablespoon cruelty, a splash of neglect. It was a recipe for pain.

We tried to stop Mary. Jess even staged another summoning with Kitty, Laurie Carmichael, and Becca Miller, "To save you, Shauna," she said to me. "To get you unhaunted." She succeeded, albeit not how she anticipated. Jess planned for Kitty to take on the curse during that last summoning, but I intervened and Jess was grabbed in Kitty's stead.

We sent Mary back into the mirror, but not before Mary spilled Jess's blood. We all knew what that meant; Mary wouldn't let Jess go until Jess died or another girl took the mark from her. It was how it had always been with Bloody Mary. It was how it would be until someone put the ghost to rest. More girls would die.

Like Anna Sasaki died.

It was hard to believe she was gone. Some days, the pain of her loss was raw, like someone branding me with a hot poker. Other days, it was a dull throb, like a bone-deep bruise. I missed Anna's intelligence. I missed her snark. I missed scribbling notes to her during math class to pass the time.

I missed *her*.

School resumed a few days after her disappearance. AMBER Alert: Anna Sasaki. The police hadn't a trace, nor would they find one: Mary dragged Anna through the mirror and into her swampy, black world.

The fog rising on the other side of the mirror. Crimson blood spraying across the glass. Too much to be nonfatal. Too much to grant any hope that Anna survived. Terror and loss and futility dropping on my head like an anvil. Grief crushing me beneath its weight.

The Sasakis would never get the closure they so deserved.

The days after the murder were a fixed reel in a movie, the same twelve-hour clip playing, rewinding, and repeating the next morning. I got up, ate breakfast with my mother, and went to school early. I didn't like being alone in the house. Every sound in the building sent me scurrying for the only weapon I knew that worked against Mary—salt. It burned her. I had boxes of it squirreled away in my closet in case she returned.

There was no reason to expect her, but Jess's tie to Mary made me uneasy. Would Jess's haunting be different because she and Mary were related? What would happen if Jess somehow allied with Mary? I put nothing past Jess. She'd sacrificed one friend to the mirror and nearly succeeded in sacrificing a second.

Jess could justify anything when she put her mind to it. Even murder.

At the end of the school day, I would go to Kitty's house until Mom got out of work. After Anna died, Mom cut her hours at her second job. It was the only good thing to come from the haunting. I loved my mom. I also loved knowing that Mary left me alone whenever Mom was near. We never quite figured out why that was, but I had my suspicions. Mary Worth loved her mother. Other mothers were safe by association.

I spent the last hour of every day alone in my room, lying in bed and gazing at the wall. My thoughts drifted to Anna, to Kitty's boyfriend, Bronx. He was a star football player before Mary pulled him through a glass window and dropped him three stories. His legs had snapped like twigs. Double casts, metal bolts, surgeries—he was lucky he'd ever walk again, never mind play sports.

Mary took so much from both of them. Thinking about my part in bringing her into this world almost always made me weep into my pillow. It would have been easy to lay it all on Jess, but I wouldn't fool myself. I'd made bad decisions, too.

Jess liked to remind me of that sometimes. She refused to fade into obscurity. Rapid-fire texts—sometimes apologies, sometimes accusations. I ignored every message. The assault died down after the first few weeks, but I'd still get the occasional plea for help. When she saw me in the halls at school—her eyes sunken in like she hadn't slept in forever, a fresh cut or scratch marring her skin—I looked away. Sometimes she followed me, calling my name. I ducked into classrooms to avoid her. I left the cafeteria if she tried to eat near me.

It wasn't just because of what she did. The cuts and bruises told me she hadn't lost Mary yet. No one near Jess McAllister was safe.

~~~

"Shauna, wait up!"

Kitty's voice sliced through the hall din. The last bell had rung, and kids were eager to exit the school. We were only a week away from summer vacation, and you could feel the anticipation in the air. The chatter was louder and more animated. The attitudes in class were more laissez-faire. I resented it. Anna's death plagued me every day, while my classmates talked about beach parties. It was too soon. I wasn't ready for life to go on.

Kitty trotted up to my locker, her book bag slung over her shoulder. Her face was flushed from gym, her heavyset body hugged by a tank top and shorts. She hadn't changed clothes from class, but then, neither of us could go into the girls' locker room. That's where Anna went missing. Kitty usually opted to change in her car. I snuck off to change in the bathrooms near the science labs, my trusty box of salt perched on the toilet tank.

Kitty swept a lock of caramel-brown hair away from her ear.

"Let's get out of here. Tennis in ninety-degree heat is not fun. I'll roll the windows down in case I stink. Sorry."

"No problem." We shouldered our way through the hallway and out the back doors. My backpack weighed fifteen thousand pounds. Finals were upon us, and though I tried to study for the tests, I couldn't focus. It was like all my textbooks had spontaneously rewritten themselves in a language I didn't understand.

"I'm avoiding the principal's office now," Kitty said as we approached her red SUV. "There's a memorial for Anna in one of the display cases. Every time I see it, I cry."

Saying Anna's name was enough to make Kitty's voice hitch. I squeezed her shoulder, doing my best to ignore the sweat slicking her skin. Kitty and Anna had been best friends since grade school. Losing Anna on top of Bronx's accident—if you can call it an accident when a ghost flings your boyfriend out a window—had ruined her. Looking at Anna's picture every day would be a special kind of torture.

"I'm sorry. At least we're almost done with school. You'll get a few months off to recoup."

Kitty tossed her stuff into the back of the car before climbing into the driver's side. "Not exactly. We're still doing that thing with Cody in Solomon's Folly."

I wasn't the only one feeling obligated to end Mary Worth. I told Kitty time and time again that I could handle it without her, that Cody Jackson had volunteered to help so Kitty could stay safe, but Kitty always threw my own words back at me: we'd walked away with our lives, but others might not be so lucky.

We had to do something.

"We started it together, we'll finish it together. For Anna," she'd say.

It was always we. It was always for Anna.

I couldn't quite look at Kitty's profile. If I'd told Jess no all those weeks ago, if I'd been less of a pushover...

"It's okay, Shauna."

She brushed the back of my hand, her fingers tan next to my pasty, befreckled skin. It wasn't absolution, but it was enough. Kitty put the key in the ignition, opening the windows and sunroof of the truck. A breeze swept in, pushing the oppressive heat away.

As soon as Kitty inched from the parking spot, a green Ford Focus sailed around the line of cars and stopped in front of us. Kitty slammed on the brakes. My hand gripped the dash as I peered down the expanse of the SUV's hood only to find myself staring at Jess McAllister. So blond. So perfect with that narrow nose and big blue eyes. So *injured*. A ragged cut bisected her right cheek and top lip. I'd passed her in the hall just yesterday and the cut hadn't been there.

How'd she explain that to her family? A fight? A bear encounter? She tripped and fell on a shovel?

My pulse pounded in my ears.

She shouted something that the end-of-school-day chaos drowned. I shook my head and looked away, but she shouted again. And again. It wasn't until Kitty threw the truck into reverse that Jess's voice finally penetrated.

Read it, Shauna.

Read what? My phone had no messages. She hadn't given me anything in school. But Jess did know my locker combination. She used to help herself to my stuff all the time. As Kitty peeled from the parking lot to get away from our once-upon-a-time friend, I started digging through my bag. Jess was bad at things like *boundaries* and *personal space*. Why would that change now that we weren't friends?

It only took a minute for me to find the photocopied pages held together by a red paper clip. They were wedged into my English textbook between the cover and the first page. She'd written a note across the back in her familiar hen scratch:

Her last letter was dated the day before her death certificate. This was written the next day. How did Mary die?